Stacey Kennedy is a *USA*
writes romances full of heat,
Stacey lives with her hus children in
southwestern Ontario. Most days you'll find her enjoying the outdoors or venturing into the forest with her horse, Clementine. Stacey's just as happy curled up indoors, where she writes surrounded by her lazy dogs. She believes that sexy books about hot cowboys can fix any bad day.

Also by Stacey Kennedy

Lone Wolf In Lights
The Devil In Blue Jeans

Discover more at afterglowbooks.co.uk

THE REBEL WITH BROKEN STRINGS

STACEY KENNEDY

afterglow BOOKS

First Published in Great Britain 2025 by
Afterglow Books by Mills & Boon, an imprint of HarperCollins*Publishers* Ltd
1 London Bridge Street, London, SE1 9GF

www.harpercollins.co.uk

HarperCollins*Publishers*
Macken House, 39/40 Mayor Street Upper,
Dublin 1, D01 C9W8, Ireland

The Rebel with Broken Strings © 2025 Stacey Kennedy

ISBN: 978-0-263-39762-8

1125

This book contains FSC™ certified paper and other controlled sources to ensure responsible forest management.

For more information visit: www.harpercollins.co.uk/green

Printed and Bound in the UK using 100% Renewable Electricity at CPI Group (UK) Ltd, Croydon, CR0 4YY

For the rebels.

Prologue

The hotel room, bathed in amber light, revealed rumpled sheets and discarded clothing. Gunner Woods sat on the edge of the unmade bed, his shirt hanging open. His fingers clutched the edge of the mattress, knuckles white against the dark blue sheets, while warmth spread through his chest—a feeling so intense it blurred the line between pleasure and pain.

Aubrey Hale, a woman he'd only met five days ago, knelt before him on the carpeted floor, her blond hair catching the light from the bedside lamp. Her hands gently ran up his thighs—a strange moment of tenderness in the midst of what they were doing. The contradiction of it made his throat tighten. Her mouth, meanwhile, moved with deliberate purpose over his throbbing cock, drawing a low groan from deep within him.

"Just like that," he murmured, his drawl thickened by desire. "Darlin', just like that."

His hand found its way to her hair, fingers threading

through the silky strands. He didn't guide her, didn't need to. Aubrey knew exactly what she was doing.

"Christ," he whispered, watching the gentle rise and fall of her head, the occasional flash of blue when she looked up to gauge his reaction. "You're gonna be the death of me."

She hummed against him, the vibration making his toes curl inside his boots—the only article of clothing he still wore besides his unbuttoned shirt.

The hotel room had been Aubrey's idea. "Neutral territory," she'd called it, texting him the room number after his show tonight. He'd been surprised—their previous encounters had always happened on his turf, like they were following some unspoken rule. First in his tour bus in Atlanta, then in the temporary apartment he'd rented because he couldn't get enough of her. But tonight, something had shifted between them.

Maybe something had changed in him.

Her hands slid up his thighs, pressing into the muscle as she took him deeper. His head fell back, eyes closing as the sensation overwhelmed him. Behind his eyelids, he saw flashes of their first night together in Atlanta—her eyes meeting his while she stood in the crowd, singing to his song. He'd had security bring her backstage after that. Those eyes... They haunted him. He needed to know the soul behind them.

He remembered how she'd lingered that first night, how conversation had flowed like good whiskey, smooth with just enough burn. He'd invited her onto his tour bus, half expecting rejection.

But she'd surprised him. Just as she surprised him now, pulling back slightly to look up at him.

"You're thinking too much," she said, her voice husky. Her lips shined in the low light, slightly swollen. "I can tell."

He managed a strained laugh. "Hard to think at all with what you're doing."

"Liar." She pressed a kiss to his inner thigh, the gesture surprisingly tender. "You're always composing something in that head of yours. I can see it in your eyes."

She was right. Even now, lyrics were forming—fragments about hotel rooms and whiskey glasses, about a woman whose touch felt like coming home even when home is the last place he deserved to be.

"Just thinking about how this wasn't exactly what I expected when you texted," he admitted.

A smile played at the corners of her mouth. "Disappointed?"

"Christ, no." His hand cupped her cheek, his thumb tracing her lower lip.

Aubrey sat back on her heels, considering him. In the gap between them, the air felt charged, weighted with unspoken complications. She rose slightly, bringing her face level with his. Her eyes—those expressive blue eyes that give away more than she thought—searched his. "I came here tonight because I wanted to stop pretending."

"Pretending what?" he dared to ask.

"That this is just physical between us. That I don't think about you when you're not around." She pressed her forehead against his, her breath warm against his lips. "That

I'm not scared of what you make me feel, even though we have known each other less than a week."

The confession hit him like a shot of pure oxygen—dizzying and essential. His hands cupped her face, and he kissed her with all the desperation he normally poured into his music. She tasted like the whiskey they'd shared at the bar and something uniquely Aubrey—something that reminded him of possibility. And none of it made any sense. How could they be this connected after such a short time?

When they broke apart, both breathing hard, Aubrey slid back down to her knees. But there was a difference now—a shift in the atmosphere. This wasn't just about physical release anymore. It was about connection. About surrendering.

Gunner watched her, committing every detail to memory—the way her hair fell forward over her shoulder, the determined set of her jaw, the gentle strength in her hands. She was beautiful in a way that made his chest ache, in a way he knew he didn't deserve after all the mistakes he'd made.

But Aubrey didn't see him as the famous country star struggling with sobriety. When she looked at him, he felt like the man he wished he could be—someone worthy of a woman like her. Because Aubrey didn't know the shake of his hand wasn't from control, but from his need for another fix.

Her mouth engulfed him again, and he lost himself in the sensation. His fingers tangled in her hair, not guiding but connecting, needing the anchor of her as pleasure built at the base of his spine. She pressed against his stomach, steadying him as she increased her pace. Her other hand worked in rhythm with her mouth, creating a force that drove him to the edge faster than he'd like.

"Aubrey," he warned, his voice strained. "Darlin', I'm close."

She made no move to pull away. Instead, her eyes locked with his, and the raw intimacy in that gaze—the acceptance, the want—threatened his control. His body tensed, and he pulled away before she could finish him.

"Come here," he said, voice rough.

She rose, moving with the practiced grace of someone comfortable in their body. He took in the sight of her—still fully dressed in jeans and a simple blue top that matched her eyes, but looking thoroughly affected, nonetheless. Her chest rose and fell rapidly, and there was a slight tremble to her hands that betrayed her composed expression.

He reached for her, fingers hooking into the belt loops of her jeans to pull her closer. "Your turn."

Her lips curved into a smile that was both shy and wicked—a contradiction that made his spent body stir again.

"What plan do you have in mind?" she asked, stepping between his knees.

"Darlin'," he drawled, his hands sliding up to her waist, "I plan on making you forget your own name. And getting you naked."

He swiftly stripped her out of her clothes until her stunning naked body was exposed, his own personal playground.

In one fluid motion, he rose from the edge of the bed,

his hands finding Aubrey's waist with a certainty that made her breath audibly hitch, and he lifted her. The transition from standing to airborne happened so quickly that a small, startled sound escaped her—half laugh, half gasp—as he deposited her onto the rumpled sheets with deliberate care.

"Warn a girl next time," she breathed with a laugh.

Gunner wasn't laughing. His cock throbbed painfully as he stood above her, shrugging off his open shirt. His eyes never left hers.

"Turn over," he told her, his voice a low command that had her shivering.

Aubrey complied, rolling onto her stomach, then lifting herself to her hands and knees. Gunner removed his boots, his belt buckle clinking as it hit the floor.

The mattress dipped as he joined her on the bed. His hands slid up her sides. "God, you're beautiful," he murmured, his palms sliding down her bare back. His calloused fingertips—hardened from years of guitar playing—found delicious friction against her smooth skin.

He positioned himself behind her, his body a warm presence against her back as he aligned himself along the length of her. His arms circled her waist, pulling her against his chest so they were spooned together on their knees. His lips found the sensitive spot where her neck met her shoulder.

"You feel so good," he breathed against her skin. One hand slid up to cup her breast while the other drifted lower to her sweet soaking wet heat. "So ready for me."

Aubrey arched into his touch, her body responding with eagerness. "Gunner," she whispered, her voice catching as his fingers found her clit. "Please."

He pressed a kiss to her shoulder blade. "Please what, darlin'? Tell me what you want."

She gasped. "I want you inside me. Now."

He smiled against her skin before he withdrew briefly to retrieve protection from his discarded jeans, but then he was back, his hands returning to her hips as he positioned himself.

The first push of his body into hers drew matching sighs from them both. Aubrey's fingers clutched at the sheets. Gunner paused, allowing her to adjust, his forehead resting against her shoulder blade.

"You drive me wild," he murmured, his accent thickening with desire. His hips began a slow, deliberate rhythm that had her pressing back against him, silently asking for more.

One of his hands slid from her hip to her stomach, then lower, his fingers finding the exact pressure and pace that made her thighs tremble. The other arm locked around her waist, holding her steady as their movements grew more insistent.

The sheets rustled beneath them alongside their increasingly labored breathing. Aubrey moaned, louder... and louder yet.

"That's it," he encouraged, his voice rough with restraint. "Let me hear you, Aubrey. Don't hold back."

"Harder," she gasped, pushing back against him. "Please, Gunner."

He complied, his thrusts becoming more forceful, more determined. The headboard began a rhythmic tap against the wall that in any other circumstance might cause him to stop. Now, it only added to the building tension coiling tight in his groin.

"Look at you," he breathed, reverence in his voice. "Taking me so well. So fucking perfect."

The room filled with the sounds of their passion—skin against skin, breathless encouragements. Gunner lost track of time, lost himself in the sensations. His fingers worked against her sensitive flesh while his body filled her completely.

"I'm close," she warned.

His rhythm faltered slightly before he found a new, more determined pace. "Together. Want to feel you come around me."

His words seemed to push her closer to the edge. Aubrey reached back, her hand finding his hip, nails digging into his flesh as she urged him deeper. Their bodies moved in perfect sync now, as if they'd been dancing this particular dance for years instead of days.

"Yes." She gasped as the first wave hit her. "Gunner, yes—"

Her body tightened around him as pleasure exploded through him. He made a sound—half groan, half her name—as he followed her over the edge. His arm tightened around her waist, holding her against him as they rode out the aftershocks together.

For several long moments, they remained locked together, both trembling with the intensity of their shared release. His forehead rested against her shoulder, his breath hot and uneven against her sweat-dampened skin. His arms held her securely, as if afraid she might vanish if he loosened his grip.

Slowly, carefully, he guided them down to the mattress, still connected, now lying on their sides. He pressed gentle kisses along her shoulder and neck.

"You okay?" he murmured against her ear.

Aubrey laughed. "Totally okay." She turned to face him. "Satisfied to my very bones."

Christ, he loved how sexy she looked after he'd had her. He kissed her then, soft and unhurried.

She watched him closely, tracing the curve of his lips with her thumb. "What happens now?"

The question Gunner had been avoiding since their first night together. The question that was growing more insistent with each encounter. *What* does *happen now?* He was a musician on a North American tour, trying to pretend he wasn't barely hanging on and losing himself more and more each day; she was a chef in Atlanta. Their paths had no business crossing.

Yet here they were, naked and tangled in hotel sheets, looking at each other like they'd discovered something precious and unexpected.

"Now," he said slowly, making the decision as the words formed, "we stop pretending there isn't something magical between us. We see where it goes."

The smile that broke across her face was like sunrise back in his hometown, Timber Falls—gradual, then brilliant, illuminating everything in its path. He pulled her closer, his kiss conveying everything words could not.

But then that overwhelming urge returned, insistent and demanding.

He dropped a kiss on her forehead and pulled back. "I'll be right back." His gaze lingered on her features—the soft curve of her cheek, the smoothness of her skin and the way her lips were swollen. She was a stark contrast to the shadows that lurked within him, a bright flame illuminating the dark corners of his soul. For a moment, he allowed himself the dream of waking up like this every day—without the loneliness clawing at his heart.

With a sigh, he slid from the bed. Padding across the room, he entered the bathroom and flicked on the light. The harsh fluorescence revealed his reflection in the mirror—a man marked by the passage of too many hard-earned miles.

Staring into his own blue eyes, he saw the faintest echoes of the man he used to be before he lost himself somewhere along the way. His reflection haunted him. He gripped the porcelain sink, the coolness of the surface grounding him as he fought the swell of emotions threatening to capsize him.

Aubrey, with her fierce independence and her tender heart, had unwittingly staked a claim on his soul. She lay in the bed, a picture of peace and vulnerability, her presence filling the room with a warmth he couldn't outrun. His chest tightened, the realization crashing over him like a relentless wave: he was terrified of wanting her to stay.

He knew too well the danger lurking in the depths of that desire. He was not the man she deserved—not anymore. His past was a tangle of mistakes and regrets, of women in his bed and gone the next day, his present a constant battle with demons that wouldn't ever quiet. The pain in his leg a reminder of the day that changed everything for him.

With a heavy heart, he turned to the drawer next to the sink. There, in the dim half-light, he found the small bottle. The pills rattled softly, a grim reminder of the chains he had yet to break. His hand trembled as he unscrewed the cap, the familiar white tablets a stark contrast against his tan, calloused palm. He tossed two back, feeling them catch momentarily in his throat, and washed them down with a swig of water from the glass he kept there for this very purpose.

As the pills dissolved, so too did the brief flicker of hope he'd felt in Aubrey's arms. He was still the same man, fighting the same battles. And though her light had pierced his darkness, he feared what might happen if she stayed close enough to be consumed by it.

One

The cold, dark Montana night cast long shadows across Timber Falls Ranch as Gunner stood rooted to the spot, his heart hammering against his ribs. The tips of his ears were frozen, his eyes were fixed on the silhouette of Aubrey, framed in the warm glow of the porch light, after the ranch's annual Christmas Eve party. The sight of her hit him like a physical blow, stirring up memories of their incredible week together that had haunted him for a couple years now.

His fingers twitched, aching for the familiar weight of a guitar to ground him that always got him through the nervousness of going on stage. Instead, he clenched his fists, steeling himself for the confrontation ahead. The warm glow of the light guided him forward as he took a hesitant step, feeling the ache in his leg—a constant reminder of the ATV accident that had derailed his life and career. The injury that led to the painkillers that had soon become his only companion.

Once inside the house that belonged to his good friend—and Timber Falls Ranch owner—Jaxon, Gunner found Aubrey in the kitchen making herself another drink.

"Aubrey," he called out, his voice rough with emotion. "We need to talk."

She turned, her blond hair catching the light, and for a moment, Gunner forgot how to breathe. Those striking blue eyes widened in recognition before narrowing with suspicion. "Do you want a drink?" she asked, redirecting the conversation like she always did. Ever since she moved to Timber Falls.

"You know that's not what I want to talk about," he grumbled.

Only silence greeted him.

"Come on, Aubrey," he said after a long-suffering sigh, "stop acting like you don't remember our week together." He had confronted her three times since she had moved to town with her two best friends, Charly and Willow, and she kept playing the same game that she had never met him. "Two years ago. Atlanta. That concert. Then the week that followed."

"Not this *again*. Are you serious right now?" she retorted, finishing fixing her drink. "Gunner, whatever you think happened—"

He didn't let her finish. "I know what I saw, what we did. It was you."

"Wasn't me," Aubrey said over her shoulder, giving him a fine view of her incredible ass in her blue jeans that he could never have forgotten. "You've got it all wrong. I didn't even go to your concert."

"Then who the hell was I with?" Gunner snapped.

"God knows!" she shot back. "But it wasn't me!"

He leaned against the doorframe, crossed his arms and snorted. "That unforgettable week, your laugh, the way you moved, your goddamn moans—it's all stuck in my head, Aubrey."

"You are legit delusional," Aubrey spat, turning toward him with a fiery stare. "You need to get over this."

The denial stung, cutting deeper than Gunner had anticipated. Her words were like a sucker punch, leaving him winded. He'd known this wouldn't be easy, but he hadn't expected she'd hold out this long. The old Gunner might have retreated, seeking solace in a handful of pills. But he wasn't that man anymore. He'd done the work, gotten sober and healed the parts of himself that had needed healing. He worked at that every single day.

"I know you must hate me," he said, his voice intense, thinking back to how he'd left her naked in that hotel bed without another word from him, "but I'm not the same person I was back then. I've changed."

For a fleeting moment, something flickered in Aubrey's deep blue eyes—a hint of vulnerability that made his heart skip. But just as quickly, it was gone, replaced by a steely resolve.

"Listen, Gunner," she said, her voice softening slightly. "I don't know how many times I can say this for you to understand, but you need to drop this."

He took another step closer, close enough now to catch the faint scent of her perfume. It transported him back to that hot week together, where he swore he could still taste her on his lips. "Is that really what you want me to do?" he asked, his voice barely above a whisper. "For me to forget those days we had? To forget what we shared?"

Her breath hitched, and for a moment, Gunner thought he'd broken through her defenses. But then she squared her shoulders, her expression hardening once more.

"What I want," she said firmly, "is for you to leave me alone."

The finality in her tone left no room for argument. Gunner gave a final nod, swallowing the lump in his throat. As he turned to go, he caught one last glimpse of her face. Behind the mask of indifference, he saw a flicker of something else—regret, maybe. Or longing.

It wasn't much, but it was enough to kindle a spark of hope in his chest. He might have lost this battle, but the war was far from over.

Back outside, his boots crunched on the snow-covered gravel driveway as his breath fogged out in the frigid winter air. The sting of Aubrey's denial burned in his chest, mixing with the guilt that had always stayed on his mind since he'd left her in the hotel room. He removed his cowboy hat and ran a hand through his blond hair, exhaling slowly, before sliding it back onto his head.

"Damn," he muttered to himself, heading toward the campfire, cringing against the ache in his thigh from the two surgeries he'd endured after the ATV he'd been riding flipped and landed on his leg, breaking it in three places. The pain there was a constant reminder of how far he'd fallen. How he'd become a man he hated. A bad boy, a rebel, the tabloids had called him. But the pain didn't remind him of all he'd done wrong anymore. The pain was a reminder of how much he'd risen back up.

As Gunner approached, Eli—his childhood friend and fellow Timber Falls Ranch cowboy—looked up, concern etched in his wise green eyes, his dark hair peeking out beneath his black cowboy hat. "Everything all right, man?" Eli asked.

Gunner took a seat on the log next to Eli, grateful for the warmth of the fire. "Yeah," he lied, grabbing another beer from the cooler next to him.

Eli's girlfriend, and one of Aubrey's best friends, Willow, gave him a little smile that almost looked like pity.

Gunner cracked open his beer and took a long sip, trying to shake off the lingering tension, just as Jaxon called, "We've got some news." His sandy blond hair stuck out beneath his own cowboy hat, his hazel eyes sharp.

Gunner looked up to see Jaxon approaching the campfire, with Charly, the other woman in Aubrey's trio of best friends, striding next to him. The firelight danced across Charly's warm brown eyes and caught the highlights in her brunette hair beneath her wool beanie.

"Jaxon and I have decided not to wait too long to get married," Charly announced, her voice brimming with excitement. "We're having a small wedding right here at the ranch in the spring."

Gunner's eyebrows shot up, a grin spreading across his face, aimed at Jaxon. "Smart plan. Lock her down before she can change her mind."

Charly laughed, but Jaxon just grinned and gave Gunner a rude gesture with his finger, which made him chuckle.

Eli chimed in, his eyes twinkling with mischief. "You

know what this means, don't you, Gunner? We're at the lady's beck and call now."

Gunner laughed, tipping his cowboy hat toward Charly. "Whatever the bride needs, ma'am. Just say the word."

Dead serious, Charly said, "Oh, you boys might regret that offer."

Willow agreed with a firm nod. "Kiss your lazy Sundays goodbye."

As the group chuckled, Gunner felt a warmth in his chest that had nothing to do with the fire. This, he thought, was what it meant to belong somewhere. To be part of something bigger than himself. For a moment, his demons seemed far away, until Decker's fingers found their home on the guitar strings.

The longtime Timber Falls Ranch cowboy caught Gunner's eye, giving a subtle nod that spoke volumes. Gunner felt the familiar tug of music in his soul, something he never could resist.

Raising his beer bottle to his lips, Gunner took a long, slow sip. The cool liquid slid down his throat, removing the remainder of the tension. As he lowered the bottle, his gaze swept over the cowboys and good friends around the fire, and his breath caught.

Aubrey was making her way toward the group. His heart skipped a beat, his fingers tightening around the bottle. And holding her stare, he sang about losing himself to alcohol until love saved him.

A couple hours later, Aubrey slammed her bedroom door shut behind her, the sound echoing through the quiet farmhouse. She, Charly and Willow had renovated it after moving to Timber Falls to fulfill a dream of opening a cocktail lounge, The Naked Moose. A bar once owned by Jaxon.

A long sigh escaped her as she collapsed onto her queen-sized bed, the soft quilt a stark contrast to the turmoil raging inside her. The scent of woodsmoke clung to her hair, a lingering reminder of the campfire—and Gunner.

Her fingers curled into the fabric as she squeezed her eyes shut, trying to block out the memory of his piercing blue eyes boring into her soul. Why couldn't he just give up? More importantly, why did her traitorous body still react to him like a moth to a flame?

"Dammit," she muttered, rolling onto her back and staring at the ceiling.

Before she could spiral further into her thoughts, the door burst open. Willow stood in the doorway, her strawberry blond hair wild and her green eyes blazing with concern.

"Alright, spill it," Willow demanded, marching into the room. "What happened with Gunner?"

Aubrey propped herself up on her elbows, forcing a casual shrug. "Nothing happened. What are you talking about?"

Willow's eyebrows shot up. "Lies. Eli and I were coming into the kitchen but stopped when we heard you and Gunner talking. I know you, Aubrey. I know all your tells. You *lied* to him. You two had a week together?"

"It's nothing you need to worry about. Really." Even Aubrey heard the note of warning in her voice.

Of course, Willow ignored it. "Eli said for us to stay out of it, but that's not how our friendship works." She entered the room and perched on the edge of the bed, her gaze softening. "Talk to me, Aub. Ignoring how insane it is that fate reconnected you here, why are you pretending you don't know him?"

Aubrey huffed. There was no outrunning this. Her carefully constructed walls began to crumble. They'd been friends since they were little. Willow *did* know all her tells. Aubrey averted her gaze, focusing on the worn pattern of her quilt. "It's not…it's not what you think."

"Then tell me what it is," Willow pressed, placing her hand on Aubrey's arm. "Help me understand all this."

The weight of the secret pressed down on Aubrey's chest, threatening to suffocate her. She took a deep breath, steeling herself for the confession she'd been holding back since they'd moved to Timber Falls and Gunner walked into their bar on opening day.

"I met Gunner in Atlanta at one of his concerts," she whispered, her voice trembling. "We spent a week together, and it was… God, Willow, it was intense. Like nothing I've ever experienced before."

Willow's eyes widened, but she remained silent, encouraging Aubrey to continue.

"The chemistry between us was electric," Aubrey admitted, her cheeks flushing at the memory. "We connected on every level—physically, emotionally. It felt like…like he got me in ways no man has ever got me, you know?"

As the words tumbled out, Aubrey felt a mix of relief and

vulnerability. She'd never spoken about that week to any-one, and now that she'd started, she found she couldn't stop.

"We talked for hours, shared our dreams, our fears. And when he finally kissed me…" Aubrey trailed off, lost in the vivid recollection. "It was passionate, tender and com-pletely unforgettable."

Memories flooded her. The warmth of Gunner's cal-loused hands on her skin, the intoxicating scent of his co-logne mixed with wood, the taste of whiskey on his lips. She shivered, her body betraying her with a surge of desire.

"His touch…it set me on fire," she continued, lost in the memory. "And when he sang to me, just for me, I felt like the only woman in the world." She clenched her fists, anger rising to combat the pain he'd left her with. "But then after he talked like we were going to make things somehow work between us, he left me in a hotel room. Just like that. No note, no call, nothing. Just threw me away like a piece of trash."

Willow's hand tightened on Aubrey's arm. "Oh, honey. I'm so sorry."

Aubrey swallowed hard, fighting back tears. "It's not just about Gunner, you know? It's…it's everything."

Willow nodded in full understanding. She knew every painful part of Aubrey's past. That her father left her and her mother when she was eight years old and never came back. And that her dream job at a five-star restaurant in Atlanta had been cut short due to a narcissistic boss who couldn't keep his damn hands to himself. But Willow listened as Aubrey continued, her voice cracking, "That week with Gunner, I let all my guards down for him."

She slowly shook her head in frustration at herself. "I don't even know how he did that, considering I never let my guards down for anyone that quickly, and I hate him for that. Hate how weak it made me feel that morning I woke up and he was gone." She paused, drew in a deep breath and blew it out slowly before continuing. "So yeah, I lied to him, but obviously, my plan of denying our week together isn't working. He just won't give up."

Willow's eyes, deep and understanding, never left Aubrey's face as she listened.

"Besides," Aubrey said after a moment, "now that I know about his past addiction to painkillers, I bet he was probably high the entire week. He isn't even sure what he remembers."

A mixture of concern and doubt clouded Willow's features. "I hear you, I do. But I can't shake this feeling that you're making a mistake."

Aubrey's chest tightened at Willow's words. "How?"

"I've seen the way Gunner looks at you. That man isn't just chasing some fantasy. There's something real there, something deep."

Memories of Gunner's intense gaze flooded Aubrey's mind, but she shook her head, trying to fight the images. "He had his chance with me, and he lost it. That's all that's happening here."

Willow cocked her head, softening her voice. "What if he's genuinely trying to make amends? Maybe…maybe you should give him a chance to explain himself."

Aubrey's back straightened, the bed bouncing beneath her. "Explain what? How he used me and left without a word? How he made me feel like I was special, only to disappear?" Her voice cracked, betraying the pain she'd been trying so hard to hide. "I can't do that again. I won't let myself be that vulnerable." Men had brought nothing but pain. She was in her self-care era, and nothing would change her mind.

Willow's expression softened further. "I know you're scared of him being a massive jerk again. Lord knows, I know this. But sometimes, the things that scare us the most are the ones worth fighting for."

"No," Aubrey said sharply, shaking her head firmly. "I've made my decision. I'm protecting myself, and that's final. He'll give up eventually," she murmured, more to herself than to Willow. "He has to."

"I wouldn't be so sure about that," Willow countered. "Men like Gunner… They don't just walk away when something matters to them."

Aubrey's jaw clenched, her fingers digging into her arms. "He doesn't get a choice. I won't let him in." But even as the words left her lips, a traitorous part of her mind whispered, *What if he doesn't give up? What if he keeps fighting for you?*

She pushed the thought away, jumping out of bed to stare out the window, focusing instead on the distant mountains in the night sky. "I've made my choice, Willow. End of story."

Willow sighed. "Alright. I hear you. But just…be prepared. Something tells me he's not ready to let this go."

As Willow's footsteps faded down the hallway, Aubrey remained at the window, sighing heavily. She tried to convince herself that her resolve was unshakable, that her walls were impenetrable.

But in the depths of her heart, a flicker of uncertainty betrayed her. And she couldn't shake the feeling that Willow might be right.

Two

Gunner clutched his well-worn coffee mug the following morning, savoring the way its gentle heat seeped through his calloused hands as he stood in his cool, sparsely decorated kitchen. The first blush of dawn spilled through the tall windows, revealing the majestic, snow-capped mountains of Timber Falls—a sanctuary where the dark shadow of addiction no longer trailed his every step. His humble bungalow, nestled snugly against the rugged peaks, exuded a comforting warmth, as if the very walls embraced him in a silent, reassuring hug. Exposed wooden beams and expansive windows framed the stunning wilderness. He also had a condo in Nashville, which he hadn't visited since returning, but Timber Falls would always be his true home.

In that serene moment, the tranquil silence swathed him as thickly as the morning mist that lazily rolled over the valleys, when suddenly, the shrill ring of his phone shattered the calm. His hand, mid-gesture as it lifted for another sip of his coffee, froze in suspense. Gunner slowly turned his gaze toward the device resting on the weathered wooden table, its screen now alive with an insistent glow that revealed a name stirring a complex brew of emotions—a name that mingled promise with a hint of caution. His agent. The man who had ridden shotgun on the tumultuous roller coaster of Gunner's career, sharing in the exhilarating highs and agonizing lows alike.

"Hey, Tom," Gunner answered with a subdued greeting.

"Morning, Gunner. How's the new material coming along?" Tom's voice crackled through the line, a mixture of anticipation and concern in each syllable.

Settling himself into the timeworn kitchen chair with legs that creaked softly against the hardwood floor, Gunner exhaled slowly. "It's coming," he replied, his tone measured and reflective. He took a deliberate sip of his coffee, feeling the comforting warmth radiate through him. "You remember 'Home Town Hero'? I'm plunging back into that style…but it's fundamentally different now. Rawer. More honest and unfiltered."

A weighted pause on the other end of the line carried with it echoes of Gunner's tumultuous past—images of platinum records and sold-out arenas mingled with the bittersweet memory of sweet ballads. Unspoken, too, were the long nights drowned in pills and the mornings when every sunrise recalled the haunting darkness he had once embraced.

"Sounds promising," Tom remarked at length, his voice imbued with both hope and nostalgia. "People fell for the raw authenticity in your voice, Gunner. They'll be drawn to it again."

"Maybe," Gunner mused quietly, a deep-seated confidence simmering just beneath his reflective exterior. "I'm not rushing this process. Being away from all the noise has taught me that there's a kind of healing in the stillness. My music has grown richer because of it."

"Keep on that path," Tom encouraged warmly. "Your fans will be there, waiting, when you're ready."

"Thank you," Gunner replied, setting his coffee mug down carefully, his fingers tracing its rim as if drawing strength from its memory. Bathed in the soft morning light, he lingered on the line, each word anchoring him in the newfound belief that while his past had shaped him, it no longer controlled his destiny.

"It's like night and day with you now," Tom added with a lighthearted chuckle that bridged the distance between them. "The tabloids aren't hounding you anymore. No more wild, reckless nights or run-ins with the law. It's done wonders for your image." Yet beneath those words lay the silent truth of the man Gunner had once been—the troubled soul lost in a haze of pills and too much whiskey.

A shadow of those former days flickered deep within Gunner's mind. He inhaled slowly, drawing in the crisp, clean air of Timber Falls, letting those thoughts fade away. No longer was that his truth. Alongside that quiet healing, a pulse of pride beat steadily—an acknowledgment of how far he'd come.

"There's a certain sweetness in living life straight," he said. "I truly value this second chance."

"Just keep walking that line," Tom urged, his tone rich

with genuine approval and admiration. "People are noticing. You're winning hearts back, one note at a time."

"Glad to hear it," Gunner replied, a slow, sincere smile curving his lips as a hint of the weight from his past lifted imperceptibly.

"Stay true to yourself and to your music," Tom added firmly, his voice laden with unwavering support. "That's truly all anyone can ask for."

"I will," Gunner murmured. "Thanks, Tom. I'll be in touch if I create something worth sharing."

"I look forward to it," came Tom's warm reply.

After hanging up, Gunner allowed the newfound silence to envelop him once more. Yet, beneath the layers of hope and renewal, he still sensed an elusive void—a yearning for something profoundly meaningful, a purpose that stretched beyond music.

Taking a long, hesitant breath, he leaned farther back in his chair and his eyes wandered around the kitchen until they fell upon a burst of color on the refrigerator—a slightly crumpled flyer, its edges curled as though begging for notice. Timber Falls Afterschool Music Program and Talent Show, it declared in a bold, Western-style typeface that resonated with the twang of guitars and the shuffle of boots. He remembered how Betty—a persistent, gossip-loving older woman—had handed it to him a few days ago at The Naked Moose.

He rose slowly and walked the few paces to the fridge. His fingertips brushed the paper as he traced the outline of a guitar graphic in the corner, unwrapping its detailed invitation—a call for mentors to guide kids.

A flicker of interest ignited within him. Timber Falls had always been his home, a place where his music had once breathed life, uncluttered by the oppressive weight of fame. Now, the invitation offered him a chance to give back.

A tug stirred at the worn edges of his heart—a blend of duty and an equally strong urge to atone for the mistakes that haunted him. "Maybe this is something worth doing," he murmured softly.

His fingers brushed over the smooth surface of the flyer before reaching for his phone. He dialed the number printed on it. "Hello? This is Margaret speaking," came a warm voice on the other end.

"Margaret, it's Gunner Woods," he said, leaning against the counter. "I saw the flyer for the afterschool music program and… I'd really like to help out. I want to mentor the kids."

After a heavy pause, Margaret exclaimed, "Gunner Woods, oh, wow, that's wonderful! These young kiddos look up to you. Your experience and talent could inspire them in ways you can't even imagine."

Margaret continued, "Can you come by the community center tomorrow? I'll fill you in on all the details."

"I sure can," Gunner replied, the mix of hope and apprehension probably evident in his tone. "See you then."

"The kids will be so excited," Margaret added with a final upbeat note. "How wonderful. See you then!"

After ending the call, Gunner stepped toward the window, squinting as the bright sun cast its familiar glow over the distant mountains. In that light, he envisioned the bright, eager faces of children—faces untouched by the shadows of doubt or failure—reflecting a future he longed to embrace. Yet, even as he entertained a glimmer of redemption, he could not silence the inner voice questioning whether one act, however genuine, could ever mend the fractures of his past. For now, he clung to the hope that this conflicted step might truly be a move in the right direction.

Aubrey's fingers wrung and tapped over the worn oak of the back room desk at The Naked Moose, as if trying to escape her constant inner turmoil. Her lip trembled in anticipation with every uneven tap, each echo of the clock intensifying the stark emptiness on her laptop screen—a dull gray void that reflected the conflict roiling inside her.

A sudden digital chime shattered the silence, pulling her from her spiraling thoughts. The screen flickered into life, revealing the composed yet distant face of her lawyer, Jeffrey. His expression bore a calm professionalism that had once buoyed her through darker times, yet now seemed to underscore the bittersweet victory before her.

"Congratulations, Aubrey," he said, his smile gentle and detached, as always. "The settlement is final. You've won."

Aubrey's exhale escaped sharply—a release of the breath she'd been holding since she'd fled Atlanta's intoxicating lights for Montana's small-town life. Not long ago, she'd been working under one of Atlanta's top chefs, absorbing skills and passion. But that promise had soured when she had dared to reject his sexual advances. His dismissal, under the guise of probation, had sealed her fate, leaving her reputation tarnished in the eyes of the Atlanta industry. "It doesn't feel like winning," she murmured, the admission heavy with resentment.

"Understandable," Jeffrey replied, nodding as if weighing every ounce of her inner conflict. "This victory is a testament to your bravery. Not everyone would have fought the way you did."

"Bravery," she echoed, the word tasting strangely bitter on her tongue. Leaning back with arms drawn protectively around her, as if shielding her from her past, she admitted, "I guess you could call it that. I just couldn't let that jerk hurt anyone else the way he hurt me." The memory of Chef Bisset—adorned with a façade of culinary genius while his hands violated her trust—was a wound that never truly healed. Her only recourse had been to counter his abuse with a lawsuit that, even now, felt as much like a battle scar as it did a victory.

"Your judgment will follow shortly and be deposited into your account," Jeffrey affirmed. "Now, you're free to chase what truly matters—your passion, The Naked Moose... Timber Falls. I hope things finally work out there for you."

"Thank you, Jeffrey. I appreciate everything you did for me." Even as her lips quivered into a faint smile, the scars still felt fresh beneath the surface.

"Take care, Aubrey," he concluded.

She pressed her palms against the cool desk, staring at the ghostly space where his digital presence had just evaporated. His words, meant to soothe, had only just begun to peel away at the heavy layers of tension when darker memories intruded.

Without warning, her mind dragged her back to a searing Atlanta summer, the chaos of clanging pots, frantic chefs and the acrid scent of burnt garlic—a place where art clashed violently with abuse. Every shadow in that cramped kitchen seemed to pulse with the malignant presence of Chef Bisset, his predatory gaze lingering like a chain of unwanted memories down her spine.

A shiver snaked up her arms as she recalled the way his voice had slithered over her name, each word an unmistakable barb that chipped away at her once cherished confidence. The memory was made all the more harrowing by the stark recollection of him pinning her against cold stainless steel appliances, his crude advances stripping her of what little dignity she had left.

Then, as if the past was conspiring with the present to deepen her inner wounds, the memory morphed into another—a silhouette of her father when she was eight. Peering through the banisters, she'd watched his heavy boots collide with the wooden floor, the front door swinging open to release a rebellious gust of wind that hinted at freedom, only for him to vanish into the unknown, leaving behind the relentless tremor of a closing screen door.

Her breath caught as the old pain flared anew, splitting open unhealed wounds. But amid this tumult of haunting recollections, a tiny seed of defiance began to stir—a raw, tentative determination that struggled to overcome her conflicted heart.

Fuck them, it screamed.

Drawing in a deliberate, anchoring breath, Aubrey forced herself back into the present—back to The Naked Moose and the hard-won life she had clawed back piece by piece.

She'd won, yet the victory felt as fractured as her past—a step forward shadowed by every man who had ever wronged her.

Exhaling sharply, her breath stirring scattered papers, she rose. Squaring her shoulders, she left the office and returned to the kitchen, where the familiar clatter of sizzling pans and gleaming stainless steel battled the heaviness of her thoughts. There, Chef Miguel—a recent hire who had stepped in so Aubrey could channel her energy into her passion rather than endless cooking—moved with quiet assurance.

Miguel, with his deep-set, intense brown eyes, trendy undercut and neatly trimmed beard framing his strong jawline, exuded a warmth that contrasted sharply with her inner chill. His sun-kissed skin and crisp white chef's coat, adorned by his name in elegant black cursive, lent him an air of confident artistry.

"Settlement's done," Aubrey announced, her voice wavering between relief and lingering grief.

"Ah, congratulations," Miguel replied, his accent wrapping his words in a comforting tone. "Now, let's see that passion in your salsa verde, sí?"

In his presence, Aubrey's mind flickered between fighting her inner demons and the simple need to escape them. Approaching the prep station where knives lay among vibrant herbs, she confessed, "It's been a while since I've allowed myself to just play with flavors."

"Then let's play," Miguel grinned, with a spark of mischief and encouragement.

As the sizzle of onions filled the room and the inviting perfume of fresh cilantro nudged at her senses, her hand clutched the chef's knife with a steady determination that belied the conflict inside her. Pausing with the blade hovered over a bright tomato, a sudden flash of a past encounter stirred—a memory of Gunner's reckless kiss, the unbidden touch that sought to reduce her to a pawn of lust.

"Easy now," Chef Miguel interjected softly, his voice smoothing over the rough edges of her spiraling recollections. "That tomato has done nothing wrong."

Blinking to dispel the haze of memory, Aubrey managed a shaky chuckle as the tension unfurled like steam escaping a pressure cooker. "You're right," she conceded, rolling her shoulders in a feeble attempt to recapture her rhythm. "I got a little lost in the sauce there."

"Lost in the sauce, huh?" Miguel teased lightly, his glance warm but perceptive. "Sometimes though, getting lost is the only way to discover new flavors."

Grateful for his lighthearted banter—a brief reprieve from the relentless churn of her past—she met his eyes. In Timber Falls, survival wasn't merely about enduring the heat of her memories; it was about learning to thrive amidst it.

"Ain't that the truth," she laughed, the sound mingling with the simmering chaos around them. She finished chopping the tomatoes and put the knife down, turning to Miguel. "You're all good here?"

"I'm on it," Miguel replied.

Aubrey offered him a tentative smile as her senses navigated the organized chaos. The sound of a knife scraping against a chopping board mingled with the warmth radiating from the stoves, and even the pervasive scent of garlic felt like a bittersweet reminder of both home and change as she pushed open the swinging door to the main bar. The bar's modern industrial style clashed against the rustic charm of Timber Falls. Her eyes drifted over the exposed brick walls adorned with local art—a moose head sporting a pink feather boa and sparkly sunglasses—and the string lights weaving uncertain patterns above.

Inside, sunlight filtered through tall windows. There, behind the bar, were Willow and Charly. "I won," Aubrey declared, the words tumbling out unexpectedly. "The civil suit against Chef Bisset. It's over."

The revelation hit the room like a sudden, turbulent storm—intense and unanticipated. Charly's practiced movements faltered, and the towel in her hand fell to the floor as her eyes widened. In moments Charly encircled Aubrey, engulfing her in an embrace that was as comforting as it was overwhelming. Willow dropped the inventory clipboard and joined in, her arms wrapping around Aubrey with an intensity that spoke of both pride and concern.

"You did it!" Charly exclaimed, her voice bubbling with joy, yet her gaze held a trace of something unspoken. Pulling back slightly, she searched Aubrey's eyes as if seeking reassurance. "I always knew you would."

Willow's embrace tightened, her tone low and fierce. "You held that bastard accountable," she said, her voice resonating with pride yet edged with unresolved anger.

Aubrey's breath caught, a sharp reminder that victory often came with its own burden. "I still can't believe it," she murmured, softer now, conflicted between elation and the heavy realization of what she had endured. "It finally...feels *over*."

"And now everyone sees the truth about him," Charly added quietly. "Your win will spread, and his name will be ruined now."

Aubrey swallowed hard, fighting back the lump in her throat. In that moment, she recognized how desperately she had needed this—a *win*.

Willow pulled back slightly, her hands still resting on Aubrey's shoulders. "I'm so proud of you, Aubs," she whispered.

Aubrey managed a nod, her voice failing her as she struggled to keep her composure. She would have to call her mother later, when she wasn't so sure her tears would betray her. The past year—a collage of humiliation, doubt, and leaving everything behind—flashed in her mind, a reminder that even victories left scars.

Taking a steadying breath, Aubrey let the familiar air of The Naked Moose fill her lungs. "Thanks for being there through all of it," she said.

Willow rolled her eyes in an affectionate, knowing manner. "You say that like it was ever in question," she retorted, though her smile betrayed her seriousness.

Charly squeezed Aubrey's hand briefly. "We always

knew you'd come out on top, even if it felt impossible," she said gently.

A shaky laugh escaped Aubrey. "Well, I'm glad you were so sure, because I was full of doubts." She opened her arms eagerly, drawing Willow and Charly into a tight embrace. "Love you guys," she murmured.

"Love you too," they replied in unison.

"Now, I think it's time to celebrate," Aubrey said. "And I've got a new recipe for you to try."

Willow's hands rubbed together. "Oh, goodie," she replied.

Aubrey retreated behind the bar. She measured bourbon into a shaker and mixed in a generous pour of huckleberry syrup, watching as it bled into the whiskey. Finishing off with a gently bruised sprig of sage, she presented a drink that shimmered with hues of purple and gold.

"Alright, cheers to putting the past behind us," Aubrey announced, sliding the glasses across to Willow and Charly, the act of sharing the drink both a celebration and an unspoken confession of vulnerability.

They lifted their glasses in a quiet toast. After the first sip, there was a charged pause.

"Wow," Willow eventually said, eyes alight but also searching. She examined the glass as if expecting the drink to reveal something more. "This is amazing," she noted.

Charly's delighted sound came with a subtle note of awe. "I love it. You're a genius, Aubrey," she said.

"I actually agree with you," Aubrey replied. "This is divine."

At that moment, a middle-aged woman clad in a denim

jacket stepped up to the bar, her curiosity mingling with cautious optimism. "Whatever that is, I'll have one too," she said, nodding toward the sample.

"Coming right up," Aubrey assured her, pouring another glass.

The woman took a sip and exhaled a satisfied sigh. "You gals are onto something here. First time in, but it won't be the last," she remarked warmly.

Aubrey allowed the woman's approval to settle into her chest like a soothing balm. She didn't have Atlanta with its glossy promises, but here, amid the blend of celebration and healing, there was a spark of something deeply sweet too.

Three

The next morning, sweat beaded on Gunner's brow, mingling with the earthy scent of horse and leather that clung to him like a second skin. As he finished cooling down the colt after a long training ride in the indoor arena, his mind wandered to the stage of the last arena he'd played, to the glint of spotlights and the roar of a crowd he feared he'd never hear again. He shoved the thought away, refocusing on the young quarter horse he currently trained for Jaxon's ranch.

He'd grown up riding at the ranch every summer, along with Jaxon and Eli, under Jaxon's father's guidance. Any memory at the ranch was a good one, but it wasn't the life Gunner had imagined for himself. It wasn't filled with music, and the deep ache in his chest wouldn't let him forget that fact.

"Easy there," he murmured, his voice a low rumble as the colt shifted restlessly beneath his touch. "We're done, bud."

With a final pat to the colt's flank, Gunner dismounted

and then gathered the reins and led the horse from the indoor arena to the weathered red barn. The familiar creak of the door brought a wave of nostalgia washing over him, memories of simpler times before fame and addiction had nearly destroyed everything he held dear.

As he stepped inside the barn, the wintery wind battering against the windows, Gunner's eyes fell on a familiar figure. Jaxon stood in one of the stalls, adjusting the saddle on the spirited young mare he was training for a lady out in California.

"Good ride?" Jaxon asked.

Gunner nodded. "Uneventful." Which was how Gunner liked his horses. In his youth, he'd loved the horses that had spunk, but after his ATV injury, he couldn't risk getting injured again. "How's the new filly coming along?"

Jaxon chuckled, patting the horse's neck. "She's got too much fire." He glanced over his shoulder and winked. "Just how I like them."

Gunner snorted and began untacking the colt. Even if the ranch didn't fulfill him like playing arenas did, he knew the value of this place. He swallowed hard, thinking of the countless nights Jaxon and Eli had sat with him through the shakes and sweats of withdrawal after he'd come home, washed up and a full-blown addict. They'd never judged, only supported.

"Listen, Jax," Gunner began, his voice rougher with emotion than he intended. "I'm going to mentor some of the local kids for an afterschool music program that ends in a talent show."

Jaxon left the stall, locking it behind him. His brow

was drawn, likely in response to the emotion Gunner had failed to hide. "Yeah? That's great, man."

Gunner set the saddle down on the rack. "It's good, for sure, but it will cut into my training time. The talent show is a month away, and word on the street is that practice will be in the afternoons after the kids get done school."

Jaxon paused, his head cocking. "You've got three horses in your roster right now?"

Gunner nodded. "This colt is nearly ready to be sold. The other two are just getting started."

"All right," Jaxon said. "I'll give Decker the other two you're starting, just keep finishing this guy. A morning ride is doable?"

"Yup," Gunner agreed. "Thanks for this. This music program… I know it sounds like a small thing, but it feels like it's the right thing to do."

He couldn't help but think about how far he'd come. For the past two years, he'd done the work. He went to rehab and got the pills out of his system. He continued therapy after that. He kept in contact with his sponsor if he felt his mood shift. But this felt like something *new*. Something that he needed to do. From the depths of addiction to standing here, ready to give back to the community that had supported him through his darkest times.

Jaxon gave a firm nod, his eyes full of understanding. "I get it. And I think it's a great idea. This town's always been about community, and what you're doing? That's the heart of it right there." He hesitated for a moment, considering, then added, "Listen, if you need any help with the show, I'd be happy to pitch in. Maybe donate some guitars or other instruments if the kids need 'em."

Gunner felt a rush of gratitude wash over him. "That's generous of you. I'm sure the kids would appreciate it."

"Just keep doing what you're doing," Jaxon replied with an easy smile. "These kids need someone like you to look up to, someone who's been through the fire and come out stronger on the other side."

As Gunner stood there, surrounded by the familiar scents of hay and leather, he felt a sense of purpose settling over him. It wasn't the roar of a stadium crowd or the thrill of a hit song, but somehow, it felt even more meaningful. This was his chance to make a real difference, one kid at a time.

And that felt better than drowning in his own damn misery.

Leading his horse down the aisle, Gunner approached Jaxon and clapped him on the shoulder. "Thanks again."

Jaxon just smiled and went back into the mare's stall.

With all that settled, Gunner returned his focus to his horse and brought him back out to pasture, stepping into the late morning sun. Once he'd closed the gate and watched the colt gallop toward the other horses at the hay bale, he turned toward his truck. He squinted, adjusting to the brightness of the snow.

As he approached his truck, he caught sight of Eli leading a chestnut mare in the nearby paddock. Eli had been a professional bull rider until he'd lost his sister and moved back home, but now he coached young bull riders, also training a horse or two for Jaxon when time allowed.

"Heading out?" Eli called.

Gunner raised a hand in acknowledgment. "Yeah, going into town for a bit."

"Bring me back a coffee?"

"Will do." Gunner climbed into his truck, the familiar creak of the door a comfort to his ears.

As he pulled away from the ranch, snow kicking up behind his wheels, his mind wandered. The drive into town was as familiar as an old song, every bend in the road etched into his memory. But as he entered the rustic town square of Timber Falls, his heart rate picked up.

The Naked Moose came into view, its sleek black modern windows a silent reminder that it was still hours from opening. Gunner's grip tightened on the steering wheel as memories flooded his senses. *Aubrey.* That week in Atlanta. Every touch, every whisper, every breathless moment came rushing back.

"Damn," he muttered, pulling to a stop at the red light directly in front of the bar. His eyes traced the outline of the old stone building, imagining Aubrey inside, her blond waves catching the light as she moved with purpose behind the bar.

"It was her," he whispered to himself, the confession hanging in the air of his truck cab. Occasionally, he questioned whether the fog from his pill addiction might have caused him to mistake her identity… He shook his head and said to himself, "I'd know those blue eyes and smile anywhere."

The light turned green, but Gunner hesitated, his foot hovering over the gas pedal. Part of him wanted to wait, to march into that bar the moment it opened and confront

Aubrey…*again*. But he knew better. This wasn't a country song where grand gestures always paid off. This was real life, and Aubrey was as complex and guarded as they came.

With a sigh, he pressed the gas, leaving The Naked Moose behind. But as he drove on, the memory of Aubrey lingered, as intoxicating as the pills he'd sworn off. His mind raced as he navigated the familiar streets of his hometown. The upcoming wedding of Jaxon and Charly loomed in his thoughts—a perfect opportunity disguised as a celebration. Aubrey couldn't avoid him then.

On the edge of town, he pulled into the community center parking lot and cut the engine with a decisive twist. The faded brick building stood before him, a far cry from the glittering stages he'd once commanded.

He climbed out of his truck and strode through the double doors, the scent of lemon cleaner and musty books hitting him like a wave. A whirlwind of activity greeted him, centered around a petite woman with wild, graying curls.

"Mr. Woods!" she exclaimed, rushing over with outstretched hands. "I'm Margaret, the coordinator. We're absolutely thrilled to have you on board!"

Gunner clasped her hand. "Ma'am, the pleasure's all mine. These kids deserve a chance to shine."

Margaret beamed, her words tumbling out in a breathless rush. "Oh, they'll be over the moon! A real country star, right here in our little town. Now, about instruments…"

"Actually," Gunner interjected smoothly, "Jaxon Reed from Timber Falls Ranch offered to donate some instruments. Figured it might help."

Margaret's eyes widened, her already frenetic energy

kicking into overdrive. "Donated instruments? Oh, that's marvelous." She waved him to follow her toward a cluttered bulletin board, gesturing at a wrinkled sheet of paper pinned haphazardly among flyers and schedules. "This is our practice schedule. Take a look."

Gunner ambled over, his eyes scanning the list of names. Some familiar, some not. His gaze caught on "Emily Winters, age 8, working on singing 'Jolene'," and he felt a smile tug at his lips at her great song choice.

"Five times a week, huh?" he mused, running a calloused finger down the timetable. "That's a commitment."

"Is it too much?" Margaret's brow furrowed. "We can always adjust—"

"No, ma'am," Gunner interrupted, his voice gentle but firm. "It's perfect. These kids deserve our best."

As he stood there, studying the names of children he'd soon be mentoring, a surreal wave washed over him. How had he ended up here? Just two years ago, he'd been chasing his next hit—both on stage and off. Now he was volunteering at his hometown's afterschool music program, his mind filled with thoughts not of fame, but of giving back.

And of Aubrey. Always Aubrey.

Margaret patted his arm. "They sure do, honey."

Gunner squared his shoulders, pushing thoughts of his past—the highs, the lows, the stage lights and the darkness—to the back of his mind. *One step at a time, Woods*, he reminded himself. *You've got songs to teach, a girl to win over, and a whole lot of making up to do.* He turned to Margaret again. "Alright, Margaret," he said, flashing that trademark grin. "Where do we start?"

★ ★ ★

Later that afternoon, the bell above the door chimed as Aubrey stepped into Rustic Romance, the quaint wedding planning boutique nestled between a charming bookstore and a cozy café on Timber Falls' Main Street. The scent of lavender and fresh flowers wafted through the air, mingling with the aroma of vanilla candles. Charly and Willow followed close behind, their eyes widening at the elegant displays of wedding invitations, centerpieces and delicate lace samples adorning the walls.

"Welcome, ladies." A petite woman with curly red hair bounded toward them, her emerald eyes sparkling with enthusiasm. "I'm Poppy, and you must be the bride-to-be." She extended her hand to Charly, who blushed and nodded.

Aubrey felt a twinge of envy as she watched her friend's face light up. She pushed the feeling aside, reminding herself that she was there to support Charly, not dwell on her own romantic shortcomings and how literally far away from getting married she was.

Those were dreams of the past. After her father's abandonment, her failed relationships and Chef Bisset, she was just over men alltogether.

"It's so wonderful to meet you, Poppy," Charly said, her voice warm with excitement. "These are my best friends, Aubrey and Willow."

Poppy clapped her hands together. "Oh, my goodness, I'm just thrilled to bits! Planning a wedding for one of Timber Falls' famous families. It's like a dream come true!"

Aubrey couldn't help but raise an eyebrow. "Famous family?"

Poppy laughed, a tinkling sound that filled the shop. "The Reed family is practically royalty around here. Everyone's been waiting for years to see which lucky lady would finally snag Jaxon's heart."

Charly's cheeks flushed an even deeper shade of pink.

"So, Poppy," said Aubrey, her voice perhaps a touch too bright, "what kind of ideas did you have in mind for Charly and Jaxon's big day?"

Poppy's eyes lit up at Aubrey's question. "I'm so glad you asked. I think holding the ceremony at the Timber Falls Ranch in May like you've suggested would be absolutely perfect. Can't you just picture it?" She gestured expansively, her enthusiasm infectious. "The wide-open sky, the rolling hills and that gorgeous old barn as a backdrop. It's like something straight out of a Hallmark movie."

Charly's eyes widened, a dreamy smile spreading across her face. "That does sound beautiful," she admitted softly.

Poppy bustled over to a bookshelf laden with thick binders. "Let me show you some ideas," she called over her shoulder, pulling out several books. "I'm thinking maybe a blend of rustic charm and elegant touches. String lights, mason jars—but with some glam accents to really make it pop."

As Poppy flipped through the pages, pointing out various designs, Aubrey found her attention wandering. Her gaze drifted to the window, the quaint Main Street of Timber Falls visible beyond. It was so different from the bustling cityscape she'd left behind in Atlanta. Willow and Charly had adjusted so well to small-town living, but Aubrey still felt like she'd left her dreams behind in the big city. She missed the sounds, the people, how alive the city was. In Timber Falls, everything was so slow—and a little boring if she was honest with herself.

Poppy's voice cut through Aubrey's reverie. "Oh! Speaking of Timber Falls Ranch, you all must know Gunner Woods then? Now there's another hot commodity!" She leaned in and waggled her eyebrows. "Any of you ladies know if he's single? I mean, a voice like that, those soulful blue eyes…"

Aubrey's stomach clenched, her fingers gripping the edge of her chair. "I wouldn't know," she said, her voice tight. She could feel Willow's questioning gaze on her, but she kept her eyes fixed on the wedding designs spread before them.

"Really?" Poppy pressed, oblivious to Aubrey's discomfort. "I thought you're all friends, no?"

Aubrey's mind raced, memories of their week together threatening to overwhelm her. The warmth of Gunner's touch, the intensity in his eyes, the bitter sting of waking up alone… She swallowed hard, forcing a neutral expression. "We don't exactly swap relationship stories," she managed, hoping her voice sounded steadier than she felt.

"Well, if he's available, maybe I'll have to stop by The Naked Moose myself," Poppy said with a wink. "A girl can dream, right?"

Aubrey bit the inside of her cheek, tasting blood. She wanted to scream, to tell Poppy that Gunner wasn't worth her time, that he'd break her heart without a second thought. Instead—because where in hell had this jealously come from?—she forced a tight smile. "I'm sure he'd be flattered," she said, her voice dripping with barely concealed sarcasm.

Charly, sensing the tension, cleared her throat. "So, Poppy, about those spring wedding ideas…"

"Oh, yes," Poppy said, and got to sharing her ideas.

After she was done, Poppy handed over the books and added, "I do think a spring wedding is totally doable. Just browse through these binders and discuss with Jaxon what theme you're leaning toward."

"I can do that," Charly said, rising from her seat. "Thank you so much, Poppy."

"Good," Poppy said. "The most important thing at this point is choosing a caterer. Since we're on a tight schedule, I'll call around today and get you a few tastings. Can you do tomorrow?"

"Yes, tomorrow morning," Charly said.

"Goodie," Poppy said. "I'll send that list over to you tonight."

As they gathered their things, Aubrey took a deep breath, reeling in her emotions. She'd have to do better if she was going to survive this wedding—and Gunner's presence in Timber Falls.

Once they all said their goodbyes to Poppy, the bell above the door chimed as Aubrey stepped out onto the snow-covered sidewalk. She inhaled deeply, the crisp mountain air helping to clear her head. But the reprieve was short-lived.

Charly's gentle voice broke the silence as she turned to face Aubrey. "What in the world is going on with you?"

she asked. "You looked like you were about to combust in there every time Gunner's name came up."

Aubrey's stomach clenched. She forced a laugh, but it sounded hollow even to her own ears. "It's nothing."

Willow nibbled her lip, glancing down.

Charly's eyes narrowed, her arms folding across her chest. "Bull. I've seen you handle a kitchen full of demanding customers without breaking a sweat. This is about him, isn't it?"

Aubrey's fingers tightened around the strap of her purse. She glanced around, relieved to see the street was relatively empty. "Can we not do this here?"

"Tell me what is going on, Aubrey," Charly insisted. She set her gaze on Willow. "What do you two know that I don't? Stop keeping secrets. We *never* do that."

Aubrey took a deep breath, her eyes darting between her friends. There was no avoiding this anymore. The words tumbled out in a rush. "We had an incredible week together a couple years ago after one of his concerts." Her cheeks burned with the admission.

Charly's eyes widened, but she remained silent, waiting for Aubrey to continue.

"Willow heard Gunner and I talking about it, so that's why she knows about it," Aubrey explained.

"Well, to be exact," Willow interjected quietly. "I heard Gunner talking about it, and you denying that it was you that was with him for that week."

"I thought we had something special." Aubrey's voice cracked. "But then he left one morning. I woke up alone, and he was gone. No note, no explanation. Nothing." She swallowed hard, fighting back the sting of tears. "And that's all I need to know about Gunner Woods."

Willow's face darkened with anger, but Charly's expression remained thoughtful. "Oh, Aubrey," Charly said softly, squeezing Aubrey's hand. "I'm so sorry."

Aubrey shook her head, swallowing back the emotion. "There's nothing to be sorry about. It happened. He showed me how he treats a woman in a relationship, and because of that, I refuse to let him in again."

Charly nodded, her eyes filled with understanding. "Of course, I can understand that. Hell, I'm a bit surprised how nice you've been to him."

Aubrey shrugged. "At this point, he's not even sure it was me, because he likely wasn't even sober then. It's just better if we let this be. I can forget all about it. I've moved on, and I'm mature enough to be friendly with him."

"I totally get not wanting to open that door again," Willow said softly.

Snow began falling in big flakes as Charly cocked her head. "Would you be okay working alongside him on wedding things?"

Aubrey straightened her shoulders, forcing a smile that she was sure didn't quite reach her eyes. "Like I said, don't worry about me, Char. I can handle Gunner Woods. And I can certainly be just friends with him. It's ancient history."

But as she said the words, Aubrey couldn't quite silence the small voice in her heart that whispered, *Liar.*

Four

Long after the dinner rush had ended, the bar hummed with anticipation. Surrounding her, a handful of early customers lounged on the plush leather stools, nursing the Smirking Ballerina cocktail she'd created as this week's feature.

She strode forward, a tray of beers in her hands, her heart quickening as she approached the stage where Gunner and his band were setting up for tonight's performance. His presence still affected her, no matter how much she tried to deny it, and that just annoyed her to hell.

"Here you go, boys," she said, distributing the drinks to the band members. Her voice caught as she turned to Gunner, extending a cold beer. "And for you." She'd used to hesitate to hand him a beer, knowing his struggle with past addiction. But his vice wasn't booze, it was pills. Once she knew that, she treated him like everyone else, knowing she'd want the same if it were her.

Gunner's fingers brushed hers as he took the bottle,

sending a jolt through her. "Thanks, darlin'," he drawled, his blue eyes all but smoldering. "Appreciate it."

Aubrey forced a smile, trying to ignore the way his low voice made her knees weak. "Just doing my job," she told him, which only made him grin.

As she turned to leave, a man who appeared to be in his fifties approached. He had graying hair, round glasses and kind brown eyes that exuded warmth.

Gunner said, "Tom, it's so good to see you, man."

"Back at you," Tom said, and the two men hugged.

When Tom leaned away, he held on to Gunner's shoulders. "Things good?" he asked gently.

Gunner hesitated and then nodded. "Yeah, I'm good."

Aubrey's curiosity piqued at his long pause. She busied herself with wiping down a nearby table, straining to hear.

"I'm feeling good," Gunner continued. "I'm staying strong and keeping up with the physical therapy to keep the pain away."

Realization dawned on Aubrey. This must be Gunner's substance abuse counselor. She felt a twinge of guilt for eavesdropping but couldn't bring herself to walk away. She knew his past addiction must always weigh on him, but hearing the vulnerability in his voice made it all too real. She wanted to go to him, to offer comfort, but she held back. Getting close to Gunner was dangerous territory. Her fingers trembled slightly as she continued to wipe down another table, her ears still attuned to Gunner's conversation.

"I've been writing again," said Gunner, his voice tinged

with cautious hope. "It's helping, you know? Channeling all those feelings into something positive."

Tom responded warmly. "That's fantastic, Gunner. Music has always been your lifeline."

Aubrey's breath caught in her throat. She'd heard Gunner's songs before, but now she understood the depth of emotion behind them. Her eyes flickered to his strong hands as they absently strummed his guitar, wondering how many demons those fingers had battled.

"It's hard when the past creeps up," Gunner admitted, his shoulders sagging slightly. "Especially when I think about how I've let people down."

The raw honesty in his voice made Aubrey's heart clench. She found herself wanting to reach out, to tell him he hadn't let her down. But the memory of their one passionate week and the complications it brought stopped her cold. She couldn't risk being hurt at the expense of anyone else anymore.

Tom patted him on the shoulder. "You're doing the work, Gunner. That's what matters."

As the conversation wound down, Aubrey retreated behind the bar, her mind a whirlwind. She'd been so determined to keep Gunner at arm's length, to protect herself from the intensity of her feelings for him. But now, with more of a glimpse into the battles he fought daily, she felt her resolve weakening.

"Dammit," she muttered, closing her eyes briefly. How could she reconcile her growing empathy for Gunner with her need for self-preservation? The urge to comfort him warred with her instinct to maintain distance.

Gunner's rich laugh drifted across the room, and Aubrey's eyes snapped open, drawn to him like a magnet. Their gazes locked for a moment, and she saw a flicker of vulnerability beneath his easy smile.

"Get it together, Hale," she muttered to herself, tearing her gaze away only to have it drawn back moments later when Tom headed back to the table he sat at with two companions.

She watched Gunner from across the room as he sat on a stool on the stage, guitar cradled in his lap, those strong, calloused hands fine-tuning the strings with a tenderness that made her breath catch.

Why was this all so damn confusing?

Following Aubrey's line of sight, Willow sidled up next to her, polishing a whiskey glass. "He's really come a long way from that YouTube video we saw, hasn't he?" she said, a note of pride in her voice.

Aubrey swallowed hard, nodding. "Yeah, seems like it." The video was the very last show he'd done a couple years ago. He was out of his mind high and aggressive and smashed his guitar on the stage before storming off.

"I mean, look at him up there," Willow continued, oblivious to Aubrey's internal struggle. "Focused, sober, ready to perform. It's just awesome."

"Mmm-hmm," Aubrey hummed, desperately searching for a change of subject. Her eyes landed on the cocktail menu. "So, about those new featured drinks we're rolling out this weekend…"

Willow raised an eyebrow, clearly catching on to Aubrey's deflection. "Right, the cocktails. What've you got in mind?"

As Aubrey launched into a description of her latest concoction, which she'd named Rose Kiss, she couldn't help but steal another glance at Gunner. Their eyes met briefly, and she felt that familiar pull, the one she'd been fighting since that first night his eyes met hers in Atlanta. She clenched her jaw, determination warring with desire.

But then her heart skipped a beat as a petite redhead entered the bar and sauntered up to the stage, her eyes fixed on Gunner like a lioness stalking her prey. Poppy's form-fitting dress and stride screamed confidence.

"Well, hello there, handsome," Poppy purred, leaning against the stage. "You must be the famous Gunner Woods I've heard so much about."

Gunner's eyes crinkled as he flashed that heart-stopping smile. "Guilty as charged," he said, setting his guitar aside. "And you are?"

"Poppy, Charly's wedding planner." She twirled a strand of hair around her finger. "Which means we'll be spending a whole lot of time together soon."

Aubrey's grip tightened on the glass she was polishing, her knuckles turning white. She tried to look away, but her eyes kept darting back to the scene unfolding before her.

"Is that so?" Gunner replied, his voice a low rumble that sent shivers down Aubrey's spine. "I've heard you do some amazing work."

Poppy gave a sensual smile. "I can do many amazing things."

Gunner raised an eyebrow in response.

Unable to bear another second, Aubrey slammed the glass down and stormed past Willow into the kitchen. Her chest heaved as she braced herself against the cool metal countertop, trying to regain her composure.

"Get it together, Aubrey," she muttered, closing her eyes. "He's not yours. He was never yours."

The kitchen door swung open, and Aubrey's eyes snapped open to find Gunner standing there, amusement etched across his face, causing her sudden glare.

"You okay, darlin'?" he asked, taking a cautious step forward, his voice laced with concern.

Aubrey straightened, folding her arms across her chest defensively. "I'm fine. Shouldn't you be out there entertaining your new friend?" Her words were sharp, but her eyes betrayed a flicker of something deeper.

Gunner's eyebrows arched in amusement, a knowing smirk dancing at the corners of his lips. "Now, now. Is that jealousy I detect in your voice?" he teased, his tone light yet probing.

"You wish," Aubrey retorted with a scoff, though even she could hear the wavering in her own voice, a lack of conviction that belied her true feelings.

He moved in closer, the space between them charged with an almost palpable tension. "There's nothing out there I want," he murmured softly, his voice a gentle caress. "What I want is right here."

Aubrey's breath hitched, caught in her throat, her resolve melting under the intensity of his steady gaze. "Gunner, I..." she started, her words faltering as the air around them crackled with an electric, fragile anticipation.

Gunner's eyes sparkled with playful mischief as he leaned in, his proximity wrapping her in the warmth of his presence. His voice dropped to a teasing, low drawl. "It's alright, sweetheart. If it bugs you to see me talkin' to other women, you can just say so." He grinned, his smile turning devilish. "Hell, I'd be lyin' if I said it wouldn't bother me to see you with someone else."

Aubrey's cheeks flared with heat, a blush creeping across her skin. "I am not jealous," she insisted with a hiss, even as her heart raced traitorously within her chest, betraying her words.

"Sure, darlin'." Gunner chuckled, his gaze lingering on her face, tracing every bit of her features. "Whatever you say."

She turned away abruptly, her fingers busying themselves with the task of organizing the bottles on the closest shelf, a futile attempt ease the emotions inside her. "Don't you have a show to prepare for?" she mumbled, her voice a little steadier now.

The muted sounds of the bar began to seep through the kitchen door—the excited chatter of the crowd gathering for Gunner's set.

His eyes flicked toward the noise for a brief moment before returning to Aubrey, his expression softening. "You're right," he said quietly, his voice filled with a promise. "But this conversation ain't over, Aubrey. Not by a long shot."

Once he'd left, Aubrey allowed herself a moment to breathe. She could hear the crowd growing restless, their energy palpable even from the kitchen. Steeling herself, she pushed through the swinging door, back into the main bar area.

The Naked Moose was beginning to become alive with electricity. More people were arriving to put their work-week behind them. Aubrey's gaze went straight to Gunner, his presence magnetic as he adjusted his guitar strap and stepped in front of the microphone, his band ready behind him. Then her focus went to Poppy, all but drooling on his shoes, and she rolled her eyes, heading toward Charly and Willow behind the bar. She had work to do, and she wasn't going to let some country singer distract her, no matter how much those sexy, smoldering blue eyes drew her in.

Five

After the school day ended for the children the following afternoon, Gunner had already completed his physical therapy routine for his leg and put in his training ride in the morning, when he swung the double doors of the community center open, flooding the dim hallway with late afternoon sunlight. The schedule was slightly demanding with the daily volunteering during the week, but there were quite a few kids to mentor, and Gunner needed the distraction. His mind had been on Aubrey all morning—and that small shift he felt between them last night. Her jealously had been rich in the air, and he got it. He would have had an issue with any guy drooling all over her. A crack in her resolve had formed, and he wouldn't miss his chance to fill that space with the million apologies he owed her until she stopped keeping him out. As he entered the community center —a single expansive room with a stage and a small kitchen to one side—his worn cowboy boots echoed on the linoleum floor.

"Gunner, hello," Margaret called. "Please come meet the kiddos."

"Hi, y'all!" Gunner called out. "Hope I ain't too late to join this little hoedown."

While Margaret hurried off to wrangle some more of the children up, a chorus of excited squeals erupted as a swarm of children rushed toward him, their faces beaming with unbridled joy. Gunner's heart swelled, and damn, did this feel good, the idea of giving back to the community that had given him a great home.

"Gunner! Gunner!" A freckle-faced boy tugged at his sleeve. "Will you sing for us? Pretty please?"

Gunner chuckled, ruffling the boy's hair. "Now, hold your horses there, partner. We've got plenty of time for singing. First, let's see what kinda talent we've got brewin' in this room."

As he scanned the bustling space, his gaze settled on a small figure hovering at the edge of the stage. A young girl, no more than twelve, clutched a wrinkled sheet of paper to her chest like a shield. Her wide eyes darted around the room, never settling on one spot for more than a heartbeat.

"Give me just a minute," he told the boy, noticing the guitar near him. "Get warmed up and I'll be right back."

Gunner's chest tightened. Lord, if that wasn't the spitting image of him at his first county fair. He remembered all too well the debilitating fear, the cotton-dry mouth, the legs that felt like they might give out at any moment.

He started toward her, his mind racing. *How do I put her at ease without scaring her off?* The last thing he wanted was to overwhelm the poor thing. As he approached, he noticed her knuckles were white from gripping the paper so tightly.

"Hey there," he said softly, crouching down to her eye level. "What's your name?"

The girl's eyes snapped to his face, a flicker of recognition passing over her features. "Emily," she barely whispered.

Gunner's heart ached for her. He understood the prison of stage fright, how it could steal your voice and leave you feeling helpless. But he also knew the indescribable joy of breaking free from those chains.

"Tell you what," he said gently. "Why don't we make a deal? You show me what you've got there, and I'll tell you about the time I fell off stage trying to do the electric slide in cowboy boots."

Emily's shy smile gave Gunner the encouragement he needed. He gestured toward the stage. "C'mon. Let's give that stage a try, shall we?"

As they walked toward the platform, Gunner felt a familiar tightness in his chest. The spotlight, even when dim, had a way of bringing back memories—both exhilarating and terrifying.

"Alright," he said. "First things first—let's take a deep breath together." He demonstrated, filling his lungs slowly and exhaling. Emily mimicked him, her shoulders relaxing slightly.

Gunner smiled. "That's it. Now, I'm gonna tell you something I've never told anyone else." He paused, making sure he had her full attention. "You know, the first time I performed at the Grand Ole Opry, I was so scared I nearly threw up on my boots."

Emily's eyes widened, surprise and curiosity replacing some of the fear. "Really?" she whispered.

"Really." Gunner chuckled, placing his hand over his heart. "I was shaking like a leaf in a tornado. But you know what? I closed my eyes, thought about why I love music, and just…let it flow. Sometimes," he continued, his voice thick with emotion, "the bravest thing you can do is just show up and be yourself."

Emily nodded and then she took a hesitant step forward. The wooden stage creaked beneath her feet, and she flinched.

Gunner felt a surge of protectiveness wash over him. "You're doin' great," he murmured, his eyes locked on hers. "Let's try a little warm-up, alright? Just you and me."

He guided her through a simple vocal exercise, his rich baritone filling the air. "Just like that," he encouraged, watching as Emily's lips parted, her voice barely audible at first.

As they continued, Gunner couldn't help but marvel at the raw talent hidden beneath her shyness. It reminded him of a young songbird, wings trembling on the edge of flight. He'd been there once, teetering between fear and dreams.

"That's it, Emily," he said, his voice warm with pride. "Now, let's try your song. Don't worry about being perfect, just feel the music."

Emily's fingers tightened around her sheet music as she began to sing, her voice a mere whisper. Gunner leaned in, harmonizing softly, creating a cocoon of sound around them.

"You've got this," he whispered between verses.

As Emily's voice grew stronger, Gunner felt a spark of something he hadn't experienced in years—pure, unadulterated joy in the music. He pushed aside thoughts of his faded career, focusing instead on nurturing the fragile confidence blooming before him.

As the music drifted away, Gunner smiled, seeing her looking much more relaxed. "You did really great, Emily. Take five, and we'll pick up where we left off." A break always helped him after facing something that scared him.

He stepped off the stage, running a hand through his hair. That's when he noticed her—a familiar woman standing off to the side, her gaze fixed on Emily with a mixture of pride and worry etched across her face. "Sarah?" She'd been in the same high school, but a couple years ahead of him.

"Hey," she said with a warm smile. "I see you met my daughter, Emily. I can't thank you enough for what you're doing."

Gunner's lips quirked into a gentle smile. "It's my pleasure. Emily's got a real gift."

Sarah's eyes clouded with concern. "That's just it. She's so talented, but her confidence…" She trailed off, glancing at her daughter.

A familiar ache bloomed in Gunner's chest. He knew all too well the weight of expectations and self-doubt. "I understand," he said softly. "Truth is, I've been where Emily is. Scared to let my voice be heard." He paused, memories of his own struggles with addiction and fame flashing through his mind. "But I promise you, I'm gonna do everything I can to help her find her voice."

Sarah's eyes welled with tears. "You don't know what that means to us."

Gunner placed a reassuring hand on her shoulder. "I'll work with her one-on-one, if that's alright. Sometimes, all it takes is someone believing in you to make all the difference. We'll get her feeling great going into the talent show."

As Sarah nodded gratefully, Gunner felt a surge of determination. This wasn't just about mentoring anymore. It was about redemption—for Emily, and maybe, just maybe, for himself too.

After he grabbed a glass of water, he strode back onto the stage, his boots echoing against the worn floorboards. He surveyed the group of young hopefuls before him. Emily stood at the edge, still clutching her sheet music like a lifeline. He gave her the glass of water and then focused back on the group.

"Alright, y'all," Gunner said, clapping his hands together. "Time to shake things up a bit. We're going to have ourselves a little hoedown."

He caught Emily's startled gaze and winked. "Don't you worry. This ain't about perfect pitch. It's about feeling the music in your bones." He started a slow, steady clap, the rhythm pulsing through the community center. "C'mon now, everybody join in. Let's get this party started!"

As the other kids enthusiastically followed his lead, Gunner noticed Emily's hesitation. He moved closer, never breaking the rhythm. "Just like that, Emily. Feel it in your feet first. Let it climb up through your body."

Emily's foot began to tap tentatively. Gunner grinned, thinking, *That's it. Baby steps.*

"Now, let's add some vocals," he called out. "Don't worry about the words. Just let out whatever sound feels right."

Emily's lips parted, a barely audible hum escaping. Gunner's heart swelled with pride. He'd coaxed that same tentative sound from his own throat years ago, in a dingy Nashville bar, where he'd first dared to dream of stardom.

As the session progressed, Gunner watched Emily closely. Her voice, initially a whisper, began to gain strength. The tightness in her shoulders eased, and a hint of a smile played at the corners of her mouth.

"That's it, Emily!" Gunner encouraged. "You're finding your groove. Remember how this feels."

He thought back to his own mentors—especially his grandfather—the ones who'd believed in him before the fame, before the fall. *I owe it to them to pay it forward*, he mused, a bittersweet pang in his chest.

The closing notes of the group performance faded, leaving a buzzing energy in the air. Gunner's heart swelled with pride as he surveyed the beaming faces of the young performers. His gaze settled on Emily, her eyes bright with newfound confidence.

"Alright, y'all," he called, his voice carrying across the room. "That's a great start for today. We'll break things down to individual sessions starting tomorrow."

Laughter filled the space as the kids began leaving the stage.

Gunner watched as Emily and her mother gathered their

belongings, the little girl's eyes still sparkling with excitement. He sauntered over, his boots clicking against the polished floor of the community center.

"Heading out?" he asked with a smile.

Sarah nodded, her hand resting protectively on her daughter's shoulder. "We are. Thank you so much. This meant the world to Emily."

Gunner tipped his cowboy hat. "The pleasure's all mine." He crouched down to Emily's level, his voice softening. "You keep practicing those exercises we talked about, alright? I expect to hear that beautiful voice of yours even stronger next time."

Emily nodded shyly. "I will. Promise."

As they turned to leave, Gunner called out, "See y'all tomorrow." He watched them go, Emily's small hand in her mother's, and he smiled.

Well, I'll be damned, he thought, running a hand through his hair. *This feels better than any standing ovation I've ever had.*

The next morning, Aubrey exhaled deeply, feeling the last traces of tension melt away as she rolled up her yoga mat. The warmth from the heated room clung to her skin, a comforting embrace after the intense session. She caught her reflection in the full-length mirror, noticing the healthy flush in her cheeks and the serene gleam in her eyes.

"Thanks for the class, Deb," Aubrey said. "I needed this today."

Deb smiled warmly. "Glad you could make it. See you next time."

After saying her goodbyes to the other attendees of her weekly hot yoga class, Aubrey left the living room-turned-gym and stepped out into the refreshing air. The coolness provided a much-needed relief for her overheated skin.

Sliding into her car, she cranked up the heat and began the drive back to the farmhouse. The winding country roads stretched before her, endless fields of snow-dusted grass on either side. She gripped the steering wheel tightly, her peaceful mood from yoga slowly evaporating.

As the old farmhouse came into view, Aubrey felt her stomach clench. The flowered wallpaper and creaky porch were a far cry from her sleek Atlanta condo. She parked and sat for a moment, staring at the house that she, Charly and Willow had renovated from top to bottom. But both Charly and Willow had wanted to keep the farmhouse as close to its original state as possible. Aubrey would have gutted it and replaced everything old with modern luxuries.

The thought of Willow potentially moving in with Eli down the road sent a conflicting wave of emotions through her. On one hand, she would miss living with Willow. She'd already lost Charly, who moved in with Jaxon at the ranch. On the other, it meant she might finally have a chance to move into town and get out of these dusty country roads where she simply didn't fit in.

"It's just temporary," she reminded herself, trying to summon some of the calm from her yoga session. "Soon, you'll be back in civilization."

But even as she said the words, a small voice in the back of her mind whispered that maybe, just maybe, Timber

Falls would never feel like home. Which was simply terrifying, since it was all she had.

She quickly squashed that overwhelming thought, grabbing her yoga mat and heading inside. She had a busy day ahead, and dwelling on her conflicted feelings about this place wouldn't do her any good.

When she pushed open the farmhouse door, the familiar creak accompanied her entrance. She made a beeline for the kitchen, her throat parched. As she reached for a glass, the sound of footsteps made her turn.

"Hey there, hot stuff," Willow greeted, her wavy hair catching the morning light as she entered. "How was yoga?"

Aubrey poured herself some orange juice and took a long sip, savoring the tart sweetness. "Sweaty. Intense. Exactly what I needed."

Willow leaned against the counter, her eyes twinkling. "Well, hope you're ready for more intensity. Charly's picking us up in forty-five for the caterer tastings."

"Sounds good," Aubrey said. "Any idea what we're in for?"

"Knowing Charly? Probably enough food to feed half of Timber Falls." Willow chuckled. "Oh, and don't forget your discerning palate. We're counting on those chef skills of yours."

Aubrey felt a familiar pang at the mention of her former career. "I'll do my best," she said, forcing a smile. "Better go get ready then."

"Be quick," Willow said, moving to fix herself a coffee.

As Aubrey headed to her room, her mind drifted to the

potential sale of the farmhouse. The extra cash could help her find a place in town, somewhere that didn't constantly remind her of how far she'd fallen from her old life.

Standing before her closet, Aubrey surveyed her options. "Practical, but stylish," she muttered, pulling out a pair of dark-wash jeans and a soft, cream-colored sweater. She added a statement necklace and ankle boots.

Once she'd showered and finished getting ready, she caught her reflection in the mirror. The woman staring back at her looked…*different*. Just nothing like the dream-chasing woman from Atlanta. Harder. Lost. So damn confused.

She reached up, smoothing the lines between her eyes away. She glanced to her lips, missing her smile that used to come so easy. She stared into her dark gaze again and saw each and every hurt she'd endured. Her father. Chef Bisset. Boyfriend after boyfriend walking away. And Gunner…the one that hurt most. Because she'd believed him, that he cared, and she was so stupid to have done that. She'd only known him a week.

But the truth was there, written in every hard line of her face. She missed the young girl she'd once been, who didn't know people were so cruel.

Sick of her thoughts, she sauntered back into the kitchen, her heeled boots clicking against the weathered wood floor. The aromas of freshly brewed coffee and toasted bread enveloped her, a comforting contrast to the crisp winter air seeping through the farmhouse's old windows.

Willow stood at the counter, her waves cascading over her shoulders as she spread jam on toast. She glanced up, a warm smile lighting her face. "Just in time. I made us a quick bite."

"You're a lifesaver," Aubrey said, reaching for a mug. "I swear, if I had to face Charly's boundless morning energy on an empty stomach, I might snap."

Willow laughed, the sound rich and genuine. "God forbid we unleash hangry Aubrey on unsuspecting caterers."

Aubrey raised an eyebrow, fighting a grin. "Hey, my discerning palate comes with a price."

As they leaned against the counter, munching on toast and jam and sipping coffee, Aubrey felt a familiar warmth bloom in her chest. As much as Timber Falls didn't feel like home, being with Willow did.

"So," Willow said, "on a scale of one to 'I'd rather eat glass,' how excited are you for today's tasting extravaganza?"

Aubrey snorted. "Let's call it a solid 'mildly intrigued with a side of trepidation.'" She paused, her voice softening. "But honestly? It'll be nice to be around food again. To see someone creating something...special."

Willow reached out, squeezing Aubrey's arm. "You could do more of that at the bar, you know? More than just apps and cocktails. We'd just have to find a way to make it work."

Before Aubrey could retort that it wasn't as easy as Willow suggested, the sound of tires crunching on gravel cut through the quiet morning. Charly's arrival.

"Showtime." Willow grinned and grabbed her coat.

Aubrey took a deep breath, straightening her shoulders. "Let's do this."

As they gathered their things, excitement and apprehension swirled in Aubrey's stomach. She followed Willow to the door, and then stepped outside, her breath forming small clouds as she walked toward Charly's car. But her steps faltered as her eyes landed on an unexpected figure in the passenger seat. Gunner, looking far too comfortable for her liking, flashed her a lazy grin through the window.

"Ugh. Why?" Aubrey muttered under her breath, her eyes narrowing.

As they approached, Charly rolled down her window, her warm eyes sparkling with barely concealed excitement. "Morning, ladies! Hope you don't mind our extra passenger."

Aubrey forced a smile. "Don't mind one bit."

As she slid into the back seat, Gunner turned, his eyes locking with hers. "Hello, darlin'." There was a hint of challenge in his voice.

Aubrey's heart raced, a mix of irritation and something else she refused to name. This day had just gotten a whole lot more complicated.

The car rumbled to life, carrying them through the snow-dusted streets of Timber Falls. Aubrey found herself hyperaware of Gunner's presence in the front seat, his broad shoulders and tousled hair visible just beyond the headrest and beneath his cowboy hat.

"So, Gunner," she said, unable to resist needling him, "I didn't realize wedding planning was part of your...diverse skill set."

He turned, a wry smile playing on his lips. "There's a lot you don't know about me, Aubrey. I'm full of surprises."

Their eyes met briefly, a spark of electricity passing between them. Aubrey quickly looked away, her cheeks warming.

"I'm sure," she muttered, focusing on the passing scenery.

Charly's voice broke the tension. "Aubrey, didn't you mention wanting to try that new fusion place in Deer Point?" Deer Point was a bigger city not too far away.

One Aubrey was wholeheartedly considering moving to after Willow moved out. "Oh, yeah," Aubrey replied, grateful for the distraction. "I heard their Thai-inspired barbecue is to die for."

Gunner chuckled. "Sounds like a culinary identity crisis if you ask me."

Aubrey's eyes narrowed on the back of his head. "And what would you know about culinary innovation, Mr. Beer-and-Pretzels?"

"Hey now," he said, turning to face her again. "I'll have you know I've dined in some of the finest establishments from Nashville to L.A."

Their banter continued, a delicate dance of wit and barely concealed attraction. Aubrey found herself both irritated and intrigued by Gunner's quips, each retort revealing a depth that had snagged her when they'd first met.

As they pulled up to the caterer's, a quaint storefront with Timber Tastes emblazoned on the window, Aubrey's professional instincts kicked in. The aromas of freshly baked bread and simmering spices wafted through the air, instantly transporting her back to her days in Atlanta's bustling kitchens.

"Alright, folks," she said, her voice taking on a no-nonsense tone. "Let's see what they've got."

Stepping inside, they were greeted by a whirlwind of activity. Chefs in crisp white jackets bustled about, putting finishing touches on an array of appetizers and entrees. Aubrey's eyes widened, taking in the vibrant colors and artful presentations.

Charly and Willow were now talking to the caterer, who was instructing them to begin tasting the menu they'd proposed.

"Now this," Aubrey murmured, more to herself than anyone else, "is what I'm talking about." Her fingers itched to grab a tasting fork, to sample the delicate balance of flavors she could already imagine dancing on her tongue. For a moment, she forgot about Gunner, about her complicated feelings towards Timber Falls, about everything except the culinary masterpieces before her.

As she reached for a beautifully plated crostini, she caught Gunner watching her, an unreadable expression on his face. Aubrey broke eye contact first, turning her attention back to the food. She lifted the crostini to her lips, closing her eyes as she savored the blend of flavors.

"Mmm," she hummed appreciatively. "The balance of the goat cheese with the fig compote is perfect."

Gunner leaned in. "I'm more of a meat and potatoes guy myself, but even I can tell this is somethin' special."

Aubrey arched an eyebrow. "Oh? And here I thought your palate was limited to beer and regret."

His lips quirked into a half smile. "Like I keep saying, there's a lot you don't know about me, darlin'."

As they moved through the tasting stations, their banter softened, replaced by genuine discussions about the food. Aubrey found herself surprised by Gunner's insightful comments.

"You know," he said, gesturing to a delicate salmon appetizer, "this would be perfect for the talent show's reception."

Aubrey paused mid-bite. "Talent show? What talent show?"

Gunner's eyes lit up. "The one I'm helping mentor for some of the local kids. It's for an afterschool music program that ends in a talent show."

"You're mentoring an afterschool music program?" Aubrey couldn't keep the surprise from her voice.

He nodded, a hint of pride in his voice. "Figured I might as well put my experience to good use."

Aubrey felt something shift inside her. Her image of Gunner as just another egotistical, self-absorbed musician was beginning to crack. "That's...actually really great, Gunner."

He shrugged, but she could see the pleasure in his eyes. "These kids have real talent. They just need someone to point them in the right direction. Feels good to give back to the community that's been so kind to me."

As they continued tasting, Aubrey found herself sneaking glances at Gunner while eating the rich chocolate torte, seeing him in a new light. She thought, *This is the Gunner I knew...* The kind man. Not the rebel the tabloids talked about who broke guitars and went through women like used socks. Not the man who walked out on her. The man she had spent an unforgettable week with. She'd liked this man. *A lot*, her heart reminded her.

At her silence, he raised an eyebrow at her. "Got something on your mind?"

She shook her head. "Just how dang good this torte is."

A warm smile swept across his face. "I can't argue with you on that."

Six

The snow-covered long grass went by in a blur as Gunner, sitting in the passenger seat next to Charly, pulled up to Timber Falls Ranch after dropping Aubrey and Willow off at the bar. Glancing out the window and spotting some of the mares with their foals out in the field, he smiled to himself, missing the banter with Aubrey already. He'd already gotten a crack to form in her impenetrable walls. Now he just had to smash that wall down entirely.

Once they'd parked at the house, they both stepped out of the car, Charly balancing two takeout containers in her arms. The frigid breeze nipped at Gunner's cheeks, a stark contrast to the warmth of the car.

"Here, let me help." He reached for one of the containers and grinned as he added, "Wouldn't want you dropping the things standing between you and an important decision, now, would we?"

Charly had been giving him that same tense look since he first saw her this morning. "Thanks," she said.

He suddenly realized that Charly probably hadn't been aware of his history with Aubrey before, but for some reason she certainly knew now. He knew he needed to prove himself—not just to Aubrey, but to Charly and Willow as well.

Gunner shut the car door behind him, glancing around the ranch. Cowboys moved with purpose, their breath visible in the cold air as they went about their daily tasks.

Movement caught his eye, and he spotted two familiar figures emerging from the distance. "Look," he said, nudging Charly.

She followed his gaze, her expression softening as she watched the two men approach on horseback. The powerful animals moved with grace through the snow, their own breath creating small clouds in the frigid air. Behind them, the vast herd of horses dotted the landscape.

"Quite a sight, isn't it?" Gunner murmured.

Charly nodded. "It's beautiful," she agreed, watching as Jaxon and Eli drew closer.

When they were only a few feet away, she held up the takeout container, a grin playing on her lips.

"Hey, cowboy," she called out, her voice warm and playful. "I've got a little wedding dilemma that needs your expertise."

Jaxon's eyes twinkled with amusement as he dismounted and then closed the distance between them. "Oh, yeah? And what might that be?" he asked, before dropping a kiss on her lips.

Charly presented the container she held. "Two caterers, both delicious." She gestured toward Gunner's container too. "I just can't decide which one to choose for our big day. You need to break the tie."

As Jaxon reached for the lids, Gunner let out a low chuckle. "Good luck with that. I've been tryin' to help her decide all morning."

Jaxon quirked an eyebrow at Gunner. "And? What's the verdict?"

Gunner shrugged. "Hell if I know. They're both incredible. Might just have to flip a coin on this one."

Charly rolled her eyes. "Some help you are! I thought you'd have a more refined palate, what with all your fancy tours and green rooms."

Gunner chuckled. "When you've lived off gas station burritos and whiskey for months on end, everything else tastes like gourmet."

Charly just shook her head at him and then said to Eli, "You have to help decide too."

Eli's eyes lit up as Charly offered her container to him, and he reached for a sample. "Don't mind if I do," he said, popping a bite into his mouth. His expression morphed from curiosity to pure bliss. "Damn, that's good. Might need another taste to be sure, though."

As Eli eagerly dug into Charly's container, Jaxon chuckled and downed another sample from Gunner's.

"You know," Jaxon mused, "I think I'm partial to Gunner's one."

Eli nodded emphatically, his mouth still full. "Mmm-hmm, that's the winner right there."

Charly threw her hands up in mock exasperation. "Oh,

sure! You guys make it look so easy. I've been agonizing over this all morning."

Jaxon wrapped an arm around her waist, pulling her close. "That's 'cause you overthink everything. Sometimes you just gotta go with your gut."

"Says the man who spent three hours deciding on new cowboy boots last month," Charly retorted, but her eyes danced with affection.

He ignored her and kissed her cheek before she stepped back, laughing, the sound light and carefree. "I'll call Poppy and let her know we've made our choice." She stood on her tiptoes, pressing a quick kiss to Jaxon's lips. "Thanks for the help."

As soon as Charly entered the house, Jaxon turned to Gunner, a suspicious glint in his eyes.

"So, what in the hell is going on?" Jaxon said, holding the reins in his hand as his horse patiently stood waiting. "You gonna tell me the real reason you're suddenly so invested in wedding catering?"

Gunner frowned. "What're you talkin' about? Charly said you wanted me to pitch in and go."

Jaxon chuckled, unconvinced. "Uh-huh. And I suppose Charly just happened to insist on bringing you along for no reason at all? There's something going on here. What is it?"

A muscle twitched in Gunner's jaw. He removed his cowboy hat and ran a hand through his hair. "Look, I'm not quite sure why she wanted me to tag along, but I have a feeling it might be about Aubrey."

"Aubrey?" Jaxon pressed, his tone gentle but persistent. "Why?"

Gunner's shoulders tensed. He could feel Jaxon's knowing gaze boring into him, peeling away the layers of bravado he'd carefully constructed. Part of him wanted to deflect, to throw out a joke and change the subject. But there was something in Jaxon's demeanor—a quiet understanding, free of judgment—that made Gunner's defenses start to crumble.

"Because, I…ah… I'm trying to right a wrong. I…" Gunner began, his voice catching. He cleared his throat, trying again. "I messed up. Bad. And I don't know how to fix it."

Jaxon's expression softened. He clapped a hand on Gunner's shoulder. "Start at the beginning. We're all ears."

Gunner took a deep breath. "It was in Atlanta, 'bout two years ago, before my last show when everything fell apart," he began, and even he could hear the emotion heavy in his voice. "I was playing a show, and there she was—Aubrey. Damn near took my breath away."

He paused, sliding his cowboy hat back into place. "We got to talking after the show, and…hell, I ain't never felt a connection like that before."

Jaxon nodded him on, his eyes reflecting understanding. "So what happened?"

"We spent a week together. It was…perfect. I gave her hope that we were more than a quick fling. But come one morning, I panicked. Left her there sleeping, with nothing, not even a sorry excuse for a note." He drew in a deep breath, blowing it slowly, shame overwhelming him. "I convinced myself it was for the best. That I was too much of a mess, with the addiction and all. That she deserved better."

Jaxon's eyebrows shot up, surprise and understanding dawning on his face. "So that's why Aubrey's been acting so cold around you," he mused, pieces of the puzzle falling into place. "She recognized you when she moved to town."

Gunner nodded miserably. "Yeah, and now she will barely acknowledge my existence. Not that I blame her."

Jaxon whistled slowly. "What're the chances of even meeting again? Especially in your hometown?"

"Right," Gunner agreed. "She kept playing that it wasn't her and I was with someone else. For a while, I thought maybe she was right. Like the odds of us connecting again were just impossible, but I know it's her. I couldn't forget her if I tried."

Eli, who had been silent until now, cleared his throat. His intense eyes flickered between Gunner and Jaxon. "I, uh… I overheard something on Christmas Eve," Eli admitted, his voice gruff. "You and Aubrey were arguing in Jaxon's kitchen. Didn't mean to eavesdrop, but…"

Gunner's heart hammered in his chest. "What'd you hear?" he asked.

Eli shifted uncomfortably. "Enough to know there's a whole lotta hurt between you two."

Gunner ran a hand over his face, regret heavy on his shoulders. Taking a deep breath, Gunner turned to face his friends fully. "Look, that mornin' I left… I was scared outta my mind," he confessed, his voice barely above a whisper. "Not of Aubrey, but of myself. Of what I might do to her." He paused, swallowing hard. "I was so lost in my addiction then." Gunner shook his head. "I couldn't bear the thought of dragging her into my mess. Of unintentionally hurting her like I was hurting."

The weight of his words hung in the air, mingling with the steam of their breath.

"So I ran," Gunner admitted, his eyes fixed on the distant mountains. "Convinced myself it was the right thing to do. But seeing her again, knowing what I threw away…" He trailed off, emotion thick in his voice. "It's got to mean something that she moved to Timber Falls. That we found each other again. And I won't run from it this time."

Jaxon's breath formed a small cloud in the cold air. "What are you going to do now, then?"

Gunner's gaze swept across the snow-covered ranch, once again taking in the bustling activity of the cowboys in the distance. When he looked back at Jaxon and Eli, he felt a new fire in his gut. "I'm gonna do whatever it takes to remind Aubrey of what we had that week together," he declared, his voice gaining strength with each word. "Of what we could have. I know I messed up, but I'm not that same scared idiot anymore." He took a deep breath, squaring his shoulders. "I've fought my demons, and I'm still fightin' 'em every day. But Aubrey…she's worth the fight. Worth every damn bit of it."

Jaxon studied Gunner for a long moment, then nodded, a small smile tugging at the corners of his mouth. "Alright then," he said simply, clapping a hand on Gunner's shoulder. "You fight for her, and we'll be here to help in any way we can."

Eli gave a firm nod. "Damn straight."

Late in the afternoon, the sun slanted through the windows of the bar, casting light across the polished bar top.

Aubrey's hands moved with practiced efficiency as she stacked the last of the clean glasses.

"Thanks for coming in, Frank," she called out to a departing patron. "Tell Marge I said hello."

"Will do," he called in return, heading outside.

As the door swung shut behind Frank, Aubrey allowed herself a moment to breathe, her shoulders relaxing slightly. The quiet of the empty bar was a stark contrast to the bustling energy of just an hour ago. She couldn't help but feel a twinge of pride at how smoothly things had run, even as her mind raced ahead to the evening preparations.

The jingle of the doorbell interrupted her reverie, and Aubrey looked up to see Betty's familiar figure silhouetted in the doorway. You couldn't mistake the purple curls and sunshine demeanor. A genuine smile spread across Aubrey's face, chasing away some of the lingering fatigue. Betty had become very close with Willow, but Aubrey appreciated her too. She was the grandmother of The Naked Moose that everyone loved to be around.

"Right on time, as usual," Aubrey said, already reaching for a shaker and various bottles. "I've got something special for you today."

Betty settled onto her usual stool, her eyes twinkling with anticipation. "You know I'm always game for your experiments, honey. What's on the menu this time?"

Aubrey's hands moved swiftly, measuring and pouring her latest concoction. "It's got local huckleberry vodka, fresh lemon juice and a touch of lavender syrup," she explained, a hint of excitement creeping into her voice.

As she worked, she found herself relaxing into the familiar routine. Betty's presence always brought a sense of comfort, reminding Aubrey of the community she'd found here in Timber Falls, even if she was missing the big city.

"Sounds divine," Betty said, leaning forward to watch Aubrey's technique. "You've got quite the talent, you know. This place wouldn't be the same without you."

Aubrey felt a flush of pleasure at the compliment, even as a part of her wanted to deflect it. "Oh, I don't know about that," she said, giving the shaker a final, vigorous shake. "I think The Naked Moose would do just fine without me. Willow and Charly run the show here." They'd even hired Miguel to handle the small menu of food they offered, so now Aubrey was more freed up to focus on the cocktail menu, which they were becoming known for.

With a flourish, she strained the vibrant purple cocktail into a chilled glass, garnishing it with a sprig of fresh lavender. "Here you go," she said, sliding it across to Betty. "Let me know what you think."

As Betty took her first sip, Aubrey found herself holding her breath, a familiar mix of pride and anxiety swirling in her chest. It was more than just a drink; it was a piece of herself, offered up for judgment.

Betty's eyes widened as she savored the drink. "Oh my, Aubrey, this is divine! What do you call it?"

"Lavender Twilight," Aubrey replied, a small smile playing on her lips. "I thought it might be nice for the summer evenings."

Betty nodded approvingly, then leaned in conspiratorially. "Speaking of twilight romances, have you seen Willow and Eli lately? Those two are practically glowing."

Aubrey smiled. "I have. It's...it's really something, isn't it?"

As she absently polished a glass, Aubrey's mind wandered to her friends. Willow, who'd been through so much, now seemed to radiate happiness. And Eli, once so tormented, looked at peace for the first time since Aubrey had known him. "They deserve it," Aubrey said softly. "After everything they've been through..."

Betty's keen gaze settled on Aubrey. "And what about you, dear? Any chance of finding your own cowboy to ride off into the sunset with?"

Aubrey let out a sharp laugh, shaking her head. "Me? No, I think I'll leave the sunset rides to Willow and Eli. I'm more of a...sunrise and strong coffee kind of girl."

But even as she deflected with humor, Aubrey felt a familiar ache in her chest. Her life was nowhere near where she'd thought it'd be nearing thirty years old. She busied herself with wiping down the bar, avoiding Betty's knowing look.

"Besides," Aubrey continued, her tone lighter than she felt, "relationships and I don't exactly have the best track record. I think I'll stick to what I'm good at—making drinks and keeping this place running."

Betty leaned forward, her weathered hands clasping Aubrey's. "Now, you listen here, honey. Good men are like fine whiskey—they're out there, but you've got to know where to look and when to take a sip."

Aubrey's lips quirked into a half-smile. "And what if I've already had my fill of bad whiskey?"

"Then you know better what to avoid," Betty countered, her eyes twinkling. "It's all about timing. The right man will come along when you least expect it."

"Maybe," Aubrey conceded, not wanting to disappoint Betty. But inside, her walls remained firmly in place.

The jingle of the bell cut through their conversation, drawing Aubrey's attention. Her breath caught as Gunner strode in, carrying his guitar, his presence filling the room like a chord struck on his guitar. But he wasn't alone.

A young girl, no more than twelve, strode next to him, her eyes wide with wonder. Behind them, a woman—clearly the girl's mother—followed, her expression a mix of gratitude and admiration.

Aubrey's heart skipped a beat as she watched Gunner lean down, murmuring something to the girl that made her giggle. His rugged features softened, those soulful eyes crinkling at the corners.

"Well, I'll be," Betty whispered, echoing Aubrey's thoughts. "Looks like our resident country star's got a softer side."

Aubrey couldn't tear her gaze away. This was a side of Gunner she'd never seen—gentle, nurturing, almost…paternal.

"I wonder what that's all about," Aubrey mused, her curiosity piqued despite herself. She watched as Gunner guided the pair to a table, his hand resting protectively on the girl's shoulder.

For a moment, their eyes met across the room. Gunner's lips curved into a slow, easy smile that sent a jolt through Aubrey's system. She quickly looked away, busying herself with glasses, all too aware of the heat rising in her cheeks.

But her brow furrowed as she tried to piece together the puzzle before her. What was Gunner doing with this girl and her mother? The tenderness in his interactions seemed so at odds with the brash, confident performer she knew.

"It's not his kid." Charly's warm voice cut through her musings as she sidled next to her.

Aubrey raised an eyebrow, curiosity getting the better of her. "Oh?"

Charly leaned in. "That's Emily and her mom, Sarah. Gunner's mentoring Emily for the afterschool music program. Can you believe it? He's helping her overcome stage fright."

Aubrey's eyes widened. "Really?"

"I know, right?" Charly grinned. "Turns out he's got quite the soft spot for kids."

As Aubrey processed this information, her gaze drifted back to Gunner. He was leaning in, demonstrating something on his guitar, Emily watching with rapt attention, holding on to hers.

"Interesting," Aubrey murmured.

Shaking herself from her reverie, Aubrey reached for the pitcher of homemade iced tea she'd prepared earlier. "I should probably get them something to drink," she said, more to herself than to Charly.

As she fixed their drinks, Aubrey found herself hyper-aware of Gunner's presence. The way his voice carried, low and melodic, as he explained chord progressions. The gentleness in his touch as he adjusted Emily's fingers on her guitar neck.

Approaching the table, Aubrey plastered on her best hostess smile. "Thought y'all might be thirsty," she said, setting down glasses of tea. "It's my own special blend."

Gunner looked up, those rebellious eyes catching hers. "Thanks, Aubrey," he said, his voice warm.

Something in his tone made her pause, a flicker of…something…passing between them. Aubrey swallowed hard. "It's my pleasure," she managed, her voice steadier than she felt. As she turned to leave, she heard Emily's shy "Thank you."

Back behind the bar, Aubrey found herself stealing glances at the unlikely trio. The easy camaraderie, the patient explanations, the proud smile on Gunner's face when Emily got something right—it all painted a picture so different from the man she thought she knew. A man that was so unlike her father, who had no part in her life whatsoever.

Twenty minutes later, Gunner rose from his seat, guitar in hand, and gestured toward the small stage at the far end of the bar. "Ready to give it a shot?"

Emily hesitated, her fingers tightening around her own instrument. "I… I don't know if I can," she whispered, eyes darting nervously around the mostly empty bar.

Aubrey found herself holding her breath, watching the scene unfold.

Gunner knelt beside Emily, his voice low but carrying in the quiet. "Remember what we talked about? It's just you and the music. Everything else fades away." He gestured toward the bar. "And the only people here are my friends. You can trust them all."

As Emily nodded and took a shaky step toward the stage, Aubrey's heart clenched. She recognized that fear, that overwhelming self-doubt. How many times had she felt it herself, facing a new challenge after school and in an unfamiliar kitchen?

The pair settled onto stools on the stage, adjusting their guitars. Gunner started a simple melody, his fingers dancing over the strings with practiced ease. He nodded to Emily, encouraging her to join in.

The girl's first few notes were hesitant, barely audible. But as Gunner's steady rhythm continued, Emily's confidence grew. Their guitars blended, creating a sweet harmony that filled the air.

Aubrey leaned against the bar, mesmerized. She'd heard Gunner perform countless times, but this was different. The gentleness in his eyes, the patient nods as Emily found her rhythm—it all made a warmth spread through her chest.

As the impromptu duet continued, Aubrey found herself torn. The walls she'd built around her heart, reinforced by past hurts and disappointments, suddenly felt less impenetrable. *"What if…?"*

She shook her head, trying to dismiss the thought. But as Gunner's eyes met hers over Emily's bowed head, a familiar spark of connection passed between them. For just a moment, Aubrey allowed herself to see the man before her now, instead of the one that left her naked and alone in the hotel room.

And if she was honest with herself, she liked what she saw.

Seven

One week later, on a Sunday—the only day the bar was closed—Aubrey found herself gazing out the passenger window while Willow drove, watching the rugged terrain roll by. The winding road stretched before them, a ribbon of asphalt cutting through the snow-dusted Montana landscape. The vastness of it all still took her breath away, so different from the crowded cityscape she'd left behind in Atlanta, and that she missed with an ache that just wouldn't quit.

"Earth to Aubrey." Willow's voice cut through her thoughts. "You've been awful quiet this morning. You okay?"

Aubrey turned, forcing a smile. "Just taking in the view. It's beautiful out here, in its own way."

Willow raised an eyebrow before focusing back on the road. "But?"

"But nothing," Aubrey said quickly.

Too quickly.

She sighed, relenting under Willow's knowing look.

"It's just…sometimes I still feel like a fish out of water, you know? Like I don't quite belong the way you and Charly have settled in here so easily."

Willow reached over and squeezed her hand. "You belong with us, Aubs. Just give it a little more time."

Warmth bloomed in Aubrey's chest. *This* was why she'd traded skyscrapers for mountains. The lifelong bonds she'd formed with Charly and Willow weren't anything she was willing to trade. Even when she'd moved to Atlanta, the end goal was always to get enough experience and then end up together. Aubrey just never expected that to be in a place like Timber Falls.

"You're right," she said softly. "Besides, I don't know what I'd do without you and Charly."

"Probably be bored out of your mind," Willow quipped, a grin playing on her lips. "Speaking of which, you ready to try a little canter today on our ride? Eli said you're totally ready to go a little faster."

Aubrey groaned playfully. "God help me. Remember last time? I think he forgets I can barely trot."

They dissolved into laughter, recalling Aubrey's last riding lesson with Eli, where she'd trotted just fine but couldn't seem to stop. He had way more confidence in her riding ability than she did, but at least she wasn't falling off.

The ranch soon came into view, a sprawling expanse of weathered wood and open pastures. Even from a distance, Aubrey could make out the flurry of activity—their friends milling about, cowboys leading horses from the stables.

Willow pulled up to the main house, barely putting the car in Park before Aubrey was out the door. The brisk wind nipped at her cheeks as she strode toward the group, drinking in the familiar faces and welcoming smiles.

"There you are!" Eli called out, waving enthusiastically. "We were starting to think you'd both chickened out—bunch of city girls."

Aubrey rolled her eyes but couldn't keep the grin off her face.

Willow called, "In your dreams. We're tough cookies and can handle the cold."

Aubrey slipped her hands into her mitts, not totally sure about that. The day was sunny, but bitterly cold.

A chorus of good-natured jeers and laughter erupted from the group. Aubrey felt herself relax, slipping easily into the warm embrace of friendship. This was her family now, chosen and cherished, and she told herself again that she just had to get used to it.

She *would* get used to it.

As the cowboys began leading out the horses from the barn for their ride today, with Charly in tow, the crunch of gravel under tires drew Aubrey's attention. A sleek black pickup rolled to a stop, and her breath caught as Gunner stepped out, his cowboy hat tipped low over those piercing eyes. But he wasn't alone. Emily and her mother emerged from the truck next.

Aubrey's stomach twisted as she watched Gunner help Sarah down. "Well, isn't that cozy," she muttered under her breath, unable to quell the flicker of jealousy that ignited in her chest.

"Did you say something?" Charly asked, appearing at her side.

Aubrey shook her head, forcing a smile. "Just talking to myself."

As Willow chatted with Charly, Aubrey couldn't tear her eyes away from Gunner. He was laughing at something Sarah said, looking more relaxed than Aubrey had ever seen him. *Ugh*. She turned away. She really had to stop looking his way.

"You okay?" Willow asked…*again*.

Aubrey blinked, realizing she needed to pull herself together. "Yeah, I'm fine."

"Great," Willow said, a knowing smirk on her face. "Come on, let's go say hi."

Before Aubrey could protest, they were walking toward the newcomers. Gunner's eyes met hers, and for a moment, the world seemed to stop. There was a flash of something in his gaze—tenderness, maybe even longing—before he quickly looked away.

"Gunner," Aubrey said, proud of how steady her voice sounded.

Gunner tipped his hat, a ghost of a smile on his lips. "Darlin'."

The endearment, casual as it was, sent a shiver down Aubrey's spine. She turned to Emily and Sarah, determined to ignore the effect Gunner had on her. "Hi, we didn't officially meet the other day. I'm Aubrey."

As introductions were made, Aubrey couldn't help but steal glances at Gunner. What was his relationship with Sarah? And why did she care so much?

The sound of hooves on packed snow pulled Aubrey from her thoughts. It was time to mount up. As she approached the horse she rode every week, a beautiful chestnut mare named Jester, she paused, taking in the breathtaking landscape before her.

The ranch stretched out in a winter wonderland, snow-capped mountains framing the horizon. Pristine white fields glittered in the sunlight, broken only by the dark silhouettes of pine trees. It was a far cry from the bustling streets of Atlanta, and yet…

"It's something else, isn't it?" Gunner's voice was low, close enough that she could feel the warmth of his breath.

Aubrey nodded, not trusting herself to speak. She might not love everything small-town living had to offer, but the majestic views were something else.

But then Emily called out to Gunner, breaking the spell. Aubrey turned back to the horse that Decker was holding still for her and pushed away the conflicting emotions swirling within her. She had a ride to focus on, after all. "Thanks," she told Decker.

He tipped his hat. "Enjoy the ride, ma'am."

As she swung into the saddle, Aubrey zipped up her coat all the way, bringing her scarf up over her face to keep her warm.

Soon, the rhythmic clip-clop of hooves on the snow-dusted trail filled the air as the group set off, their breaths puffing out in small clouds in the wintery air. Aubrey found herself relaxing into the gentle sway of Jester's gait, the tension in her shoulders easing with each step.

"So, Aubrey," Willow called out from a few paces ahead, "ready to admit that country life isn't so bad after all?"

Aubrey rolled her eyes but couldn't suppress a grin. "Don't push it. I still miss decent sushi."

Laughter rippled through the group, and Aubrey felt a warmth bloom in her chest that had nothing to do with the exertion of riding. For a moment, her worries about the bar, her past in Atlanta and even the confusing presence of Gunner faded into the background.

"We've got fish in the lake," Eli chimed in, atop his black horse. "Slap it on some rice, and voilà! Montana sushi!"

"I'd pay good money to see you try that," Aubrey shot back, her competitive streak flaring.

As the banter continued, Emily's mother, Sarah, guided her horse alongside Jester. "Don't beat yourself up about it too much," she said with a warm smile. "I remember when I first moved here as a teen. Quite the culture shock."

Aubrey nodded. "It's…different. But not in a bad way, I guess."

Sarah's gaze drifted to where Gunner was riding ahead, deep in conversation with Emily. "Speaking of different," she mused, "it's wild seeing Gunner back in town. Did you know he was quite the rebel back in high school?"

"Oh?" she asked, aiming for nonchalance but knowing she'd missed the mark.

"Oh yeah," Sarah continued. "He was a couple years behind me, but everyone knew Gunner Woods. Everyone knew he was bigger than this town."

As Sarah spoke, Aubrey found herself studying Gunner, on his horse next to Emily's gray pony, and trying to reconcile the man she'd met in Atlanta with this small-town rebel who was brave enough to chase his dreams and catch them.

"I guess it wasn't a huge surprise when he hit it big," Sarah added. "Some people are just destined for the spotlight, you know?"

Aubrey hummed noncommittally, her mind whirling. She'd known Gunner was famous, of course, but hearing about his roots stirred something in her. A curiosity, perhaps. Or something deeper she wasn't quite ready to name.

Sarah leaned in, her eyes twinkling with mischief. "You know, if I were even remotely interested in men, Gunner would be at the top of my list. That voice, those eyes…" She fanned herself dramatically, then burst into laughter. "But I'll leave that to someone else. My wife would have my head!"

Aubrey chuckled, a genuine smile tugging at her lips. Sarah's easy humor was infectious, chipping away at the walls Aubrey had carefully constructed around herself. And now she knew Sarah and Gunner weren't a thing at all, and that brought more relief than she thought necessary.

"Speaking of," Sarah continued, her tone softening, "it's good to see him looking more like himself these days. When he first came back to town…" She trailed off, shaking her head.

Aubrey's grip on her reins tightened. "What do you mean?"

Sarah's gaze turned distant, as if looking back through time. "Oh, honey. Everyone could tell he was a shell of himself. Exhausted, lost…like he'd left pieces of himself scattered across every stage in America. It broke my heart to see the guy I remembered looking so…hollow."

A lump formed in Aubrey's throat. She swallowed hard, her mind conjuring tormented images of Gunner, not the charming musician she'd met in Atlanta, but a man worn down by the weight of fame and expectations.

"But now," Sarah continued, her voice brightening, "it's like watching the old Gunner come back to life. That spark in his eye, the way he carries himself… It's good to see. This town, it has a way of healing people, you know?"

Aubrey nodded, her mind whirring as she guided her horse along the snowy trail. Sarah's words echoed in her thoughts, painting a picture of two Gunners—the charismatic man she'd met in Atlanta and the broken one who'd slipped away in the morning. Her heart clenched, realizing the possibility that the real Gunner might be a blend of both, complex and layered.

Lost in her musings, Aubrey barely registered the shift in conversation until Eli's booming voice cut through her reverie.

"C'mon, Gunner! You can't hold out on us forever. When are you gonna grace us with that famous jambalaya of yours?"

Gunner chuckled, shaking his head. "You're relentless, man."

"Famous jambalaya?" Aubrey asked, her chef's instincts kicking in.

Looking back over his shoulder, Gunner's gaze met hers. "It's my grandma's recipe," he said, his voice warm. "But I'm biased to how good it is."

"Don't let him fool you," Eli interjected. "It's the best damn jambalaya this side of the Mississippi."

Aubrey raised an eyebrow. "Is that so?" she called out, her voice carrying a playful challenge. "Let's see if your culinary skills match your musical talents."

Gunner's lips quirked into a half smile. "Is that a dare, Miss Hale?"

"You bet it is," Aubrey replied, a smirk playing on her lips. "Impress me with your dinner, if you can."

He chuckled again, the sound low and rich. "Challenge accepted, darlin'."

For the rest of their ride, and then as they guided their horses back toward the ranch, Aubrey's mind whirled. What was she doing? Wasn't she supposed to be avoiding him? Yet here she was, practically inviting him into her world.

"Don't get too excited," she said, when the trail brought their horses nearer to one another, trying to mask the emotions flaring within her. "I've got pretty high standards, you know."

Gunner steered his horse closer toward her. "I wouldn't expect anything less from you, Aubrey."

The use of her name sent a tremor through her. "Just remember," she whispered, "I'm not easily impressed."

His eyes searched hers, filled with an intensity that made her breath catch. "Maybe that's exactly why I want to try."

A couple hours later, the aroma of sautéing onions and bell peppers filled the farmhouse kitchen as Gunner expertly wielded a wooden spoon, his movements smooth and assured. He inhaled deeply, savoring the familiar scents that reminded him of lazy Sunday afternoons spent with his grandmother. The sizzle of andouille sausage hitting the hot pan brought a smile to his face.

He'd dropped Sarah and Emily back off at home before heading to the grocery store. His eyes roamed over the fresh ingredients spread across the butcher-block island—plump tomatoes, fragrant garlic and a colorful array of spices. His fingers itched to start chopping and dicing, to lose himself in the rhythmic motions of cooking. It felt good to be creating something again, even if it wasn't music.

The sound of laughter drifted in from the living room, and soon the kitchen was filled with the boisterous energy of his friends. Willow perched on a barstool while Aubrey leaned against the counter, her eyes sparkling with amusement at something Eli had said.

"Smells amazing in here," Jaxon commented, inhaling deeply.

Gunner chuckled, tossing a dish towel over his shoulder. "My grandma's recipe never disappoints."

"I agree, it smells delicious," Charly teased, nudging Aubrey with her elbow. "Looks like you've got some competition in the kitchen."

Aubrey rolled her eyes good-naturedly. "Please. I could cook circles around this country boy."

"Is that another challenge, darlin'?" Gunner drawled, raising an eyebrow. His gaze locked with Aubrey's, and for a moment, the air between them crackled with unspoken tension.

Willow cleared her throat, breaking the moment. "As fun as a cook-off sounds, we've got more pressing matters. Like why my socks are still damp after two cycles in the dryer." She turned to Eli and Jaxon. "Our dryer has been acting up for weeks. You guys know anything about appliance repair?"

Jaxon puffed out his chest. "I'm basically a mechanical genius. Lead the way, milady."

Eli just rolled his eyes.

As the group filed out of the kitchen, Gunner found his gaze drawn to Aubrey. She lingered for a moment, her expression unreadable. He wondered what she was thinking, if she ever thought about that night in Atlanta. The memory of her soft skin and breathy sighs haunted him still.

He shook his head, forcing himself to focus on the task at hand. He had a lot to make up for, and a home-cooked meal was just the beginning.

"So," Aubrey began, "where'd you learn to cook like this? Didn't peg you for a culinary expert."

Gunner glanced over his shoulder, a slow smile spreading across his face. "There's a lot you don't know about me."

Aubrey snorted, but Gunner spotted the slight upturn of her lips.

"Enlighten me then," she said. "What's the secret to your kitchen prowess?"

"My grandmother, actually. Spent a lot of time with her growing up. That woman could make a feast out of thin air."

Aubrey took a seat on the stool. "Yeah? What was she like?"

"Picture a five-foot-nothing spitfire with a wooden spoon in one hand and sheet music in the other." He chuckled. "She'd have me up at dawn, picking fresh tomatoes from her garden. Said a man who couldn't feed himself wasn't worth his salt."

"Sounds like quite a woman," she murmured.

He nodded, his eyes meeting hers. "She was. Taught me more than just cooking. Said music and food both came from the soul. If you didn't put your whole heart into it, folks could taste the difference."

Aubrey's eyes softened. "Well," she said, her voice light, "let's hope you were paying attention. I've got high standards for my jambalaya."

Gunner's lips quirked. "Trust me, darlin'. I aim to exceed 'em." His hands moved deftly as he diced tomatoes, his knife a blur against the cutting board. Desperate for her to know him better, he said, "She passed away after I'd just left for Nashville, and that's when my folks began traveling. They actually split their time between here and Costa Rica these days."

Aubrey's eyebrows shot up. "Costa Rica? That's quite a change from Montana."

He chuckled. "My dad always said he'd retire somewhere without snow. Turns out, he meant it." He gave her a quick smile. "They come back every summer, though. Stay in our old family home on the east side of town."

"Must be nice," she murmured, "having roots like that."

Gunner glanced up. "It is," he said softly. "Especially after... Well, the road can get mighty lonely."

Aubrey cocked her head, and Gunner swore she looked at him like she wanted to reach out, to offer some kind of comfort. Instead, she busied her hands, pulling at the lint on her pants.

"What about you?" Gunner asked, his tone deliberately light. "Got family back in Atlanta?"

Aubrey tensed, her chest tightening. "No, my mom is in Ann Arbor, Michigan, where I grew up with Charly and Willow," she said after a moment. "She's a teacher. Third grade."

"Bet she's proud as punch of her chef daughter," Gunner said with a grin.

Aubrey's smile didn't quite reach her eyes. "She is. We talk every Sunday evening." She paused, her voice growing thick with emotion. "I miss her lasagna nights. The way the whole house would smell like garlic and oregano."

Gunner watched her for a moment, then asked gently, "And your dad? Is he back in Ann Arbor too?"

She shifted on the stool. When she spoke, her voice was flat, devoid of emotion. "No. He's...not in the picture. Hasn't been since I was eight."

The kitchen fell silent, save for the bubbling of the jambalaya. Gunner was swallowed up by a mix of empathy and something deeper—a flash of guilt that Aubrey didn't quite catch. He set down his knife, wiping his hands on a nearby towel.

"Aubrey, I'm sorry. I shouldn't have pried," he said, taking a step toward her.

She shook her head, still not meeting his eyes. "It's fine. Ancient history."

But Gunner wasn't letting it go. He moved closer, until he was standing just a few feet away from her. "No, it's not fine." He reached out on instinct to touch her arm, then thought better of it. "I'm sorry, Aubrey," he continued. "Not just for bringing up painful memories, but for...for leaving you that night in Atlanta. I was a coward, and I hurt you. I've regretted it every day since."

Aubrey's arms crossed over her chest. But this time, she didn't deny their night together, didn't brush him off. "I don't know what you want from me, Gunner," she said.

"I want a chance," he told her. "A chance to make things right, to show you who I really am. If you'll let me."

She huffed. "Friends?"

He'd take that for now. "Yes, friends."

"I can do that," she finally said.

Gunner's heart was pounding so loudly, he was sure Aubrey could hear it. Her fiery eyes held his, and he could hardly believe it when he found her leaning in, drawn by an invisible force that had pulled them together once before.

Suddenly, the silence ended, shattering the moment. "Good Lord, it smells heavenly in here." Willow's voice rang out, followed by the thunderous footsteps of the rest of the group.

Aubrey jerked back, her cheeks flushing as she busied herself with looking at her pants again. Gunner cleared his throat, running a hand through his tousled blond hair.

As everyone crowded around the stove, exclaiming over

the aromatic dish, Aubrey snuck a glance at Gunner. He caught her eye, a small smile playing at the corners of his mouth, and she smiled back.

"Alright, folks," Gunner announced, clapping his hands together. "Let's go play cards while this simmers for a little while."

"Yes," Willow said. "And I've got a movie for us later."

They moved in a chaotic dance, pouring drinks and grabbing cards, heading to the living room. His eyes found Aubrey's before she headed out of the kitchen. As their gazes met, he felt a silent promise, a question left hanging in the air.

What now? Gunner wondered. *Friends*, she'd offered. But could they ever just be friends?

Eight

The dying embers cast a warm, flickering glow across the room as Aubrey's eyes fluttered open. Disoriented, she blinked away the remnants of sleep, her gaze sweeping over the cozy yet disheveled living room. Blankets and pillows were strewn haphazardly, evidence of the movie night that had clearly ended while she slept. The absence of her friends' laughter and chatter struck her, replaced by a hushed stillness broken only by the occasional crackle from the fireplace.

Though as her gaze landed on Gunner's sleeping form sprawled across the couch, her breath caught. His chest rose and fell in a slow, steady rhythm, one arm draped carelessly over his midsection while the other dangled off the edge. The fading firelight played across his features, softening the lines of his face.

God, he's gorgeous, Aubrey thought, allowing herself a moment to drink in the sight of him. Even in sleep, there was something magnetic about Gunner Woods. It was the same pull she'd felt that night in Atlanta, before everything had gone sideways.

She shook her head, trying to wash away the memory. *This is dangerous territory, Aubrey. You know better.*

But as her gaze traced the curve of his lips, slightly parted in sleep, she couldn't help but wonder what might have been if things had gone differently. If he hadn't left her alone in that hotel room, waking up to nothing.

The ache of that rejection still stung, even after all this time. Yet seeing him like this, vulnerable and unguarded, stirred something within her that she'd thought long buried.

She sighed softly, conflicted emotions warring inside her. Part of her wanted to wake him, to confront him about that night and demand answers. Another part wanted to simply curl up beside him, to feel the solid warmth of his body next to hers.

Instead, she sat up slowly, her muscles protesting as she pushed herself upright on the makeshift bed. She rubbed her eyes, wiping away the last vestiges of sleep as reality seeped in.

Her gaze darted around the room, taking in the empty spaces where her friends had been. No sign of Charly's infectious laughter, Jaxon's easy smile, Willow's comforting presence or Eli's steady demeanor. They were gone, leaving her alone with…

Gunner.

As if on cue, he stirred on the couch, his eyes fluttering open. Their gazes locked, and Aubrey felt a jolt of electricity course through her. Recognition flickered in his eyes, followed by a mix of surprise and something deeper, more intense.

"Aubrey," he murmured, his voice husky with sleep.

She swallowed hard, her heart hammering in her chest. "Gunner," she replied, barely above a whisper.

The silence stretched between them, heavy with unspoken words and shared memories. Aubrey's mind raced, recalling their passionate night in Atlanta, the bitter sting of waking up alone and now, this unexpected time alone.

"I guess we're the last ones standing," Gunner said, breaking the tension with a wry smile.

Aubrey nodded, tucking a strand of hair behind her ear. "Looks like it," she agreed, trying to keep her voice steady. "I didn't mean to fall asleep."

"Neither did I," he admitted, sitting up and running a hand through his tousled hair. The movement drew Aubrey's attention to the lean muscles of his arms, and she quickly averted her gaze.

This is ridiculous, she chided herself. You're not that starry-eyed girl anymore. But even as she thought it, she couldn't deny the pull she still felt toward him.

She cleared her throat, pushing all that aside. "So, uh, where did everyone go?" she asked.

He chuckled, the sound low and warm. "Honestly? I have no idea. Last thing I remember was the opening credits." His eyes twinkled with amusement. "Guess I'm not as fun as I used to be—can't even stay awake for a movie night."

A soft laugh escaped her lips. "Well, if it makes you feel

any better, I didn't make it much further." She shook her head, smiling. "Some party animals we are."

Their shared laughter eased some of the tension, but Aubrey couldn't shake the heightened awareness of his presence. She watched as he stretched, his muscles flexing beneath his shirt.

He glanced at his watch, his expression shifting. "I should probably head out," he said, moving to stand up. "It's getting late."

Aubrey felt a sudden pang of...something. Disappointment? Concern? She wasn't quite sure. "Wait," she found herself saying, surprising even herself. "It's late. Just stay."

Gunner paused, his eyes searching hers. "You sure?" he asked, his voice soft.

Aubrey nodded, her practical side taking over. "We've got plenty of blankets, and the fire's still going," she said, ignoring the flutter in her stomach.

He hesitated, his eyes flickering between Aubrey and the couch. A moment passed, charged with unspoken possibilities, before he slowly sank back onto the couch. Aubrey's heart skipped a beat as she watched him settle in, his broad shoulders relaxing against the cushions.

"Thanks," he murmured, his voice a low rumble that sent a shiver down her spine.

Aubrey lay back down on her side, pulling the blanket up around her. The fire crackled softly. In the dim light, she swore she could see the questions in his eyes, mirroring her own curiosity and apprehension.

Taking a deep breath, she steeled herself. "Can I ask you something?" she began, her voice barely above a whisper.

He turned to face her fully, his eyes intense. "Anything, darlin'."

Her heart raced. She'd imagined this conversation a hundred times, but now that the moment was here, words seemed to fail her. She bit her lip, wrestling with how to phrase the question that had haunted her since that night.

"It's just…" she started, then paused, searching for the right words. "Why did you leave me like you did?" she finally asked.

Gunner's eyes widened before he sat up. "So, it was you? You're admitting it?"

Aubrey snorted. "Oh no," she quipped, her tone lighter than she felt. "You don't get to turn this around on me. I'll answer that after you explain yourself."

He chuckled, a deep, rich sound that sent a warmth through Aubrey's chest.

"Fair enough," he conceded, his eyes crinkled with amusement and something deeper. "I suppose I owe you that much."

Aubrey hugged her pillow, bracing herself for his explanation.

His expression grew serious, his gaze drifting to the dying embers of the fire. "It all started with an ATV accident," he began. "I was being reckless, a stupid rebel, I guess…" His fingers absently traced a line along his leg, drawing Aubrey's attention. "The accident left me with a nasty scar, right here," he said, gesturing to his thigh. Then his expression grew somber. "That scar was just the beginning," he continued, his voice dropping to almost a whisper. "The pain… It's bad sometimes. I turned to pills, thinking they'd help me cope while I was on tour."

Her heart ached at the raw vulnerability in Gunner's voice. She wanted to reach out, to offer comfort, but remained still, sensing he needed to get this out.

"Before I knew it, I was in deep," he confessed. "The addiction took everything—my music, my sense of self. I was empty. A shell of who I used to be."

The weight of his words hung heavy in the air between them.

"Then I saw you," he continued. "That week in Atlanta, it was like a jolt of electricity. For the first time in years, I felt like I'd woken up again, if that makes any sense at all."

Aubrey found herself leaning in, her eyes never leaving his.

"Our week together," he went on, "it was more than just a fling. It was…normal. Happy. Everything I'd been missing."

A bittersweet smile tugged at Aubrey's lips. "Then why did you leave?" she asked.

Gunner's eyes clouded with regret. "I was scared," he admitted. "Terrified, actually. I felt something real with you, and it made me realize how far I'd fallen. I couldn't bear the thought of dragging you into my mess."

Her breath hitched. "So you ran?"

He gave a slow nod. "I ran. From you. From myself. From seeing what a fucking mess I'd become. I hated the man those pills made me. I came back home within a week, faced my demons, got help. Started the long road to healing." A shaky breath escaped him as his gaze locked on to Aubrey's with an intensity that made her breath catch. "I never thought I'd see you again," he whispered. "But here you are, in my hometown of all places. It feels like…"

"Like what?" Aubrey prompted, her heart thundering in her chest.

"Like fate," he said. "Like the universe is giving us a second chance."

Aubrey's heart skipped a beat. She wanted to believe him, but the memory of waking up alone in that Atlanta hotel room still stung. "Gunner, I—" she began.

He rose and he came to sit close to her. "I know I hurt you," he interrupted, his eyes never leaving hers. "And I know I've got a lot to make up for. But I swear to you, I'm not the same man I was back then. I want to earn your trust back."

His words hung in the air between them, heavy with promise and possibility. Aubrey found herself torn between the urge to guard her heart and the desire to let him in.

Her breath caught in her throat as he sat mere inches from her, the heat radiating off his body wrapping around her like a warm embrace. Her mind reeled, memories of their night in Atlanta flooding back with startling clarity—the taste of whiskey on his lips, the feel of his calloused hands on her skin, the way he'd made her feel more alive than she had in years.

She swallowed hard, her voice barely above a whisper. "I… I tried so hard to forget."

His eyes bored into hers, filled with an intensity that made heat spiral through her. "Darlin', some things are too powerful to forget."

Her gaze dropped to his lips, full and inviting. Her heart thundered in her chest with longing and trepidation. She knew she should turn away, maintain the walls she'd so carefully constructed. But the magnetic pull between them was undeniable, and she couldn't hate him for why he walked away.

A ghost of a smile crossed his lips. His gaze searched hers, an ocean of longing and something deeper, a need for acknowledgment. "I'll give you the kiss your eyes are begging me for," he whispered, his voice husky with restrained desire. "But I need to hear you say it, Aubrey."

She swallowed hard, her heart hammering against her ribs. "Say what?"

His hand cupped her cheek, his thumb tracing her lower lip. "I need you to say that night in Atlanta... It was you. What we had, what we felt, it was real."

Aubrey closed her eyes, memories of that night in Atlanta washing over her. The heat of his touch, the electricity of their connection, it had been undeniable then, just as it was now. She opened her eyes, finding Gunner's face mere inches from hers, patient and expectant.

"It was me," she admitted, her words barely audible. "And it was real. God help me, it was real."

His eyes widened, relief and desire darkening their depths. "Aubrey," he breathed her name on his lips.

In an instant, the space between them vanished. Gunner's mouth claimed hers, urgent and tender all at once. She melted into the kiss, her hands grabbing the soft fabric of his shirt. The taste of him—woodsy and something uniquely Gunner—overwhelmed her senses.

Their lips moved in a dance of rediscovery, each stroke of tongue and gentle nip rekindling the fire that had smoldered between them so long ago.

"I've dreamed about this," Gunner murmured against her lips, his hands framing her face. "About you."

Aubrey pulled back slightly, her breath coming in short gasps. "Gunner, I, we can't just…"

He silenced her with another kiss, softer this time. "We can be whatever we want to be. No more runnin'."

She searched his face, finding sincerity etched in every line. "I'm not the same person I was that night," she whispered, vulnerability lacing her words.

Gunner's thumb traced her cheekbone. "Neither am I. But this—us—it's still here. Can't you feel it?"

Aubrey nodded, unable to deny the electric current humming between them. She leaned in, initiating the kiss this time, pouring the longing she'd felt into the connection. As Gunner's arms encircled her, drawing her closer, she allowed herself to hope that maybe, just maybe, they could heal each other's wounds.

His fingers trailed down Aubrey's neck, tracing her collarbone before settling on the top button of her blouse. His eyes, dark with desire, searched hers for permission.

"Are you sure?" he whispered, his voice husky.

Aubrey's heart raced. "Yes," she breathed, surprised by the steadiness in her own voice.

With deliberate care, Gunner unfastened the first button, pressing a soft kiss to the newly exposed skin. Aubrey shivered, her nerves singing at his touch.

"You're beautiful," he murmured, his lips brushing against her throat as he worked on the next button.

Her fingers tangled in his hair as each piece of clothing fell away. His kisses mapped a trail of fire across her skin, from the curve of her shoulder to the valley between her breasts.

"Gunner," she gasped, overwhelmed by the sensations he was evoking.

He looked up, his eyes meeting hers. "Tell me what you want, darlin'."

The vulnerability in his gaze matched her own, she was sure, and Aubrey felt a surge of courage. "I want you," she whispered. "All of you."

Gunner's response was a low growl as he captured her lips once more, his hands roaming her body with new-found urgency. She arched into his touch, every nerve aflame with desire.

As his lips traced a path down her body, her thoughts scattered. She surrendered to the moment, to the connection that had haunted her too.

Her world narrowed to a pinpoint of exquisite sensation as Gunner slid between her legs and his mouth found her most sensitive spot. Her fingers clutched at the blanket beneath her, a soft moan escaping her lips.

"Oh, God," she breathed, her head falling back as waves of pleasure coursed through her body.

His touch was both intense and passionate, his tongue moving in rhythmic patterns that left her gasping. Her mind raced, torn between the physical ecstasy and the emotional intensity of the moment.

This is so much more than Atlanta, she thought hazily. So much more than she ever imagined.

"Gunner," she panted, her voice barely above a whisper. "I—"

He looked up, his eyes dark with desire. "Let it all go," he murmured.

His words, coupled with the renewed focus of his attention, sent Aubrey spiraling over the edge. Her climax crashed over her like a tidal wave, release flooding every cell of her body.

As the aftershocks subsided, she found herself reaching for him, an urgent need to reciprocate overwhelming her. Her fingers fumbled with the buttons of his shirt.

"My turn," she said, her voice husky with emotion.

Gunner's lips quirked into a smile. "Take your time. We've got all night."

Her hands explored his newly exposed skin, tracing the contours of his chest and abs. She marveled at the familiar yet thrilling sensation of his body under her fingertips.

"You know," she murmured, pressing a kiss to his collarbone, "I've dreamed about this more times than I care to admit."

Gunner's breath hitched. "Aubrey, I—"

She silenced him with a kiss, pouring all her pent-up longing into the connection. As she continued to undress him, she felt a sense of coming home, of finally allowing herself to embrace the connection they'd forged that night in Atlanta, and that she'd been running from since she arrived in Timber Falls.

Her heart raced as she watched Gunner reach for his

wallet. Her gaze followed his movements, transfixed. She reached out, gently taking the condom from him. "Let me," she whispered.

As she rolled the protection onto his thick hard cock, his hands settled on her hips, his touch both steadying and electrifying. Aubrey could feel the slight tremor in his fingers, urgency claiming her.

"You're sure about this?" he asked with emotion heavy in his voice.

Instead of answering with words, she shifted, positioning herself above him. She paused, savoring the moment of connection, before slowly sinking down onto him. The sensation was overwhelming, filling her completely.

"Oh, God," she breathed, her eyes fluttering closed.

Gunner's grip on her hips tightened. "You are so damn beautiful," he said softly.

She opened her eyes, meeting his gaze. The intensity she found there nearly took her breath away. Slowly, she began to move.

Her body responded to the rhythm of his, their movements becoming more urgent and synchronized. Their skin slick with sweat, they moved harder and faster, lost in the ecstasy of pleasure. It rose and rose until she was trembling and fighting the scream trying to tear from her lips, and he was bucking and jerking and groaning his release beneath her.

For a moment, they lay entwined, hearts pounding, trying to catch their breath. She raised her head to look at him, and he smiled at her with a tenderness she had never seen before.

He chuckled. "I can hear you thinking from here."

She slid off him and lay on her side, propping herself up on one elbow, studying his face in the flickering light. "I'm just…processing, I guess," she admitted softly.

His hand came up to tuck a stray strand of hair behind her ear. "Regrets?" he asked, a flicker of uncertainty in his eyes.

"No," she said quickly, surprised by how true it felt. "It's more like…where do we go from here?"

A slow smile spread across his face. "Well, we could start with breakfast. I make a mean stack of pancakes."

Aubrey couldn't help but laugh, the tension in her chest easing. "I'm being serious."

His expression sobered, and he reached out to cup her cheek. "So am I. I know we've got a lot to figure out, so let's just figure it out, okay?"

She sighed, leaning into his touch. "Okay."

Nine

As the first rays of dawn filtered through the curtain the next morning, Gunner's eyes fluttered open. The warm cocoon of Aubrey's bed enveloped him, a stark contrast to the chill Montana air outside the window. He blinked, orienting himself in the unfamiliar room until his gaze landed on Aubrey's sleeping form beside him and he was instantly reminded how they'd ended up in her room at some point last night.

He couldn't take his eyes off her. She was breathtaking, her hair splayed across the pillow, her face softened by sleep. His heart swelled with a tenderness that caught him off guard. He wanted to trace the curve of her cheek, to feel the silk of her skin beneath his fingertips, but he held back, not wanting to disturb her peaceful sleep.

Lord, she's somethin' else, he thought, a mixture of awe and desire coursing through him. The memories of last night—which had kept on going long after they'd left the couch—flooded his mind, sending a pleasant tremble down his spine.

He knew he'd promised her breakfast, but he found himself reluctant to leave the bed. It had been so long since he'd felt this…*content*. The nagging voice of his addiction, always lurking in the background, was blessedly silent.

With a quiet sigh, he carefully began to slide himself out of the tangle of sheets and limbs. Aubrey stirred slightly, a small furrow appearing between her brows. He froze, holding his breath until she settled back into sleep.

Once free, he stood and stretched, his muscles pleasantly sore from their nighttime activities. He located his jeans and shirt and pulled them on, then padded silently to the door, pausing to look back at Aubrey one last time.

A mix of emotions swirled within him—contentment, anticipation, a touch of uncertainty. What did last night mean for them? Would Aubrey regret what had happened this morning?

Having no answer to that now, he took a deep breath and grabbed the door handle. With one last glance at Aubrey's sleeping form, he turned the knob and stepped out into the hallway.

As he eased the door closed, he found himself face-to-face with Willow, her eyes dancing with amusement. A smirk played at the corners of her mouth as she leaned against the railing, blocking his path.

"Well, well," she drawled. "Looks like someone didn't stay on the living room couch last night."

Gunner felt a flush creep up his neck, but he met her

gaze with a crooked grin. "What can I say? I'm direction-
ally challenged before my mornin' coffee."

Willow's eyebrow arched. "Uh-huh. And I'm sure Aubrey was just…giving you directions?"

Before Gunner could retort, the door to Willow's bedroom swung open, revealing Eli. The former bull rider's
intense eyes swept over the scene, a hint of amusement
softening his usually guarded expression.

"Mornin'." He glanced between Gunner and Willow,
a ghost of a smile tugging at his lips. "I'm gonna put on
some coffee. Want some?"

Gunner nodded gratefully, relief washing over him at
the change of subject. "Hell yes." He stepped past Willow
and followed Eli down the staircase and into the kitchen.
Willow trailed behind. As Eli busied himself with the
coffee maker, Gunner found himself drawn to the stove.

"How 'bout some pancakes?" he asked. "Do you have
all the ingredients?"

"We do," Willow said, and she fetched him the ingredients.

As Gunner began making the pancakes and Willow
began frying up bacon, a comfortable silence settled between them. It felt easy, natural, as much as Gunner felt
with Jaxon and Eli.

"So," Willow said, breaking the quiet, "are you planning on sticking around Timber Falls for a while?"

Gunner paused, considering. The question carried more
weight than its casual delivery suggested. Willow was worried about Aubrey. "I have no plans to leave anytime soon,"
he replied softly.

"Well, then, that's good," Willow said with a smirk.

Just then, Charly breezed into the kitchen, her hair tousled from sleep. Apparently, she had stayed over in her old room last night. She stopped short at the sight of Gunner, her eyes widening slightly.

"Well, this is a surprise," she said, recovering quickly. "I thought you'd have hightailed it out of here by now."

Gunner grinned, pouring the pancake mixture into the pan. "And miss out on all this charming company? Not a chance."

Charly shook her head, laughing as she poured herself a cup of coffee.

"He came out of Aubrey's room this morning," Willow said.

Charly chuckled. "Oh, is that so?"

"Mmm hmm," was the only reply Gunner was going to give.

The sizzle of bacon filled the kitchen as Willow flipped the last strips and Gunner had a stack of pancakes made. He inhaled deeply, savoring the smoky aroma, when a soft creak from the hallway caught his attention. His heart skipped a beat as Aubrey appeared in the doorway, her presence instantly transforming the room.

She stood there in an oversized T-shirt and flannel pajama bottoms, her hair an absolute mess from sleep. But it was her eyes, those striking eyes, that captivated him. They sparkled with shyness and warmth that made his chest tighten.

"Mornin', darlin'," he drawled, unable to keep the admiration from his voice. The world around him seemed to fade, leaving only Aubrey in sharp focus.

Without a second thought, and letting everyone there know the new development between them, Gunner crossed the room in three long strides. His hands found her waist, pulling her close as his lips met hers in a passionate kiss. Aubrey melted into him, her fingers threading through his hair.

Time stood still as they lost themselves in the embrace. His mind raced with a jumble of emotions—desire, tenderness, and a surprising sense of rightness. When they finally broke apart, he rested his forehead against hers, drinking in her closeness.

"Well, good morning to you, too," Aubrey whispered, a shy smile playing on her lips.

Gunner became acutely aware of the silence that had fallen over the kitchen. He turned, still keeping an arm around Aubrey's waist, to find their friends staring at them.

"I, uh…" he started, suddenly feeling like a teenager caught necking behind the barn. "The pancakes are ready. Eat up."

The group settled around the breakfast table, plates piled high with crispy bacon and golden pancakes. Gunner couldn't help but steal glances at Aubrey, marveling at how natural it felt to have her by his side. The silence stretched, thick with unspoken questions, until Eli cleared his throat.

"So," Eli said, his eyes twinkling with mischief, "are we gonna address the bull in the room, or do I gotta spell it out?" He gestured between Gunner and Aubrey with his fork. "You two seem awful cozy this mornin'. Anything you'd like to share with the class?"

Gunner felt heat creep up his neck. He opened his mouth to respond, but Aubrey beat him to it.

"Well, Eli," she said, her voice steady and confident, "if you must know, Gunner and I are...exploring things, as I'm sure you could plainly tell." She reached for Gunner's hand under the table, giving it a squeeze. "It's new."

Gunner's heart soared at her words. He'd been worried she might shy away, put up those walls he'd seen her build around herself. But here she was, asserting their connection without hesitation.

"Exploring, huh?" Eli chimed in, a grin spreading across his face. "Is that what we're calling it these days?"

Laughter erupted around the table, breaking the last of the tension. Gunner felt a surge of gratitude for this found family, their easy acceptance warming him from the inside out.

Charly cleared her throat, drawing attention away from the newly minted couple. "As heartwarming as this is," she said with a wry smile, "I'm glad we're all here, because we've got some business to discuss." She turned to Aubrey, her eyes sparkling with excitement. "The bar's numbers are looking great this month. That new cocktail menu you came up with is really bringing in the crowds, and even with hiring Chef Miguel to take over for you there, we're doing great."

Aubrey smiled, chewing her pancake. "That's fantastic news!"

As the women dove into a spirited discussion about the

bar's future, Gunner found himself marveling at Aubrey's passion. Her eyes sparkled as she gestured animatedly, describing flavor combinations that made his mouth water.

"Another thing on our plate is entertainment for the wedding," Charly said, seamlessly shifting gears. "Can you help with that, Aubrey, as well as handle the caterer since that's right up your alley?"

Aubrey nodded. "Of course."

Eli added, "Well, we've already got one thing sorted. Our very own country superstar can provide the music, right, Gunner?"

All eyes turned to Gunner, and he felt a familiar flutter of nerves in his stomach. It had been a while since he'd performed for more than the regulars at The Naked Moose. But as he looked around at the expectant faces of his friends, he knew he couldn't say no.

"I'd be honored," he said, his voice thick with emotion. "Though I might be a bit rusty. It's been a while since I played for a larger group."

Aubrey squeezed his hand under the table, her touch grounding him. "You'll be amazing," she whispered, her faith in him shining through her words.

"I do appreciate the offer," Charly said. "But Jaxon really wants you to enjoy the wedding, not play at it."

Gunner leaned back in his chair, a crooked smile playing on his lips. "You know, I might be able to do you one better than just me and my guitar," he said. "We can use the band I've been playing with at the bar, but I know someone who would be perfect. Her name is Jessie. She's on tour right now, but she'll be done by the time the wedding rolls around."

Charly's eyes widened with excitement. "Are you serious? That would be incredible!"

"Damn straight," Gunner replied, winking at her. "I'll reach out to her."

As the others chattered excitedly about the possibilities, Gunner smiled. It had been a long time since he'd felt this...useful. This wanted. He caught Aubrey's eye across the table, and the pride shining in her gaze made his heart skip a beat.

Eli pushed back from the table, his chair scraping against the floor. "As much as I'd love to sit here and enjoy the conversation and the warmth, I've got work to do." He turned to Gunner, a glint of mischief in his eyes. "I'm headed to the ranch, if you want a ride."

Gunner nodded, rising to his feet. "Count me in."

As they started clearing the table, Gunner found himself marveling at how natural it all felt. The easy banter, the sense of purpose, the way they all moved around each other like a well-oiled machine. For a moment, he let himself imagine a life like this—waking up to Aubrey every morning, sharing breakfast with friends, heading out to work at the ranch instead of chasing the next big hit.

It was terrifying. And exhilarating.

"You coming, Woods?" Eli called from the doorway, keys jingling in his hand. "Or are you gonna stand there daydreaming all day?"

Gunner shook himself out of his reverie. "I'm right behind you," he replied, grabbing his cowboy hat from the counter. He turned back, finding Aubrey at the sink. As she began to scrub a plate, he closed in on her.

"Forgot something," he murmured, his voice a low rumble even to his own ears.

Aubrey's breath hitched. "Oh? And what might that be?"

Instead of answering, Gunner brushed her hair aside and pressed his lips to the sensitive spot just below her ear. The kiss was tender, a stark contrast to the passionate encounters they'd shared last night.

"That," Gunner whispered against her skin.

Aubrey leaned back into him. "You're going to be late," she managed.

Gunner chuckled and said, "Worth it," before sliding his hat on his head and heading out the door.

Ten

Later that night, the firelight flickered and played along the walls of Gunner's living room. Aubrey, weary from a long day, was happy that she had a night off tonight. Cocooning herself in a large armchair near the dancing flames, she wrapped her knees close and watched as Gunner's fingers moved deftly over his guitar strings. The tune he played was raw and unrefined—simply him, free of performance or artifice; there was no audience, no spotlight, just his unguarded vulnerability. The days seemed to pass quickly as Aubrey and Gunner made the most of their time together, balancing Aubrey's shifts at the bar with Gunner's volunteer work.

God, he was gorgeous.

When he paused to fix a tuning peg, her eye noticed a crinkled, yellowed piece of paper peeking out from his guitar case. "What's this?" she murmured, reaching out tentatively.

Gunner shot a glance over his shoulder, and for an instant, his jaw tightened as an emotion flashed behind his eyes—a mixture of warning and plea that she couldn't decipher. "Just an old photo," he replied quietly as his fingers grazed an accidental, lingering note that seemed laden with extra meaning.

With careful gentleness, Aubrey opened the picture and let her thumb trace its creases as if trying to ease the sting of old memories. Though faded, the image clearly showed a young Gunner—maybe six or seven years old—sitting next to an older man whose kind eyes and weather-beaten face radiated warmth; they both held guitars and smiled. "Is this your grandpa?" she asked softly, her touch along the edge of the photo delicately caressing what once was.

Gunner fell silent. He set his guitar aside and leaned forward, elbows resting on his knees as his eyes remained fixed on the shifting flames. Finally, his voice emerged, rough yet measured: "Yeah. That was the summer he taught me to play." He drew in a long, heavy breath before continuing, "He was the first person who ever made me feel like I was good at something. More than just... good—worthy."

She sat quietly, letting the silence between them deepen. "He used to say that music wasn't about chasing perfection; it was about sharing your truth, even if it hurt," Gunner went on, locking his eyes with hers and causing something to tighten painfully within her chest. "I stopped visiting him after I got signed. I kept promising myself I'd find the time, you know? But I never did. And then he was gone." His hands clenched into fists under the soft light, the slight tremor in his voice betraying deeper wounds that simple words couldn't mend.

Without thinking, Aubrey slid off her chair and knelt beside him. She reached out and took his hand, their fingers intertwining in a grasp that was both tender and conflicted. The warmth of his skin reminded her vividly of what she longed for, yet it also stirred the fear of dismantling the walls she had so carefully erected. As she gently rested her forehead against his thigh, she realized with painful clarity how deeply she cared for every flawed, scarred part of Gunner.

When she pulled back slightly, he began to strum his guitar again. Her gaze wandered back to the old photo, where genuine smiles and a palpable bond leaped from the sepia-toned memories. "Tell me more about him," she urged softly.

For a long moment, Gunner's fingers hovered uncertainly over the strings. The pause was heavy with unspoken memories until he finally said, "He was more than just family to me. He taught me about life, about love and about the soul of music. When we played together, it was like we were speaking in a secret language meant only for us. His lessons weren't solely about chords and melodies— they were about staying true to yourself, to the music and to the people you cherish." Each word painted a richer picture of the man Gunner hoped to become—a man forever tethered to his grandpa's wisdom, yet haunted by the loss of that guiding spirit. In the intermingling of past and present, Aubrey saw not only the acclaimed, mysterious artist but also a wounded soul still aching for healing.

She understood completely. She herself carried broken pieces of a soul she wasn't sure would ever fully mend.

Eventually, Gunner let his fingers rest on the guitar, leaving a resonating note hanging in the air. His eyes drifted back to the lively flames. "When I was a kid, we'd sit on the porch together, watching the sunset. He taught me the value of honest work—the kind that leaves your hands rough and your soul quietly satisfied." Gunner's voice shimmered with memory.

Aubrey absorbed the details: the way his jaw tensed on certain words, how his broad shoulders seemed to curl inward, as if trying to contain the ache. "Grandpa had this way of making things simple, you know?" he said. "He'd work sunrise to sundown, and no matter how busted up his hands got, he'd still find time to make up stories or whistle old hymns. I think he believed if you just kept moving, kept doing, nothing bad could get too close."

But there was more, something swirling just beneath the gentleness—a storm brewing in Gunner's faraway gaze.

"Then came Nashville," he continued, each word dragged through bitterness. "The music started out like the best high I'd ever known. I thought I'd finally found a way to honor him. I wanted to make him proud, like maybe he'd hear my song on the radio and know it was me."

He laughed, sharp and self-deprecating. "But somewhere along the line, it stopped being about music. Or him. Or even me. The spotlight turned everything urgent and desperate, and suddenly I didn't know who the hell I was without it. I got lost." The line of his mouth hardened, his eyes distant. "I traded my roots for painkillers and a badge—a badge that said 'Famous,' even if I couldn't look in the mirror anymore."

Aubrey's hand hovered for a moment before she let it rest quietly on his knee. She didn't squeeze, didn't force comfort, just offered warmth and presence. The gesture made Gunner shiver, and some small, battered part of Aubrey's heart shivered, too. She understood wanting to run or escape pain.

He looked down at her hand, then at her. For a second, the old Gunner flickered back—a boyish, crooked grin, a flash of what might be hope. "I used to think if I just played the songs loud enough, numbed the pain down deep enough, I could somehow find myself again. But demons don't run. They wait. And eventually, you gotta face 'em. Otherwise, you're done."

Aubrey nodded. "You're not the only one who ever tried to run," she said, her voice steady. "But you didn't fail. You're here."

He reached for her hand, enveloping it in both of his. His touch was warm, rough with calluses, and for a blinding second Aubrey could see the boy he'd been, sitting on a porch with an old man, learning about the world one story at a time.

"Remembering him used to hurt," he said, so softly she almost missed it. "But now it doesn't. I stay sober. I'm a better man for many reasons, and he's a big part of that."

She traced her thumb along the side of his hand, memorizing the landscape of his scars and veins. "He'd be so proud of you," she whispered.

For a long moment, the world shrank to just them—and his sweet stare on her that drank her in.

"I think you're right about that," he eventually replied quietly.

Aubrey wanted to say more—wanted to tell him how her own ghosts still rattled chains, how the city lights of Atlanta haunted her even when she slept, how much it meant to be seen in this place, at this hour, by someone who understood the way pain could double as fuel. But the words tangled up inside her. Instead, she looked into his strong stare that had overcome so much, searching for a reflection of her own longing for finding her place in this world again.

Gunner offered it, unguarded, holding her gaze. "Thank you," he said, voice raw. "For listening. For sitting with me while I lay it all out."

"That's what friends do," she replied, surprised by how true it felt.

He turned her hand over and pressed his lips, chapped and earnest, to the inside of her wrist. The simplicity of the gesture—intimate, not desperate—made Aubrey's pulse stutter.

"Friends, huh?" he teased, the corners of his mouth lifting just enough to let her know he'd noticed the tremor in her hand, the catch in her breath. "You sure about that?"

She almost laughed, but it came out as a sigh. "More than friends then?"

He squeezed her hand with a gentleness that reverberated down to her bones. "Definitely more." He reached over and brushed a strand of hair from Aubrey's face.

"Wanna know something?" he asked, his voice lighter, but no less sincere.

She tilted her face to meet his. "What's that?"

"I think you're the first person I've let see me in years. Like, really see me. Not just the cowboy, or the singer, or the mess I made in Nashville." He studied her, earnest to the core. "I missed that. I missed being a whole person."

Aubrey felt her heart squeeze, tight and aching. "Me too," she admitted. "Sometimes I think I left half of myself back in Atlanta. Feels like it's still there, waiting for me to return. But the other half—she's here, trying to figure out what it means to be whole again."

He touched her cheek, gentle and reverent. "Then maybe we can help each other. If you want."

The offer was as terrifying as it was beautiful. Aubrey wanted to accept, wanted to believe she could build something honest from the wreckage of her old life. But fear clawed at her, as it always did when so many things had gone wrong before.

She hesitated, and Gunner saw it. "Hey," he said softly, "it's okay. No pressure. Just... I like sitting here with you. That's all."

Aubrey exhaled, grateful. "Me too."

"So," he said with a sly edge, "what do we do now?"

Just then, out of the blue, Aubrey's stomach rumbled— a sudden reminder of the mundane amidst the memories. Laughing, she slapped her hand against her belly and said, "If that isn't a sign that we should stop dwelling on the past and focus on the future, I don't know what is." Rising, she tugged him by the hand. "Come on," she declared.

"Where are we going?" he asked, curiosity clear in his tone.

"To eat," she answered, leading him toward the kitchen.

Gunner trailed hesitantly behind Aubrey as she stepped into the kitchen—a space adorned with weathered pine cabinets and copper pots suspended from the ceiling. His eyes drifted to the grocery bags scattered on the counter that she'd brought earlier. "That's quite a load," he observed, peeking into one with a curious wariness that probably betrayed his inner turmoil.

"I thought we could try something different today," she murmured softly, her voice laced with both hope and uncertainty.

"Different how?" Gunner asked, leaning casually yet somewhat uncertainly against the counter. He felt both weighted with missing his grandpa but also comforted, knowing he would be proud of the man Gunner was today.

Aubrey offered a tentative smile and explained, "Me cooking for you. I want to make a family recipe—my grandmother's robust beef stew. It's comforting, filled with memories…but also messy, like all our stories."

"That sounds just right, I suppose." He stepped closer. "I'm all ears…and taste buds."

"Perfect, because you're officially my sous-chef today," she declared.

Gunner rolled up his sleeves. "Alright, let me help," he said, both resolved and hesitant.

As Aubrey rummaged through a grocery bag, she mused, "Every ingredient here carries a bit of history."

Gunner chuckled softly, lifting a crisp carrot. "Really

now? Tell me about this one," he probed, his tone edged with both humor and a hint of sorrow.

Aubrey returned his smile with warmth as she began slicing an onion with practiced ease. "Carrots were my grandmother's favorite. She used to insist they sharpened her vision—even though her glasses were as thick as a whiskey bottle."

"Nice," Gunner teased while slowly peeling the carrot, each movement deliberate.

"She truly was the best," Aubrey replied, her eyes dancing with playful mischief.

"Now, the celery," she said, snapping a stalk in half with a fond sigh. "My mom used to say that life needs a bit of crunch—a reminder that we're more than just fleeting moments."

"One wise woman," Gunner agreed softly as he accepted the celery with a gentle smile. When their fingers brushed briefly as he took the knife from her, it was a fleeting contact charged with things he could never name.

"Well, like most things about her, yes—even if, sometimes, I hate admitting that to her," she quipped.

With all the ingredients prepped, their focus shifted to the stove. Gunner watched as Aubrey ignited the burner— a sharp click followed by a warm whoosh that seemed to pull at both his heart and stomach. The pan absorbed the heat, its glow painting a delicate blush across her cheeks as if hinting at the inner conflicts neither of them could fully speak of.

"Here we go," she announced, sliding the onions into sizzling oil.

"That smells like heaven," Gunner murmured, stepping closer to inhale the aroma.

"Just wait until you smell the garlic," she teased, tossing in the minced cloves. The aroma deepened—rich and earthy, bold yet somber.

His eyes followed her graceful hands as she added the bright carrots, beef and crisp celery, the vibrant hues clashing with the dark of the pan.

"Do you ever miss it?" he asked, watching her as she worked. "The chaos, the hustle of running a restaurant?"

Aubrey paused, the knife hovering midair for a breathless moment. She didn't meet his gaze. "I don't miss the pace," she finally replied, her voice brittle. "I miss what happens when all the pieces snap together. When a dish becomes more than the sum of its parts. That creation—" A low, wry laugh escaped her lips. "It's like magic, you know? I miss being the magician."

He shifted his weight against the doorframe, a slow smile creeping onto his face at her words. "You're still a magician, darlin'. Just a different kind of spell now."

Her snort surprised him and made him grin wider as she turned to face him fully, her eyes blazing with an unguarded intensity that caught him off guard. "You have no idea," she shot back, though he could sense that edge had softened just slightly between them. He noticed her hands tremble just enough as she tossed the last of the beef into the pot and felt an ache in his chest at how her lips hovered on an almost-smile.

"It's not just the food," she blurted suddenly before catching herself, embarrassment flickering across her features. "It's the people. In Atlanta, everyone was always hungry for something—sometimes actual food, some-times... I dunno. A taste of something bigger. Life was so bright there, so loud. Moving here felt like going deaf."

Gunner cocked his head. "Seems to me you still got plenty to say," he murmured softly.

"Maybe I do," she said finally; there was newfound steadiness in her voice now as if some invisible weight had lifted slightly from her shoulders. "Maybe I just needed someone to remember who I used to be and to feel like that person again."

His response came out almost reverently: "I remember, Aubrey. Even if you try to forget."

He shouldn't have been surprised by how those words made her freeze—but they did nonetheless. She glanced over her shoulder and smiled. "Thanks. I'll get there again, finding that path in my career that truly fulfills me. It just takes time."

Gunner absorbed her confession in silence, the tension in the kitchen mingling with unspoken questions. Soon, the gentle hum of the sizzling stew was interrupted by his careful query: "Mind if I ask something more personal?"

"Of course," she replied, though her tone wavered slightly.

"Tell me, what about your dad?" he inquired, setting his knife aside.

"Ain't that a loaded subject," she sighed, placing her knife down and leaning against the counter. "He just left one morning and never returned. My mom stepped in like a warrior and filled that void. He's not part of my life anymore."

Gunner moved in closer, erasing the gap between them. "Do you even know where he ended up?" he asked hesitantly, his voice tinged with remorse.

She shook her head slowly. "I don't know, and honestly, I don't care. I have so many incredible people in my life now that I refuse to waste my energy on someone who chose not to do right by me."

"Strong and resilient," he murmured, his words earnest yet conflicted. "A real fighter."

"My mom is a fighter," she whispered, reaching for another onion with hands that trembled slightly. "She was one of the reasons I survived my toughest battle back in Atlanta."

"Tell me about that," Gunner urged gently.

She hesitated, her chopping rhythm faltering as she spoke. "Just another disappointing jerk, if I'm being honest. I thought I'd found a mentor, but he turned out to be a sleaze who only wanted to get in my pants. When I said no, he wasn't too pleased."

"Did he fire you for refusing?" Gunner asked, barely able to control the fury in his voice.

"He did," she affirmed, bitterness lacing her admission. "Then he tried to sully my reputation in the restaurant world, but I fought back—legally."

Gunner nodded slowly, weighing his conflicting emotions. "You stood up for yourself, Aubrey. That takes real courage, even if it came at a high cost."

"I will get a settlement from it, but winning never felt

entirely sweet after all that," she admitted, her gaze locking with his. "It's a bittersweet victory."

"Sweet because you prevailed, bitter because it had to happen," he concluded softly. "But you're here now—stronger for it, aren't you?"

She exhaled, the weight of her past and the present seeming to seep out with the breath. "I am, but I'm still trying to figure out where I belong in all of this."

"Tell me, what did you love most about being a chef?" Gunner asked gently, hoping to help her remember all the good within the bad. That had helped him in his own journey of forgiveness.

"It's the way flavors come together to tell a story… How one dish can stir up memories and emotions," she replied in a measured, heartfelt tone.

"Sounds like music to me," Gunner mused.

"Food is my music," she confessed with a conflicted smile. "It's how I express everything I am—even when that expression is full of contradictions."

"Then let's keep cooking," he suggested warmly. "Together."

She returned his smile, and he could see her eyes flickering with both hope and hesitance. "Together."

He stepped behind her, wrapping his arms around her, and placed a gentle kiss on her shoulder. "Just in case you haven't heard it, you bring that special feeling—that meaning—to the people in Timber Falls. You know that, right?"

She leaned back into him, her voice soft and emotional. "Yeah, I know."

"It might not be as grand as the stage you had in Atlanta,

but it's important," he said, pressing another soft kiss on her shoulder. "I'm sorry for the men who let you down. And I'm even more sorry that I was once one of them."

She turned in his embrace, looking up at him with bright yet conflicted eyes. "You're not like them," she said.

"I hurt you," he admitted quietly, the remorse in his voice palpable.

"But you're here, making all that pain seem to fade away," she murmured, gently cupping his face with her trembling hands. "That means everything to me. Don't lump yourself in with those others—you're nothing like them."

"I'm still sorry," he whispered, his forehead pressed to hers, the admission heavy with regret.

She squeezed his face, drawing his lips to hers in a tender kiss. "And that only proves my point: you really are nothing like them."

Eleven

Weeks had flown by in a whirl of chilly wedding planning days and warm evenings at the bar and nights tucked into Gunner's arms. There hadn't been a night they'd spent apart since the movie night, and every single day was better than the last.

Standing behind the bar early in the morning, waiting for Gunner's friend to set up with the band to audition for the wedding, Aubrey watched the amber liquid swirl hypnotically in the glass as she added a splash of bitters. The familiar scents of oak and citrus wafted up, tickling her nose as she jotted down measurements in her dog-eared notepad.

"A little more vermouth," she murmured to herself, reaching for the bottle. "Maybe a hint of elderflower."

The tinkle of ice cubes against glass was a soothing melody, reminding her of busy nights in her Atlanta kitchen. For a moment, a pang of nostalgia threatened to overtake her, but she pushed it aside. This was her bar now, her creation. She was determined to make it shine. And she hoped that, in time, this experience would become as fulfilling as her time at the restaurant in Atlanta had been.

As she raised the glass to her lips for a taste, her phone buzzed insistently on the polished wood counter. Aubrey's heart leaped at the sight of her mother's smiling face on the screen. She quickly wiped her hands on a nearby towel and answered the call, a genuine smile blooming across her face.

"Mom!" she exclaimed, propping the phone up against the liquor bottles. "How are things?"

As her mom launched into a story about their neighbor's unruly dog, Aubrey found herself drinking in the familiar cadence of her voice, the crinkles around her mother's eyes.

Aubrey's mother leaned closer to the screen, her eyes twinkling with unmistakable curiosity. "So, honey, how is Gunner? Is he treating my girl right?"

A laugh bubbled up from Aubrey's chest. She glanced at him helping the band get the instruments ready. "Gunner is great, and yes, he treats me very well."

"Oh, sweetie," her mother cooed, "you look happy. Happier than I've seen you in a long time."

Aubrey's heart swelled. "I am, Mom. I really am."

As she told her mom about her latest adventures with Gunner over the last week, she felt a surge of excitement. "Soon, you'll finally get to meet him." She was coming to town for Charly's wedding—only a few months away now. "I'd love for you to see the bar, meet Gunner, experience Timber Falls for yourself."

"I cannot wait," her mother said, her voice warm with

affection. "Well, honey, I'm just thrilled to see you so happy. This Gunner sounds like a real catch. I can't wait to meet him and see this beautiful town you're calling home now."

Aubrey felt a lump form in her throat. "Thanks, Mom. That means a lot."

"You deserve it, sweetie," her mother added softly. "After everything you've been through, this is wonderful."

Aubrey nodded, blinking back tears. "I love you." She looked up to see Gunner waving her over to the stage. "Sorry, I need to get going."

"Okay, my sweetie, love you," her mother said.

Ending the call, Aubrey took a deep breath. She tucked her phone away, her gaze sweeping across The Naked Moose until it landed on Gunner, chatting animatedly with the band near the small stage.

Her heart did a little flip as she watched him, all easy charm and rugged good looks. Grabbing a mug, she filled it with steaming black coffee and made her way over.

"Thought you might need a pick-me-up," she said, holding out the mug.

Gunner turned, his eyes lighting up. "You're a lifesaver," he drawled, reaching for the coffee.

Their fingers brushed as she handed it over, sending a jolt of electricity through her. Gunner's lips quirked up in a knowing smile, and Aubrey felt heat rise to her cheeks. The heat had never quit between them over the weeks that had gone by. Somehow it only seemed to be growing hotter.

"Aubrey," he said, turning slightly, "I'd like you to meet an old friend, Jessie. We toured together a few years back."

The woman beside Gunner, all wild curls and smoky eyes, flashed a warm smile. "So, you're the famous Aubrey," she said, her voice rich and husky. "Gunner here hasn't stopped singing your praises since I arrived."

Aubrey raised an eyebrow at Gunner, who looked slightly sheepish. "Is that so?" she teased.

"What can I say?" Gunner shrugged, and she thought she heard a hint of pride in his voice. "When you find someone special, you want the whole world to know."

"Such a charmer," Aubrey grinned.

Gunner winked. "Always."

Jessie laughed, shaking her head at them. "How 'bout we get started."

"Please," Aubrey said, taking a seat next to Gunner at the small table.

The band took their positions on the small stage, instruments gleaming under the soft lighting. Jessie stepped up to the microphone, her presence commanding attention even before she uttered a single note.

As the first chords rang out, Aubrey felt the air in the room shift, charged with an electric anticipation. Jessie's powerful gravelly voice filled the space, raw emotion pouring from her lips as she belted out a soulful country ballad.

Aubrey's foot began tapping involuntarily to the rhythm, her body swaying slightly. She stole a glance at Gunner, noticing the way his eyes had closed, lost in the music. *God, he's beautiful when he's like this*, she thought, a warm flutter in her chest.

His eyes suddenly opened, finding hers locked on him. He smiled softly, leaned in close, his breath tickling her ear. "She's got something special, don't she?" he said, his low drawl sending a shudder down her spine.

"Mmm-hmm," Aubrey hummed in agreement, trying to ignore the way her skin tingled at his proximity. "Her voice is incredible."

The song built to a crescendo, Jessie's voice soaring as the band poured their hearts into the performance. Aubrey found herself holding her breath, completely captivated.

As the final notes faded, Aubrey's eyes met Gunner's again. "I think we just found our wedding band," Aubrey said, a smile playing on her lips.

Gunner nodded. "Couldn't agree more, darlin'," he replied, his touch sending heat flaring through her body.

As the music died down, Aubrey and Gunner applauded, and Gunner strode toward the stage. "That was somethin' else, Jess," he said.

"Thanks," she said.

Aubrey agreed, "Totally incredible. We'd love to book you for the wedding, if you're agreeable."

"Of course, I'm in," Jessie said.

"Great," Aubrey said. She glanced to Gunner. "Why don't you talk details, and I'll get back to work." At Gunner's nod, Aubrey offered her hand to Jessie. "It's really great to meet you. I can't wait to hear you play at the wedding. It's going to be fab."

"Lookin' forward to it," Jessie said, then got into a conversation with Gunner about the logistics of the evening.

Just as Aubrey strode behind the bar, the door swung open, flooding the dim bar with early morning sunlight. Poppy breezed in, her vibrant red curls bouncing with each step, clutching an envelope to her chest like a prized possession. Her eyes scanned the room, landing on Aubrey behind the bar. A grin spread across Poppy's freckled face as she made a beeline for her target.

Aubrey felt her heart warm as the whirlwind that was Poppy approached.

"Well, well, if it isn't the belle of The Naked Moose," Poppy quipped, sliding onto a barstool. "I see you've got quite the view from here." She winked, nodding toward Gunner, who was helping the band pack up.

Aubrey felt heat rush to her cheeks. "It is a nice view," she said with a laugh, grabbing the cocktail glass she was mixing earlier. "And what about you?" she deflected. "Any luck in the romance department?"

Poppy dramatically placed a hand over her heart. "Alas, my prince charming seems to be stuck in traffic. But don't you worry about little ol' me. I'm just biding my time until Mr. Right comes along…or until I can convince one of these rugged cowboys to sweep me off my feet."

Aubrey chuckled. "Well, there's certainly no shortage of those around here."

As she watched Poppy's animated gestures, Aubrey couldn't help but marvel at how quickly this force of nature had wormed her way into their lives the last couple months. When Poppy had noticed that there was a connection between Gunner and Aubrey, she, with her quirky charm, accepted that another Timber Falls heartthrob was off the market and resumed her quest for new prospects. She was a force, and a welcome one at that, which was good because, with the wedding planning in full bloom, she seemed around more often than not.

Poppy's voice snapped her back to the present. "Speaking of rugged cowboys, how's our resident country star treating you? If that man isn't writing a love song about you as we speak, I'll eat my hat."

Aubrey rolled her eyes, but couldn't quite suppress the smile tugging at her lips. "You're incorrigible, you know that?"

"It's part of my charm," Poppy replied with a wink.

Aubrey's gaze drifted to Gunner. "He's treating me very well," she admitted.

Before Poppy could respond, the door swung open again, bringing with it a gust of cool Montana air and the sound of boots on hardwood. Aubrey's gaze snapped to the entrance, where Charly stood framed in the doorway, her eyes dancing with excitement.

"Mornin', ladies," Charly called out, practically bouncing as she made her way to the bar.

"Morning," Aubrey said, gesturing to Jessie. "You just missed the show. Jessie agreed to do the wedding. You'll love her."

"Oh," Charly said, giving a quick glance to Jessie. "I knew she'd work out. Those YouTube videos were mind-blowing. I'll go say hi in a second." She turned her focus to Poppy. "What brings you by this early?"

Poppy grinned. "I've got the final invitation to show you."

Aubrey felt a surge of anticipation. She'd seen how much stress the wedding planning had put on Charly, and the completion of this milestone was clearly a weight off her shoulders.

"Well, don't keep us in suspense," Aubrey said to Poppy. "Show us."

With a theatrical flourish, Poppy slid the invitation from its envelope, holding it up like a prized artifact. Aubrey leaned in. The invitation was a work of art—delicate ivory paper embossed with a subtle pattern of pine trees, the text a rich, earthy brown.

Charly's brow furrowed slightly as she examined every detail, her eyes roving over each carefully chosen word. Aubrey found herself holding her breath, acutely aware of how much this meant to her friend. She glanced at Poppy, seeing her own nervous anticipation mirrored in the wedding planner's face.

"Well?" Aubrey prompted, unable to bear the suspense any longer. "What's the verdict, Char?"

For a moment, Charly's expression remained unreadable, and Aubrey felt a flicker of worry. Had something gone wrong? But then, a radiant smile spread across Charly's face.

"It's perfect," she breathed, her eyes welling with happy tears. "Absolutely perfect."

The tension in the air dissolved instantly, replaced by a wave of collective joy. Aubrey felt her own lips curve into a smile. "Thank God," she muttered, reaching for Charly's hand and giving it a squeeze. "I was worried we'd have to tie Poppy to a chair to keep her from redesigning the whole thing if you didn't like it."

Poppy let out a laugh, bright and melodious. "Hey now, I might just like being tied to a chair."

Aubrey barked a laugh. "Somehow I do not doubt that."

As the three of them shared a moment of laughter and relief, Aubrey's heart warmed. She couldn't forget that only a few months ago everything seemed wrong, but now, there was a brightness to her days she loved.

When the laughter faded, Poppy leaned in, her eyes sparkling with excitement. "Now, ladies, let's talk accommodations for our out-of-town guests. I've been doing some research, and I think I've found some perfect options."

"Do tell," Aubrey said.

"The Timber Falls Inn is our crown jewel, of course," Poppy explained. "It's got that rustic charm with all the modern amenities. But for those looking for a more intimate experience, I've scouted out a few adorable bed and breakfasts."

Charly nodded appreciatively. "You've really thought of everything, haven't you?"

"That's why you hired me, sugar." Poppy winked. "I've got brochures for each place, complete with pricing and availability. I figure we can include them with the invitations, make it easy for everyone."

Aubrey couldn't help but be impressed. "Poppy, you're a godsend. I don't know how we'd manage all this without you."

As Poppy beamed under the praise, the door to the bar opened yet again, bringing the familiar presence of Willow.

"Well, well," Willow said, her eyes taking in the scene

before her. "Looks like I'm interrupting a party. I've never seen the bar this busy so early in the morning."

Charly held up the invitation with a grin. "Final approval on the invitations." She pointed to Jessie. "Band has been booked."

Willow's face softened. "Amazing," she said, sliding onto a stool next to Charly.

Charly let out a deep, contented sigh, her shoulders visibly relaxing as she gazed around at her friends. The weight of wedding planning that had been pressing down on her for months seemed to lift, replaced by a warm sense of accomplishment.

"I can't believe we're almost there," she said, her voice soft with wonder. "All the big things are done. It's really happening."

Aubrey reached over and squeezed Charly's hand. "This wedding is going to be beautiful."

Charly's eyes misted over. "I couldn't have done it without all of you," she said, her gaze sweeping from Aubrey to Poppy to Willow. "I just appreciate it so much."

She trailed off, overcome with emotion. Aubrey put an arm around Charly's shoulders.

"Alright, enough of the mushy stuff," Aubrey said, keeping them on track as she'd done the past two months. "What's left on the list?"

Charly straightened, wiping at her eyes. "Well, we've still got the final fittings next week. And then there's the decorations that I want to make."

"Oh! Speaking of decorations," Poppy interjected, practically bouncing in her seat. "I had the most brilliant idea for centerpieces. We could use mason jars filled with wild-flowers and fairy lights!"

Charly's face lit up. "That sounds perfect! But it's a lot of work." She paused, head cocking. Then added, "What if we made it a group project? We could all get together, maybe even rope the cowboys into helping. Make a day of it?"

Aubrey grinned. "Count me in."

"Oh, my gosh, yes!" Poppy squealed, clapping her hands together. "More cowboys? Yes, please."

Aubrey snorted, her eyes twinkling with amusement. "Of course that's what you're focusing on."

Poppy placed a hand on her chest and said, dead serious, "As if there is anything else *to* focus on."

Twelve

The next morning, the sunlight streaming through the curtains danced across Aubrey's face, coaxing her awake. She stretched, savoring the rare luxury of a lazy Sunday morning. As consciousness fully returned, a ghost of a memory flitted through her mind—Gunner's warm lips pressing a gentle kiss to her forehead at dawn—making her heart flutter.

She eventually got out of bed and padded barefoot to the kitchen. "A day off deserves a proper breakfast," she mused, pulling ingredients from the fridge. Her hands moved with practiced ease, chopping vibrant bell peppers and whisking eggs for a frittata. The sizzle of bacon in the cast iron skillet filled the air with a mouthwatering aroma.

The coffee maker gurgled to life, its rich scent mingling with the savory breakfast smells. Aubrey took her time, setting the table with care. It was a far cry from the elegant place settings of her Atlanta restaurant days, but there was an intimacy to this simple act that touched her.

Footsteps in the hallway announced Willow's arrival. She appeared in the doorway, hair tousled from sleep but eyes bright.

"Morning, sunshine," Aubrey called out with a grin. "Perfect timing, breakfast is just about ready."

Willow inhaled deeply, a smile spreading across her face. "It smells amazing in here. You didn't have to go to all this trouble, Aubs."

Aubrey waved away the comment as she plated the frittata. "Please, you know I live for this. Besides, we deserve a little pampering on our day off, don't we?"

They settled at the table, and Aubrey took a sip of her coffee, savoring the rich flavor before setting the mug down.

Willow took a bite of the frittata and moaned in happiness. "Always so dang good." She took another bite before saying, "It's been so long since we've had a morning alone." She gave Aubrey a long stare. "How's things going with Gunner? You guys seem happy."

"You know," Aubrey began, her voice soft but steady, "I never thought I'd say this, but things with Gunner, they're really good. Better than I could have imagined."

Willow's eyes sparkled with interest. "Oh? Do tell," she encouraged, leaning forward slightly.

Aubrey felt a blush creep up her cheeks, but she continued. "I feel safe with him, which is not something I ever expected to feel again with any man." Not after her handsy boss. Or her absent father.

Willow reached across the table, squeezing Aubrey's hand. "I'm so happy for you. You deserve this."

Aubrey smiled, feeling a weight lift off her chest. She'd been holding these feelings in, afraid to jinx things by speaking them aloud. But sharing with Willow felt good. Right, even.

"Thanks. It means a lot to hear you say that," Aubrey replied, her voice thick with emotion.

Willow nodded, then bit her lip, seeming to contemplate something. Finally, she spoke. "Actually, I wanted to talk to you about something too. Eli and I have been talking about maybe moving in together."

"Wow, that's big!" Aubrey said. "How do you feel about it?"

"Excited, but also a little scared," Willow admitted. "After everything I've been through, it's a big step. What do you think?"

Aubrey considered her words carefully, knowing the weight they would carry with her friend. "Honestly? I think it's wonderful. Eli's a good man, and I've seen how he treats you. If you feel ready, I say go for it."

Willow smiled, but it looked a little sad. "But what about you alone in this big house?"

Aubrey glanced around the spacious kitchen. "I've been thinking about my own living situation lately, actually."

Willow tilted her head, curiosity evident in her expression. "Oh?"

Aubrey nodded. "I miss being in the city, and while downtown isn't really a city, it would give me a little more of that feel. If you moved out, we could sell the house and I might buy a condo in town."

"Really?" Willow's eyes widened. "That's a big change."

"I know," Aubrey replied. "This place, as beautiful as it is, it's too quiet and lonely. I want something that feels more...*me*."

Willow nodded, understanding dawning in her eyes. "You want more life."

"Exactly," Aubrey said, a smile tugging at her lips. "A place where more of the action is. Where I can walk downstairs and be surrounded by people and life."

As she spoke, Aubrey could almost see it—a modern kitchen with gleaming countertops, large windows letting in natural light.

"I think it's a great idea," Willow said, her voice warm with support. "Nothing is decided on my end yet, but we can revisit this down the road for sure."

"Agreed," Aubrey said.

They touched their coffee mugs together in a playful toast, the ceramic making a satisfying clink. As they finished the last bites of their breakfast, Aubrey felt a surge of possibility that maybe this feeling in her gut that she didn't fit in within Timber Falls would finally go away.

An hour later, showered, with a fully belly, Aubrey's hands gripped her steering wheel as she navigated the winding road to the ranch, the landscape outside transforming into a winter wonderland. Willow sat beside her, their animated chatter filling the car with warmth despite the frigid temperature outside.

"I still can't believe how much snow there is here in February," Aubrey marveled, her eyes wide as she took in the pristine white blanket covering everything in sight.

Willow laughed. "I know. It's wild."

As they rounded a bend, the breathtaking view of Timber Falls unfolded before them. Snow-capped mountains loomed in the distance, their jagged peaks piercing an impossibly blue sky. The sun glinted off frozen streams and icicle-laden trees, creating a dazzling spectacle.

"It's like a postcard," Aubrey breathed. "I never thought I'd say this, but I'm starting to understand why people fall in love with this place."

"Even at a balmy five degrees?" Willow teased.

Aubrey chuckled, shaking her head. "Okay, I could do without the arctic temperatures. But this view, it's something else."

As they approached the ranch, Aubrey's heart began to race, anticipation and nervousness fluttering in her stomach. "I wonder what Gunner's got planned for his talent show kids today," she mused, trying to keep her voice casual. He'd had this surprise excursion planned for a month now but kept the details to himself.

"Knowing him, it'll be something special," Willow replied with a knowing smile.

Aubrey agreed with a nod, pulling into the ranch's driveway, and her jaw dropped. The scene before her was like something out of a fairy tale. A crackling bonfire cast a warm glow over the snow-covered ground, surrounded by hay bales draped with cozy blankets. To one side, a quaint wooden stand was set up, steam rising from large urns of what could only be hot chocolate.

But what truly took her breath away was the magnificent black horse hitched to an old-fashioned sleigh, the horse's coat gleaming in the sunlight.

"Oh, my god," Aubrey whispered, her eyes wide with wonder. "This is gorgeous."

"No kidding," Willow agreed, stepping out of the car.

Aubrey followed, the crisp air nipping at her cheeks as she took in the thoughtful setup.

Willow gave Aubrey's arm a gentle squeeze before heading off toward the campfire, where Eli was stoking the flames. Aubrey found herself alone, surrounded by the bustling energy of the kids, along with their families.

"Aubrey!" Charly called out, waving from the hot chocolate station. "Come try some of this cocoa. It's to die for!"

Aubrey made her way over, her boots crunching in the snow. "This is incredible," she said, accepting a steaming mug. "I can't believe how much work you all put into this."

As she sipped the rich, creamy cocoa, Aubrey felt a warmth spread through her that had nothing to do with the drink.

"It's nice, isn't it?" Jaxon commented, sidling up to them. "But this was all Gunner. We're just helping."

"Amazing," Aubrey said, before saying goodbye and heading off.

As she wandered through the event, greeting familiar faces and meeting new ones, she couldn't shake the feeling of being so damn happy she could nearly burst.

Suddenly, she felt a presence behind her, and warmth enveloped her senses. Turning, she found herself face to face with Gunner, his eyes twinkling with joy.

"Hey there, darlin'." He leaned in to place a gentle kiss on her lips. "I'm glad you could make it."

Aubrey's heart fluttered, her body instinctively leaning into his. "Gunner, this is amazing. I can't believe you did all this."

He smiled, a hint of bashfulness in his expression. "Well, I wanted to do something special. For the kids and their families."

As they stood there, surrounded by the laughter and warmth of the community, Aubrey felt the last of her walls crumbling. In Gunner's eyes, she saw a future she'd never dared to dream of, right here in Timber Falls. "This is just amazing," she repeated, not sure how to word all she was feeling.

Gunner's eyes sparkled with mischief as he took Aubrey's hand, his touch sending a familiar shiver down her spine. "Say, Miss Hale," he drawled, "how'd you like to be my navigator for the sleigh ride? I promise I'll be a perfect gentleman."

Aubrey laughed, the sound bright and clear. "A perfect gentleman? Now that, I'd like to see," she teased, feeling a flutter of excitement in her chest. She squeezed his hand, her eyes meeting his. "I'd love to."

As they made their way to the sleigh, Aubrey's mind raced. How had this man, this place, become so important to her in such a short time? The thought both thrilled and terrified her. She was barely thinking about how much she didn't like small-town life anymore.

When they reached the sleigh, Gunner placed his hands on her waist, his touch gentle but sure. "Allow me, darlin'," he said, helping her climb aboard.

Aubrey settled into the seat, the worn wood smooth

beneath her. Gunner joined her, his body a solid warmth against her side.

He offered her a wool blanket. "Thanks," she said, tucking it around her.

Just then, Gunner let out a sharp whistle, and a group of excited children came running towards the sleigh. As they clambered aboard, their giggles and chatter filling the air, Aubrey couldn't help but smile.

The sleigh lurched forward as Gunner clucked softly to the horse, its hooves crunching through the snow-covered field. Aubrey inhaled deeply, the crisp winter air filling her lungs as she took in the breathtaking scenery around her.

"It's like something out of a fairy tale," Aubrey murmured, her eyes wide with wonder.

Gunner's low chuckle brushed over her. "Glad you approve. Though I'd say you outshine the view any day."

Aubrey felt a blush creep up her cheeks, still unused to his easy compliments. She turned to watch the children, their faces alight with joy as they pointed out snow-capped trees and the occasional wildlife.

"Look, a deer!" one little girl squealed, causing a chorus of excited gasps.

As Gunner guided the horse around a gentle bend, Aubrey found herself lost in thought. How different this was from the bustling kitchens and city lights she once knew. Yet, surrounded by laughter and wrapped in Gunner's warmth, she felt a peace she'd never experienced before. This was it, she realized. This was where she belonged.

"You look a million miles away," Gunner said softly, his eyes searching hers. "Everything alright?"

Aubrey smiled, surprised to find tears pricking at the corners of her eyes. "More than alright," she whispered. "I just… I never expected to find this kind of happiness here."

Gunner's arm tightened around her, and she leaned into his embrace, savoring the moment. As the sleigh glided across the snow, Aubrey felt a deep sense of contentment settle over her.

For the first time since moving to Timber Falls, she felt truly like maybe she could make this town work.

The winter sun dipped below the horizon, casting long shadows across the snow-covered pasture as Gunner, Jaxon and Eli watched the last minivan crunch down the gravel driveway.

Gunner let out a low whistle. "Well, I'd say that went better than even I expected."

Jaxon chuckled, his breath visible in the crisp air. "You're not wrong. Those kids had more energy than a rodeo bull on Red Bull."

"Speak for yourself," Eli grumbled, but the twinkle in his eyes betrayed his amusement. "I feel like I just went ten rounds with a mechanical bull."

Gunner clapped him on the shoulder. "Aw, come on now, Cole. Don't tell me the infamous bull rider's getting soft in his old age?"

As they shared a laugh, Gunner's smile felt easier. It had been a long time since he'd felt this sense of belonging, of being part of something bigger than himself. The talent show kids, their infectious enthusiasm… It all stirred something in him he thought he'd lost. A purpose.

"Alright," Gunner said, straightening up. "One last chore and we can call it a day." He turned to the mare and the sleigh.

Gunner took hold of her bridle, stroking her velvety nose. "Let's get you settled for the night, huh?"

After Eli and Jaxon unhooked the horse from the sleigh, he led the mare toward the barn, Jaxon and Eli falling into step behind him. The steady clip-clop of hooves on packed snow gave way to a hollow echo as they entered the barn, the familiar scents of hay and leather enveloping them.

Once inside, Gunner's cold fingers worked at the horse's harness, the familiar motions a soothing rhythm. As he unbuckled the last strap, Jaxon cleared his throat.

"So, uh, how're things going with Aubrey?" Jaxon's tone was casual, but there was a hint of genuine curiosity beneath it.

Gunner paused at the mention of her name, a slight smile tugging at his lips. "It's good. Real good." He ran a hand along the horse's flank, brushing away bits of snow. "She's somethin' else, you know?"

Jaxon chuckled. "I hear ya. It's nice to see you both so happy."

Gunner nodded, reaching for a brush. As he began to groom the horse, he found himself opening up. "It's different with her. Feels real."

He worked the brush in slow, circular motions, paying close attention to each spot. The repetitive movement was almost meditative.

"I used to think I needed the spotlight, the adoration

of fans," Gunner mused. "But with Aubrey? It's like I've found something I didn't even know I was missing."

"I get that," Jaxon said.

As Gunner continued grooming the horse, Eli leaned against a nearby stall. "Speaking of things you were missin'," he said, "how's the songwriting coming along?"

Gunner's hand stilled on the horse's coat, a flicker of excitement passing through him. He reached into the inner pocket of his jacket and pulled out a well-worn leather notebook, its edges frayed and pages bulging with loose sheets.

"Matter of fact," Gunner said, "it's going well." He ran his fingers over the notebook's cover. "It's like a damn floodgate opened up lately. Words and melodies just pourin' out of me."

Eli raised an eyebrow, a rare smile tugging at his lips. "That so?"

Gunner nodded, flipping through the pages filled with his messy scrawl. "It's like, for the first time in forever, I'm not trying to write what I think people want to hear. I'm just writing what's in here," he said, pointing to his chest. He paused, considering his next words carefully. "You know, I used to be so caught up in chasin' that next big hit, worrying about staying relevant." Gunner's eyes met Eli's and then shifted to Jaxon. "But now? I'm just livin' in the moment, takin' it all in. And somehow, that's making the music flow easier than ever." His mind drifted to Aubrey, to the ranch, to the simplicity of life in Timber Falls. "It's like I've finally figured out what really matters, you know? And that's what's finding its way into these songs."

"That's so damn good," Eli said.

Gunner patted the horse's neck absently, lost in thought. "I don't know what the future holds, and for once, I'm okay with that. I'm just happy. Here. Now. With Aubrey, with working at the ranch, with the talent show, with my music coming back to me in a way I never expected."

Jaxon's eyes crinkled with warmth as he clapped Gunner on the shoulder. "Man, it's good to hear you talk like that. You've come a long way since you first showed up here."

Eli nodded. "Yeah, Woods. Who'd have thought a washed-up country star would find his mojo again getting dumped from young horses?" His tone was teasing, but there was no mistaking the affection behind it.

Gunner chuckled. "Watch it, Cole. I might just write a song about a grumpy ex-bull rider with a heart of gold."

The three men shared a laugh, the sound echoing through the barn. As it faded, Gunner felt a surge of gratitude for these friendships he'd never expected to find his way back to as an adult.

"Alright," Gunner said, giving the horse a final pat. "Let's get her back to the field and call it a day."

He led the horse out of the barn and put her back in the pasture with the other mares. As they walked back toward the house, Gunner found himself hanging back a bit, taking in the scene.

The weathered barn, the sprawling fields, the distant mountains, it was all so different from the glitz and glamour he'd once chased. Yet somehow, Timber Falls was always home.

His mind wandered to Aubrey, to the way her eyes lit

up when she smiled, to the feeling of her hand in his. He thought about the kids he was mentoring, their faces beaming with pride and excitement. It was a simple life, but it was real. It was honest.

As they approached the house, Gunner realized he was smiling. The path that had led him here had been winding and often painful, but standing here now, he wouldn't change a thing. For the first time in years, he felt truly, deeply content.

He followed Jaxon and Eli into the house, a wave of warmth and enticing aromas enveloping him. The house buzzed with a comforting energy, laughter and chatter drifting from the kitchen. When he entered the kitchen, his eyes immediately sought out Aubrey, drawn to her like a magnet.

There she was. Her waves cascading over her shoulders as she bent to check something in the oven. Without hesitation, Gunner strode across the room, his heart quickening with each step.

"Now that's a view I can appreciate," he drawled, wrapping his arms around her waist from behind.

Aubrey straightened, leaning back into his embrace. "Well, hello, cowboy," she replied, laughing.

Gunner nuzzled her neck, inhaling the scent of vanilla and spice that always clung to her. "Thank you," he murmured. "For everything today. Those kids won't ever forget it."

Aubrey turned in his arms, her eyes meeting his. "I wouldn't have missed it for the world," she said softly. "You were amazing with them."

His chest tightened with emotion. "It's all thanks to you, you know," he confessed. "You make me want to be better."

A flicker of vulnerability passed over Aubrey's face, quickly replaced by a warm smile. "Come on," she said, giving him a playful nudge. "Let's eat before it gets cold."

As they all settled around the table, Gunner couldn't take his eyes off Aubrey. The way she effortlessly commanded the room, dishing out plates with the precision of a seasoned chef, stirred something deep within him. It wasn't just attraction—it was admiration, respect, and something dangerously close to love.

"This smells incredible," he said, inhaling deeply as Aubrey set a steaming plate before him.

She beamed, a hint of pride in her voice. "Just a little something I whipped up. Nothing fancy."

Gunner took a bite, flavors exploding on his tongue. "Darlin', if this is 'nothing fancy,' I can't imagine what you'd do if you were really trying to impress."

Aubrey's cheeks flushed slightly, and Gunner felt a surge of affection. He loved that he could still make her blush, this fierce, independent woman who'd seen and overcome so much.

The warmth of the conversation around the table enveloped Gunner like a familiar melody. Eli's deep chuckle mingled with Jaxon's animated storytelling, creating a harmony that filled the room.

"Remember that time we tried to wrangle old Bessie?" Jaxon grinned, nudging Gunner with his elbow.

Gunner groaned. "How could I forget? That cow had it out for me from day one."

Aubrey leaned in, her eyes dancing with curiosity. "Oh, this I've got to hear."

As Jaxon launched into the tale, Gunner found himself watching Aubrey. The way she threw her head back in laughter, the slight crinkle around her eyes—it was a side of her he was still getting to know, and he cherished every moment of it.

"You boys were something else," Aubrey said, shaking her head fondly. "Pure trouble."

Gunner's heart swelled as he winked. "Still are, darlin'. Just a little more weathered now."

Thirteen

A couple hours later, after making a quick trip back to Audrey's house, the clatter of dishes and the warm laughter of friends filled the kitchen as Gunner, Jaxon and Eli finished cleaning up after dinner. Aubrey watched from the table, along with Willow and Charly, stuffed full and finally warm again after spending all day outside.

When Gunner finally finished, wiping his hands on a towel, his eyes drifted to hers and he gestured for her to follow him into the living room.

As she reached him, he tugged her close. "Hey there, darlin'," he drawled, his voice dropping to that low, inviting tone that never failed to send a quiver down Aubrey's spine. "How about you and I slip away for a little surprise?"

"A surprise, huh?" she repeated. "What kind of surprise are we talking about?"

He chuckled, the sound rich and warm. "Now, if I told you, it wouldn't be a surprise, would it?" He extended his hand to her, his calloused fingers a stark contrast to her smooth ones. "Trust me?"

"Alright, cowboy," she said finally, slipping her hand into his. "Lead the way."

"We'll be spending more time outside," Gunner said. "Dress warm."

Aubrey nodded, savoring the heat of his body next to hers. "Okay," she replied. "But maybe you could tell me where we're going to help me get a better feel of what I should wear?" She really hated surprises.

Gunner's laugh rumbled through her. "Patience, darlin'. Some things are worth the wait."

She laughed, shaking her head, but dressed in all her warmest clothes, including a snow suit, hat and mitts, and then followed him to his truck after they said quick good-byes to the others.

Once outside, she settled into the passenger seat of Gunner's truck, her heart racing as he climbed in beside her. The engine roared to life, its low growl filling the comfortable silence between them. As they pulled away from the ranch, Aubrey stole a glance at Gunner, admiring the way the dashboard lights cast a soft glow on his rugged features.

"Now are you gonna tell me where we're headed?" she asked, unable to contain her curiosity.

Gunner's lips curved into a mischievous smile. "Now where's the fun in that?"

Aubrey rolled her eyes playfully but couldn't help the flutter in her chest. She turned her gaze to the window, watching as the familiar streets of Timber Falls gave way to winding country roads. The stars above seemed to shine brighter with each passing mile.

"You know," Gunner said softly, breaking the silence, "I used to drive these roads late at night when I was struggling when I first came home." He paused, his grip tightening slightly on the steering wheel. "Something about the open road always helped clear my head."

Aubrey felt a pang in her heart, recognizing the vulnerability in his admission. "And now?" she asked, her voice barely above a whisper.

Gunner's eyes met hers for a brief moment, filled with an intensity that took her breath away. "Now, I've got better reasons to stay grounded." He gave a small smile. "And I've learned better pain management."

As they continued their journey, Aubrey found herself captivated by Gunner's relaxed confidence. The way he effortlessly navigated the winding roads, one hand on the wheel, the other resting casually on his thigh. It was a far cry from the tortured artist she'd first encountered in Atlanta.

"You seem so much different now than when I first met you," she mused aloud.

Gunner raised an eyebrow at her before focusing back on the road. "Good different or bad different?"

Aubrey hesitated, weighing her words carefully. "Good, I think. More at peace."

A soft chuckle escaped Gunner's lips. "Funny how a small town and a certain stubborn chef can do that to a man."

As the truck climbed higher into the hills, Aubrey laughed. "I suppose that's true."

Twenty minutes later, the truck rolled to a stop in a parking lot at the edge of the cliff, the engine's purr fading into the night's stillness. He swiftly exited, his boots crunching on gravel as he grabbed wool blankets from the back. Then he rounded the vehicle and extended his hand to Aubrey, a gentle smile playing on his lips.

"May I assist you, ma'am?" he drawled, his eyes twinkling with mischief.

Aubrey couldn't help but roll her eyes, even as her heart skipped a beat. "Such a gentleman," she teased, placing her hand in his. The warmth of his touch sent a shiver through her that had nothing to do with the crisp night air.

As she stepped down, her breath caught in her throat. The view before her was breathtaking—a sea of twinkling lights from Timber Falls nestled in the valley below, mirroring the bright stars above.

"Gunner, this is…" She trailed off, at a loss for words.

He squeezed her hand gently. "I know. C'mon, the view's even better from back here."

He led her to the truck bed, where he laid out a nest of blankets. They settled in, shoulders brushing as they arranged the wool around themselves. Aubrey found herself hyperaware of every point of contact between them.

"So," she began, desperate to break the charged silence, "was this where you'd bring all the girls to impress them back in the day?"

Gunner's laugh was low and warm. "Nah, darlin'. This spot's special. I used to come here to write when I was younger. Helped me feel connected, I guess. To the town, to the music."

"And now?" she asked.

His eyes met hers, filled with an intensity that made her breath hitch. "Now, I'm hoping it'll help me feel connected to something—someone—even more important."

She smiled, inhaling deeply, the crisp mountain air filling her lungs. A profound sense of calm washed over her, seeping into her very bones. Her gaze drifted across the sleepy town below, its lights twinkling. A mix of emotions swirled within her.

"It's so quiet up here," she murmured. "Makes the world feel... I don't know, simpler somehow."

His low chuckle rumbled through her. "That's part of why I love it," he said. "Used to think I needed the roar of the crowd, you know? The bright lights, the constant rush."

Aubrey turned to face him, struck by the vulnerability in his eyes. Gunner took a deep breath, as if steeling himself.

"Truth is," he continued, his voice soft and sincere, "I thought I'd be going crazy by now, missing all that. But being home, with you..." He trailed off, obviously searching for the right words. "I've never felt more like myself."

The confession hung in the air between them, heavy with unspoken meaning.

She took a shaky breath, her voice barely above a whisper when she finally spoke. "I know what you mean," she admitted. "Timber Falls was not what I expected when I first came here. But there's something about the town that's gotten under my skin." Now she paused, struggling to find the right words. "I miss Atlanta sometimes. The energy, the constant buzz of the city. But here, I've started to find a different kind of excitement. A warmth I didn't know I was missing."

Gunner's hand found hers, his touch sending a spark through her body. "Tell me more," he encouraged gently.

Aubrey bit her lip. "Sometimes it feels like I'm caught between two worlds," she admitted. "The city girl in me craves the hustle, the opportunities. But Timber Falls, and you…" She squeezed his hand. "You've shown me a life I never knew I wanted." She glanced out toward the sleepy town. "I can't imagine a future without this place now," she confessed. "But I also can't let go of who I was before. Is it crazy to want both?"

His arm wrapped around her, pulling her closer with a gentle but firm tug. The warmth of his body enveloped her, a stark contrast to the cool night air.

"Darlin'," he drawled, his voice rich like honey, "wantin' both ain't crazy at all. It's who you are."

She tilted her head up, meeting his intense gaze. "You really think so?" she whispered, afraid to break the spell of the moment.

His lips curved into a soft smile. "I know so. Hell, look at me. I'm living proof that a man can have two hearts— one for the stage, one for home."

His words settled over Aubrey like a warm blanket, soothing her doubts. She snuggled closer, breathing in his scent of leather and pine.

"Maybe," she mused, "maybe we could build something that has room for everything we want and need."

Gunner's chest rumbled with a low chuckle. "We can have anything we want."

"Of course we can." She smiled.

They soon fell into a comfortable silence, gazing out at the twinkling lights of Timber Falls below.

Until the soft rustle of fabric broke the silence as Gunner shifted, reaching behind him. She lifted her head from his shoulder and watched, curiosity piqued, as he pulled out a well-worn guitar case.

"What are you up to?" she asked.

His eyes twinkled as he unlatched the case, carefully extracting his Gibson. "Just feeling inspired."

Her breath caught as he removed his gloves and positioned the guitar on his lap, his strong hands caressing the polished wood with a tenderness that made her heart flutter.

His fingers found their place on the strings, and he began to strum a gentle melody. The notes floated on the night air. And when he started to sing, his rich baritone sent shivers down Aubrey's spine.

"Back roads twist through little towns,
Where neon fades and stars hang down.
City lights might shine so bright,
But peace is found on country nights."

Aubrey closed her eyes, letting the tingles from the music and Gunner's voice spread through her entire being.

An hour later, Gunner's hand enveloped Aubrey's as he pushed open his heavy oak front door. The scent of pine and woodsmoke greeted them. No matter how many times she'd been here, Gunner always loved the way Aubrey's smile brightened at his house. He'd felt the same way when the designer had shown him the plans for the property. And every day since he'd moved in, he'd found a wonderful peace here.

As they moved further into the living room, he reluctantly released her hand, making his way to the river rock fireplace. "Let's get you warmed up," he remarked, crouching down to start a fire. Within minutes, the flames licked at the fresh wood.

Aubrey settled onto the plush leather couch, tucking her legs beneath her. "You always do know how to warm me up," she said, a hint of playfulness in her tone.

He glanced over his shoulder, feeling a slow smile spread across his lips. "Well now, Miss Hale, I do believe that's a compliment."

The fire crackled to life, filling the comfortable silence between them. He finally rose, brushing his hands on his jeans, her eyes meeting his with an intensity that spoke volumes.

"Penny for your thoughts?"

A blush crept up her neck. "Just appreciating the view," she admitted.

He crossed the room, settling beside her on the couch. "Do you want more of the view—" he began.

But before he could finish, she leaned in and captured his lips in a kiss that tasted of promise.

With a soft groan, he pulled Aubrey into his arms, deepening the kiss. The warmth of her mouth against his hardened his cock to steel. Her fingers tangled in his hair as his hands roamed her back, tracing the curve of her spine through her shirt. Each touch was electric, charged with desire.

"Daaaarlin'," Gunner drawled, the words grazing the space between them like a promise. He could feel Aubrey's breath mix with his, could see the way her eyes darkened, the way she trembled against him. The house around them faded to nothing—just her, him and the fire burning hotter with every second.

Nothing mattered now. All he knew was the feel of her in his arms, soft where he was hard, delicate yet strong enough to pull him under. When their lips met again, the kiss turned desperate, a wildfire sweeping through his veins. Her hands roamed his chest, fingers fumbling with his flannel shirt, brushing against bare skin with every button she freed. He felt her touch like a spark, each press of her hands driving his need higher.

"God, Aubrey," he murmured against her mouth, his hands finding her waist and pulling her closer. The curve of her body fit against his perfectly, and he didn't know how he'd ever gone a day without this—without her. He dragged his lips away, kissing down her neck, tasting her skin. She shivered, a soft sound that damn near undid him escaping her throat.

"You taste so sweet," he said, his voice roughened by the hunger clawing at him. He meant it, every word. She was intoxicating, and he couldn't get enough—would never get enough.

The world blurred as clothes fell in a tangle at their feet. Gunner's hands explored Aubrey's body, memorizing every inch, every sigh, every way she responded to him. Their bodies came together like a perfect rhythm, the air thick with need, with heat, with something deeper than he was ready to name.

Here, with her in his arms, everything else fell away. Nothing mattered but this—Aubrey, beneath him, with him, lost in him. And Gunner knew he was lost in her too.

His breath hitched as her cool fingers grazed his skin. "Aubrey," he murmured as he gently guided her toward the plush rug before the crackling fireplace. The warmth enveloped him as he sank down on top of her. Flickering firelight danced across her skin.

His calloused fingertips traced the delicate line of Aubrey's collarbone, making her shiver and him smile. "You're so beautiful," he murmured.

Her breath hitched as he removed her clothing, piece by piece. "Gunner," she whispered, her usually confident voice tinged with vulnerability. "I need you."

He smiled again, his touch featherlight as it trailed down her arm. "Ah, and you can have me." His hands, strong yet gentle, began to explore her body with careful deliberation. Each caress was a revelation, igniting sparks of sensation that made her tremble. She closed her eyes, tipping her head back, and he groaned against her neck, loving her just like this.

"You're shakin', sweetheart," he murmured.

"Please," she gasped.

He didn't need to hear more. He slid between her thighs. His eyes locked with Aubrey's as he placed a gentle kiss on her inner thigh. She shivered as he fully lowered himself, his breath hot against her sex.

With his first stroke, she gasped, her fingers tangling in his hair. "Oh, Gunner."

Each movement he made was deliberate and focused as her back arched, a soft moan escaping her lips.

When the wave of pleasure finally crashed over her, she cried out his name, her body trembling. As she caught her breath, he gave her a satisfied smile. Christ, he loved watching her unravel like that.

"Come here," she said softly, pulling him up for a deep, passionate kiss.

As their lips parted, her hand trailed down his chest. "My turn," she whispered.

He trembled now as she took him deep into her mouth, and Gunner's world narrowed to a pinpoint of exquisite sensation. His fingers tangled in her silky hair, cradling her head. The sight never lost its edge—this fierce, independent woman he'd longed for since that week in Atlanta—willingly on her knees before him nearly undid him completely every single damn time.

She poured all of her desire into her movements, and he was sure she was determined to drive him wild.

And she did. Every single time.

Heat soared through him as she bobbed her head deliciously, until he couldn't take any more.

"Sweet Jesus," he grunted, pulling away. "You're gonna be the death of me, woman."

A playful glint in her eye, she said, "Wouldn't be a bad way to go."

He chuckled, the sound rumbling deep in his chest. He cupped her cheek, his calloused thumb tracing her swollen lips. "C'mere," he murmured, gently pulling her to her feet.

The fire crackled, casting a warm glow across her body as he gently flipped Aubrey onto her knees. His movements were careful, yet urgency thrummed through his muscles. He reached for his jeans, fumbling for his wallet, extracting a foil packet.

After sheathing himself in a condom, he leaned down over her, capturing her lips from the side in a searing kiss. She tasted of a sweetness he'd always crave.

Their kisses were like fire, igniting him with an intense passion that consumed him. Breaking the kiss, he eventually gripped the base of his cock and entered Aubrey with a slow, deliberate motion that sent shockwaves through him. She gasped, her fingers digging into the blanket beneath them.

He paused. "You alright, darlin'?" His voice was husky, strained with the effort of restraint.

"God, yes," Aubrey breathed. She arched back against him, her body craving more.

"Don't stop," she pleaded.

He listened and began to move, his rhythm steady and intense. Each thrust sent sparks of pleasure coursing through his veins, awakening parts of him only she could awaken.

"God, yes—" she gasped, her pleasure seeming to build with every movement.

He silenced her with a deep, hard thrust, his movements becoming more urgent. She matched his intensity, meeting him for every thrust, their bodies moving in a perfect rhythm.

He felt the familiar tension building within her, the way her sweet body hugged him tight.

"Let go, sweetheart," Gunner whispered, his breath hot against her ear. "I've got you."

With those words, Aubrey cried out, trembling in his arms as he followed her over the edge, their bodies finding release in each other.

As the aftershocks subsided, Gunner withdrew and tucked her into his arms, holding her close.

"You've got me," she whispered.

He kissed her shoulder. "Always, darlin'. I always have you."

Fourteen

The following evening, Aubrey's heart swelled with pride as she stood at the entrance of The Naked Moose, the warm glow of the bar's lights spilling onto the wintery street. A steady stream of townsfolk approached, their excited chatter filling the air.

"Evening, Betty! Glad you could make it," Aubrey called out.

"Wouldn't miss it for the world, dear," Betty replied with a wink.

As more familiar faces passed by, Aubrey's smile grew. This was her idea from a month ago—a way to give the kids a chance to practice before the big talent show. Tonight was a private show, with only the talent show kids and family present, and the turnout was even better than she'd hoped.

"Hey there, Walt," she greeted the local hardware store owner. "Grandkids all set for their big debut?"

Walt grinned, tipping his well-worn baseball cap.

"Reckon so. Though I think I'm more nervous than they are."

Aubrey laughed, the sound mingling with the growing buzz of anticipation.

As the crowd outside thinned, Aubrey slipped inside, the familiar scents of polished wood and hints of her latest cocktail creation enveloping her. The bar was packed, a sea of flannel and denim and cowboy hats, and faces alight with excitement.

Weaving through the throng, Aubrey's trained eye scanned for any last-minute details needing attention. A loose tablecloth here, a misplaced chair there—small imperfections she swiftly corrected.

"Aubrey!" a voice called out. She turned to see Nancy, one of the regulars, holding up a glass filled with a shimmering purple liquid. "This new drink of yours? It's amazing!"

Aubrey beamed, a flutter of pride in her chest. "Glad you like it."

As she continued her rounds, Aubrey caught snippets of conversation, most praising her latest mixology experiment. The kids would be on soon, and there was still work to be done. She may have left behind the prestige of a top-tier restaurant, but here, in this moment, she felt more fulfilled than ever before.

Her breath caught in her throat as she saw Gunner approaching, his eyes shimmering with an intensity that made her heart skip. He moved through the crowd with an easy grace, his presence drawing admiring glances from the patrons.

"Aubrey," he drawled. "This is incredible. I can't believe you pulled all this together for us."

She felt a flush creep up her neck, fighting to maintain her composure. "It's nothing, really. Just thought the kids could use a little practice before the big show—and for their families to see how far they've come."

Gunner's hand brushed her arm, leaving a trail of heat in its wake. "Don't sell yourself short, darlin'. This means the world to them, and to me."

"I'm just glad I could help," she murmured, acutely aware of how close they were standing.

As they gazed at each other, the rest of the bar seemed to fade away. Aubrey felt herself being drawn in, captivated by the intensity of Gunner's gaze.

The spell was broken by a commotion near the stage. Aubrey's attention snapped to the source, her eyes landing on Emily. The young girl stood at the edge of the platform, her small hands fidgeting with the hem of her dress. Even from a distance, Aubrey could see the nervousness etched on Emily's face.

"Poor thing looks terrified," she murmured, her heart going out to the child.

Gunner nodded, his expression softening. "Stage fright's a beast, even for seasoned performers. I should get over there—she could use a little encouragement."

He approached Emily, said something to her which made her smile a little. Then he strode onto the stage, his presence commanding immediate attention. The crowd hushed, all eyes drawn to him as he approached the microphone. His eyes sparkled with warmth as he surveyed the packed bar, a slow smile spreading across his face.

"Well, folks," he said, his rich baritone filling the room, "looks like we've got ourselves a real shindig tonight." A ripple of laughter flowed through the crowd. "Y'all are in for a treat, 'cause we've got the best darn show right here in The Naked Moose."

Aubrey felt a flutter in her chest as she watched him work the crowd. There was something magnetic about Gunner when he was in his element, a charisma that was impossible to ignore.

"These kids," he continued, gesturing to the nervous young performers, "they've got more talent in their little fingers than most of us have in our whole bodies. So let's give 'em a big ol' Timber Falls welcome!"

The audience erupted in cheers and applause. Aubrey found herself clapping along, a surge of pride washing over her. This was her idea, her event, and seeing it come to life was exhilarating.

As the first young performer took the stage, a hush fell over the crowd. Aubrey held her breath, watching as a little boy no more than seven picked up a guitar almost as big as he was. His small fingers began to pluck at the strings, and a sweet, simple melody filled the air.

The silence from the audience was palpable, a collective holding of breath as everyone focused on the child's performance. Aubrey glanced around, taking in the rapt expressions on the faces of the townsfolk. There was something magical about the moment, a sense of community support that brought a lump to her throat. And this was something she realized was hard to find in a big city.

As each child took their turn, the atmosphere in the bar grew warmer, more supportive. Aubrey found herself swept up in the emotion of it all, her heart swelling with each performance. She caught Gunner's eye across the room, and he gave her a wink that warmed her from head to toe.

But Aubrey's heart started to sink as she watched Emily's turn approach. The young girl's eyes widened with panic, her head shaking vigorously as she backed away from the stage. Aubrey's protective instincts flared, but before she could intervene, Gunner was there, kneeling beside Emily, talking to her.

Aubrey's breath caught as Emily hesitated, then nodded. She watched them ascend the stage. The first chords struck her like lightning. It was the song from the cliff, the one that he had clearly been writing. Aubrey's heart clenched as Gunner's rich voice filled the air, joined moments later by Emily's tentative soprano, her confidence seeming to grow with each note. The girl's voice strengthened, twining with Gunner's in perfect harmony. All around, cell phones appeared, capturing the magical moment.

Aubrey's chest tightened again, pride and something deeper, more vulnerable.

As the song ended, a heartbeat of silence hung in the air before the crowd erupted into thunderous applause. Cheers and whistles ricocheted off the walls. Emily's eyes widened, her cheeks flushing with a mixture of surprise and elation.

Gunner's hand found Emily's shoulder, giving it a gentle

squeeze. "Take it in," he drawled, loud enough for Aubrey to hear over the din. "This is all for you."

Emily's gaze swept across the room, drinking in the sea of smiling faces and raised glasses. Aubrey felt a lump form in her throat as she watched the young girl's transformation. Gone was the shy, hesitant child from moments ago. In her place stood a beaming, confident performer.

Gunner pulled Emily into a warm embrace, bending down to whisper in her ear. Though Aubrey couldn't make out the words, she saw their impact. Emily's smile, if possible, grew even brighter, her eyes shining with unshed tears of joy.

Aubrey's heart swelled as she watched Gunner step off the stage, his hand resting protectively on Emily's shoulder. And Aubrey found herself captivated by Gunner's unexpected gentleness, a side of him she'd rarely glimpsed before.

"Well, well," a familiar voice purred beside her. "Looks like someone's falling madly in love."

She turned to find Willow sidling up next to her, a impish glint in her eyes. She playfully nudged Aubrey's ribs.

Aubrey's gaze drifted back to Gunner, a soft smile spreading across her face. She let out a quiet sigh. "It's kind of hard not to," she admitted. "Look at him."

Willow's teasing grin softened into a look of genuine warmth. "He is pretty dreamy."

As if sensing their gazes, Gunner looked up, flashing Aubrey a warm smile that sent a flutter through her chest. He was in his element, moving through the crowd with easy charm, shaking hands and clapping backs. But there was something different about him tonight—a lightness to his step, a genuine joy in his interactions that went beyond his usual stage presence.

Aubrey watched, mesmerized, as Gunner crouched down to speak with a little boy clutching a guitar. The tenderness in his expression, the way he gave the child his full attention, it stirred something deep within her.

Her heart swelled with an emotion too big to name. There was no use denying it anymore. The realization washed over her. Her feelings for Gunner weren't just a fleeting attraction or a remnant of their past encounter. They were real, growing stronger with each passing day, impossible to ignore.

As Gunner's laughter rang out across the bar, mingling with the joyful chatter of the crowd, Aubrey came to a realization she knew she could never run from. She wasn't falling in love with him—she knew she was already in too deep to ever turn back.

And no matter how much happiness filled her heart, there was a cold, harsh reminder that whispered in her heart: *But will he stay?*

Fifteen

Early the next morning, Gunner was still riding the high from the talent show preview as his calloused hands gripped Ginny's reins, guiding the mare back to the stable after the training ride through the wintery meadow. "That's it, girl," he said to her. "We've come a long way, you and me."

The horse nickered softly in response, as if agreeing with his assessment. Gunner couldn't help but smile, a sense of pride welling up in his chest. This mare had been skittish and untrusting when he'd first started working with her, but now she moved with confidence, her steps sure and steady, and Jaxon had told him a couple weeks ago she'd been sold to a young rider in Ontario, Canada, and would be shipped there in a couple weeks.

As they approached the stable, Gunner's mind wandered to his own journey. He'd come back home broken and lost, much like this horse. But here, among the rolling hills and open sky, he'd found a piece of himself he thought he'd lost forever.

"Guess we both needed a little TLC, huh?" he said, patting the horse's neck.

Gunner led the mare into the barn, removing her tack with practiced ease. His fingers worked nimbly, unbuckling straps and lifting the saddle. As he hung up the equipment, he found himself humming a melody that he'd been working on.

With the mare settled, Gunner made his way to the pasture gate and released her into the pasture. He leaned against the weathered wood, watching as she trotted out to join the other horses. The sight filled him with a quiet satisfaction, a feeling of accomplishment that resonated deep in his bones.

"Look at you go," he whispered, more to himself than the horse. "All that fear, all that doubt, gone."

As he watched the mare integrate seamlessly with the herd, Gunner couldn't help but draw parallels to his own life. He'd come to Timber Falls feeling like an outcast, a washed-up country star with more regrets than hit songs. But this town, these people—they'd healed him, helped him find his footing again.

The tranquil moment shattered as Gunner's phone vibrated in his pocket. With a sigh, he fished it out, his brow furrowing as the screen lit up with an overwhelming barrage of notifications, now that his patchy reception had evidently improved.

"What the hell?" he muttered.

Each ping echoed in the quiet of the ranch, a stark contrast to the gentle whinnying of horses and loud voices of the cowboys working the ranch. His calloused thumb scrolled through the messages, his heart rate quickening with each swipe.

"What?" he whispered.

His new song with Emily—their impromptu duet at The Naked Moose—had somehow found its way onto social media and was spreading like wildfire. Comments flooded in, praising the sweet performance, the raw emotion in their voices.

He leaned against the fence, his legs suddenly unsteady, his chest tightening with each ping from his phone. Pride swelled within him at the song's successful reception, a bittersweet reminder of the heights he'd once reached. But that pride was quickly overshadowed by a gnawing anxiety that threatened to consume him.

He gazed out at the sprawling Montana landscape. The life he'd built in Timber Falls—the stability, the sense of belonging—suddenly felt fragile.

As if on cue, his phone erupted with a familiar ringtone, slicing through his thoughts like a knife. Gunner's heart raced as he saw his agent's name flash across the screen. His thumb hovered over the screen, his hand trembling slightly.

Gunner took a deep breath, steeling himself. "Here goes nothin'," he said, his voice steady despite the storm raging within him. He answered the call, bracing for the conversation that he sensed could upend the peaceful life he'd fought so hard to build.

"Gunner, my man!" Tom's voice boomed through the speaker, crackling with excitement. "You've done it again, buddy! That song is blowing up!"

Gunner leaned against the weathered fence post, his free

hand absently tracing the grain of the wood. "Yeah, I noticed," he replied, his tone measured. "Quite a surprise."

"Surprise? It's a goddamn miracle!" Tom's enthusiasm was palpable. "Listen, I've got the label on the other line. They want you in the studio to record this so we can release it as a single."

Gunner's breath caught in his throat. The offer dangled before him like a shiny lure, tempting and dangerous. He closed his eyes, remembering the roar of the crowd, the thrill of the spotlight. But then Aubrey's face flashed in his mind.

"I don't know, Tom," Gunner said. "I've got a good thing going here."

"Good thing? Are you kidding me? This could be the comeback story of the decade!" Tom's voice rose an octave. "We need to strike while the iron's hot. I'm talking private jet to Nashville to record the song."

Gunner's mind raced. The allure of fame, of reclaiming his spot at the top of the charts, clashed violently with the peace he'd found with Aubrey. He thought of the kids he was mentoring, of lazy evenings at The Naked Moose, of all the quiet moments with Aubrey that held more meaning than any stadium show.

"I can't just up and leave," Gunner said. "I've got commitments here, people counting on me."

"People?" Tom scoffed. "This is a good thing for you, Gunner. Don't mess this up."

Gunner pressed, "I've been good here. I've been sober."

"That's great, Gunner, really," Tom replied. "Remember how it felt to have thousands of fans singing your lyrics back to you?"

His breath caught in his throat. The memories flooded back. The adrenaline rush, the adoration, the feeling of being on top of the world. His fingers itched for his guitar, longing to strum out the melodies that had been his lifeblood for so long.

"Dammit, Tom," he growled. "You're asking me to uproot my entire life here. It ain't just about the music anymore."

"I get it, I do," Tom's voice crackled through the phone. "But this could be your last shot at the big time. You really want to let that slip away? We need to ride this wave, and you need to do it now."

Gunner's jaw clenched. The demons of his past whispered seductively, reminding him of the intoxicating highs of his fame—and the devastating lows that followed. He closed his eyes, picturing Aubrey's smile, the way her eyes lit up when she laughed. It was a different kind of high, one that didn't leave him hollow afterward.

"Look," Gunner said finally, his voice intense even to his ears. "I ain't saying no. But I ain't saying yes either. I need time to think this through, to figure out what I really want."

He could almost hear Tom's disappointment through the silence that followed. "Alright, Gunner. Take some time. But don't take too long. Opportunities like this don't come around every day."

"I know," Gunner replied. "I'll be in touch."

As he ended the call, the sudden silence of the ranch

enveloped him. He slumped against the fence, the weight of the decision pressing down on him like a physical force.

"What the hell am I gonna do?" he muttered to himself.

Right at five o'clock in the evening, the community center buzzed with anticipation, a hive of excitement as Aubrey and Gunner stepped through the double doors. Children's laughter mingled with the shuffle of feet and murmur of voices.

"I can't believe how many people showed up," Aubrey breathed as she took in the packed room. Rows of folding chairs faced a makeshift stage, where three judges sat at a table, clipboards at the ready.

Gunner nodded, his gaze sweeping the crowd. "Timber Falls knows how to show up for its own."

Aubrey's chest swelled with pride as she spotted all the familiar faces in the sea of people. This was *her* community now—these were *her* people. The thought both thrilled and terrified her, if she was honest with herself.

"Look at those kids," she said, gesturing to a group of children huddled near the stage, faces flushed with nerves and excitement. "They're so brave."

Gunner's lips quirked in a half-smile. "Braver than I ever was at their age."

Aubrey turned to study him, noticing the slight furrow between his brows, the distant look in his eyes. Something was off. It had been since the moment he picked her up. She opened her mouth to ask, then hesitated. This wasn't the time or place for probing questions.

"You okay?" she settled on, keeping her tone light.

Gunner blinked, focusing on her. "Yeah, darlin'. Just got a lot on my mind."

Aubrey's stomach clenched. She knew that look, had seen it on the faces of just enough men before they walked out of her life. But Gunner was different this time, wasn't he?

She pushed the thought aside, forcing a smile. "Well, clear that mind of yours. We've got some talented kids to cheer on."

Gunner's expression softened, and he reached for her hand, giving it a gentle squeeze. "You're right. This night's about them."

As they made their way to their seats, Aubrey couldn't shake the feeling that something significant was shifting between them. But she refused to let her fears overshadow the joy of the moment. These kids deserved her full attention and support.

She settled into her chair, determined to lose herself in the magic of the talent show. Whatever storm was brewing in Gunner's eyes could wait. For now, she'd bask in all the hard work the kids had achieved.

The first act took the stage, a young boy in a sequined vest juggling colorful balls. His tongue poked out in concentration, eyes fixed on the whirling orbs. Aubrey leaned forward, her breath catching as one ball wobbled precariously.

"Come on, kiddo," she whispered, fingers crossed.

The boy caught it deftly, finishing with a flourish. Applause erupted, and Aubrey's chest swelled with pride.

"Did you see that recovery?" she gushed to Gunner. "He's got nerves of steel!"

Gunner nodded, a genuine smile spreading across his face. "Reminds me of my first time on stage. Scared as hell, I shook in my cowboy boots."

Act after act followed, each showcasing a unique talent, and all of Gunner's musical kids did their songs. One girl twirled ribbons in mesmerizing patterns, and a pair of twins performed a comedy skit that had the audience in stitches. Aubrey's heart overflowed with each performance, marveling at the courage it took to bare one's soul on stage.

Then Emily appeared, clutching the microphone stand like a lifeline. Aubrey's breath caught in her throat.

"She looks terrified," Aubrey murmured, fighting the urge to rush up and wrap the girl in a hug.

Gunner leaned close, his breath warm on her ear. "Watch this."

He caught Emily's eye and gave an almost imperceptible nod, his eyes radiating calm reassurance. The change in Emily was immediate. Her shoulders relaxed, chin lifting as she took a deep breath.

The first notes of her song wavered, barely audible. Aubrey gripped the edge of her seat, silently willing Emily to find her voice. With each passing moment, the girl's confidence grew. Her voice soared, filling the community center with a hauntingly beautiful melody.

Aubrey blinked back tears, overwhelmed by the transformation. She glanced at Gunner, seeing her own awe mirrored in his expression.

"I had no idea she could sing like that," Aubrey breathed.

Gunner's eyes never left the stage, a mix of pride and something deeper, almost wistful, etched on his face. "Sometimes all it takes is someone believing in you to unlock that hidden talent."

"Don't go making me cry, Gunner Woods," she said, reaching for his hand, squeezing it tightly as Emily's song reached its peak.

As the last chord faded, the audience erupted in cheers. Aubrey found herself on her feet, clapping until her hands stung, her vision blurred by the tears that threatened to spill over.

"Attagirl!" Gunner whooped, his face split by a grin that made Aubrey's heart skip.

She nodded, unable to speak past the lump in her throat. Emily stood frozen on stage, her eyes wide with disbelief at the crowd's reaction.

As the applause began to die down, Aubrey sank back into her seat, wiping at her eyes. "I can't believe how brave she was up there," she murmured, more to herself than to Gunner.

He leaned in close, his voice warm. "Reminds me of someone else I know."

Aubrey scoffed. "Yeah, right, I would never get up there and sing."

Gunner winked. "No, but you would move across the country, leaving everything you know."

Aubrey's cheeks flushed. She was still navigating this new phase of her life, striving to rediscover the strong person she used to be. Thankfully, she was saved from explaining all that by the emcee taking the stage. Time seemed to slow as he thanked all the participants, building suspense before announcing the winner.

"And the first prize goes to Emily Johnson!"

The crowd erupted once more. Emily's mouth fell open in a perfect 'O' of surprise before her face lit up with pure, unbridled joy. She bounced on her toes, hugging her mom before accepting the trophy with trembling hands.

Gunner was out of his seat in an instant, striding toward the stage. Aubrey watched as he scooped Emily up in a bear hug, spinning her around. His deep laughter mingled with Emily's delighted squeals, the sound wrapping around Aubrey like a warm blanket.

"You did it, kiddo!" Gunner's voice carried over the crowd. "I knew you had it in you!"

Aubrey's chest tightened as she observed the tenderness in Gunner's eyes, the gentle way he set Emily down and ruffled her hair. It was a side of him she was still getting used to—this nurturing, protective presence that seemed at odds with the rebel bad-boy image he'd once embodied.

As Emily ran to show her trophy to her friends, Gunner caught Aubrey's gaze across the room. The pride and joy radiating from him was almost palpable, and for a moment, Aubrey allowed herself to imagine a future where moments like these were commonplace. But she couldn't ignore that behind his easy smile and pride for the kids, there was tension in every line of his body.

His stare stayed on her as he approached, and when he reached her, she said, "Are you okay? You just seem…*off*."

"I… I need to tell you something," he said slowly. "Come here."

Aubrey felt Gunner's warm hand on the small of her back, guiding her toward a quiet corner near the stage. The touch sent a familiar tremor over her, but there was something different in his demeanor, a tension that hadn't been there moments before.

"Aubrey, I..." His voice trailed off, his eyes clouded with an emotion she couldn't quite place.

Aubrey's heart quickened. "What is it?"

He took a deep breath. "My agent called earlier. That song I played at The Naked Moose last week with Emily? It's gone viral. Like, millions of views viral."

The words hit Aubrey like a punch to the gut. She blinked, trying to process the information. "That's amazing. Isn't it?"

"It is." He nodded, but his smile didn't quite reach his eyes. "But it means the label wants me back in Nashville. They're talking about recording the song."

Aubrey felt the blood drain from her face. Her mind raced, images of Gunner leaving, of her being left behind once again, flashing before her eyes. She struggled to keep her voice steady. "When would you leave?"

"They want me there as soon as possible," Gunner said quietly.

Aubrey's world tilted on its axis. *As soon as possible.* She wrapped her arms around herself, feeling ice coating her veins. "I see," she managed. Inside, her thoughts were a chaotic whirlwind. *This is it, isn't it? Everyone leaves eventually. Just like Gunner did the first time. Just like my dad. Just like always.*

She forced herself to meet Gunner's gaze, searching for

any sign that this was all a mistake, that he wasn't about to walk out of her life just when she'd started to let him in. But all she saw was uncertainty that mirrored her own.

Gunner took a step closer, his gaze intense and earnest. "Darlin'," he began, his voice a gentle rumble that sent shivers down her spine. "I know this is sudden, but I promise you, we can make this work. I'm not leavin' you behind." His hand reached out, fingers brushing her arm with a tenderness that made her heart ache. "I've been thinkin' about us, about what we have here. It's special. Real special. And I'm not about to let it slip away just 'cause of some record deal."

Aubrey wanted to believe him, wanted to sink into the warmth of his words and the sincerity shining in his eyes. But doubt gnawed at her, insidious and familiar. She turned away, arms still crossed tightly over her chest.

"How can you be so sure?" she asked, hating the tremor in her voice. "Nashville's a long way from Timber Falls. And once you're back in that world..."

She trailed off, unable to voice her deepest fear: that he'd forget all about her, about the quiet life they'd been building together. Her mind raced with images of Gunner on stage, surrounded by adoring fans, while she faded into nothing more than a distant memory.

He stepped into her line of sight, his presence impossible to ignore. "Look at me, Aubrey," he pleaded softly. "I'm not the man I was before. And I'm not about to throw away the best thing that's ever happened to me."

Her gaze flickered to his face, wanting desperately to believe him. But the walls she'd built around her heart were strong, reinforced by years of disappointment and betrayal. She bit her lip, fighting back tears.

"I want to believe you," she whispered. "But I've heard promises before. They don't always hold up when push comes to shove."

The weight of her words hung in the air between them, heavy and suffocating. Silence stretched out, broken only by the distant chatter of the dispersing crowd and the muffled thump of Aubrey's heart in her chest. She stared at a scuff mark on the community center's worn linoleum floor, unable to meet Gunner's gaze.

He shifted his weight, the soft creak of his boots echoing in the quiet corner. She could feel his eyes on her, intense and searching. She wondered if he could see right through her, past the walls she'd so carefully constructed, to the scared little girl who'd been left behind one too many times.

"Please, please look at me." Gunner's voice was barely above a whisper, rough with emotion. "I know words ain't enough." He reached out slowly, giving her time to pull away if she wanted. When she didn't move, his calloused fingers gently tucked under her chin, lifting her gaze. The tenderness of his gaze made Aubrey's breath catch in her throat.

"I can't promise it'll be easy," he continued, his touch lingering on her cheek. "But I can promise I'll fight like hell to make this work. You're worth fightin' for, darlin'."

Aubrey leaned into his touch, almost against her will. The warmth of his hand seemed to seep into her very bones, chasing away some of the chill that had settled there.

His gaze was steady. "We'll figure it out together, okay? One step at a time."

His thumb brushed across her cheekbone, the gesture so achingly tender that Aubrey felt something inside her begin to crack. She wanted to believe him, wanted it more than she'd wanted anything in a long time. But the fear still lingered, a reminder that he had promised her that before. And he had lied. "Okay. One step at a time."

Sixteen

The next afternoon, Aubrey leaned against a countertop in the kitchen of The Naked Moose, thrumming with excitement as she discussed the new lunch menu with Chef Miguel. "I think the jalapeño poppers will be a hit," Aubrey said. "It's the perfect blend of spicy and creamy."

Miguel nodded, his salt-and-pepper beard twitching with a smile. "Sí, señora. It will bring the heat that cowboys crave."

Aubrey glanced at the clock on the wall, its face showing just half an hour until the lunch rush. Her heart quickened with anticipation. "I'll leave you to it," she murmured. "Please let me know if you need my help."

"I will, thank you," Miguel said.

As she pushed through the swinging kitchen doors into the main bar area, a wave of warmth washed over her. Charly and Willow stood behind the polished oak bar, their familiar faces a balm to Aubrey's soul. The sight of her friends brought a genuine smile to her lips, chasing away some of the lingering doubts that had plagued her since her talk with Gunner.

"Hey, girls," Aubrey called out, her steps light as she approached them. The bar hummed with the quiet chatter of early patrons, a few tables already occupied by regulars nursing their drinks.

Willow's eyes lit up as she spotted Aubrey. "There's our culinary genius," she teased, as she moved to pour a drink.

Charly chimed in, "How's the new menu coming along? Got any tasty surprises for us?"

Aubrey felt a surge of affection for her friends, grateful for their unwavering support. She leaned against the bar, facing them. "Oh, you bet. Miguel will wow us, as always," she replied. "But you'll have to wait and see like everyone else."

Charly's eyes sparkled with excitement as she leaned across the bar, her voice lowered. "Have you seen it yet? Gunner's video with Emily is absolutely everywhere!"

Aubrey's heart skipped a beat at the mention of Gunner's name. She tried to keep her expression neutral, but her fingers tightened into fists.

"It's incredible," Charly continued, her words tumbling out in a rush. "He's getting so much recognition again. It's like watching a star being reborn."

Willow nodded in agreement, but her eyes, sharp and observant, never left Aubrey's face. "It's great to see him back in the spotlight," she added softly, her tone measured.

Aubrey felt a storm of emotions brewing inside her. Pride warred with anxiety, joy with uncertainty. She leaned against the bar, trying to appear casual, but her knuckles were white where they gripped the edge.

"Yeah, it's something," she managed, her voice sounding strained even to her own ears. She took a deep breath, the scent of polished wood and lingering coffee grounding her. The clink of glasses and murmur of conversation from the few occupied tables seemed to fade away as she struggled to find the right words.

I should be happy for him, Aubrey thought, her chest tight. *So why does it feel like I'm losing him already?* She looked up at her friends, seeing concern and support reflected in their faces. The words she'd been holding back threatened to spill out, a dam about to break.

"What is it?" Willow asked. "And no lying."

Her eyes glistened as she finally let her guard down. "I'm terrified," she confessed, her voice barely above a whisper. "What if this is it? What if he takes off and leaves everything—leaves me—behind?" The words tumbled out in a rush.

Charly reached across the bar, her warm hand covering Aubrey's trembling one. "Oh, honey," she said softly, her eyes filled with empathy. "Gunner's not just some passing fling. What you two have is real."

Willow nodded, her hair catching the soft bar light. "And don't forget," she added, her voice steady and reassuring, "he would never leave you and not look back. Not now. I don't doubt that for a minute."

Aubrey's gaze flicked between her friends, wanting desperately to believe them. "But what if it's not enough?" she asked, her voice cracking. "What if I can't handle being with someone who comes and goes?"

Charly squeezed her hand. "You're selling yourself short, Aubs. You've faced worse and come out on top. Remember how you rebuilt your life here?"

"Charly's right," Willow chimed in. "And don't forget, communication is key. Have you talked to Gunner about this?"

Aubrey shook her head, feeling a pang of guilt. "I didn't want to rain on his parade," she admitted, biting her lower lip. "This viral video couldn't have come at a worse time," she said, her voice wavering slightly. "Things were just starting to feel…right with Gunner. And now?" She shook her head. "I don't know how we can make this work."

Her gaze darted between Charly and Willow, searching their faces for answers she knew they couldn't provide. "He's going to be pulled back into that world of touring. He won't be here with me."

She shut her eyes and breathed deep before she added, "I want to be happy for him," her voice thick with emotion. "God knows Gunner deserves this second chance. But I can't help feeling like I'm going to lose him before I've really even had the chance to…" She trailed off, unable to voice the depth of her feelings for Gunner—who'd unexpectedly stolen her heart.

Willow's eyes softened as she too reached across the bar to lay a reassuring hand on Aubrey's arm. "I know it feels overwhelming right now, but let's take a step back." Her voice was gentle but firm, grounding Aubrey in the present. "Focus on what's in front of you today, not what might happen tomorrow."

Aubrey's shoulders relaxed slightly at her friend's touch but doubt still weighed her down. She opened her mouth to protest, but Charly cut in.

"Willow's right," Charly nodded, leaning in. "The future's always uncertain, but that doesn't mean it's insurmountable. You and Gunner, you've got something special. Don't let fear rob you of that."

Aubrey's mind raced, processing her friends' words. They made sense, but the practical side of her couldn't help but fret. She bit her lip, her brow furrowing. "But how am I supposed to balance everything?" she asked, gesturing around The Naked Moose. "This place, it's my responsibility. Our dream." She paused, her voice dropping to a near-whisper. "But so is Gunner."

"You don't need that answer right now," Charly said, her hand squeezing Aubrey's tightly. "Just see how this all plays out."

See how this all plays out. That seemed simple enough. "Okay, I can do that."

"Yes, you can," Willow said, rounding the bar and wrapping her arms around Aubrey tight.

Aubrey felt a rush of gratitude towards her two best friends as Charly joined in on the hug too. They had been there for her through thick and thin, always offering their unwavering support. She took a deep breath, trying to calm her racing thoughts.

As she exhaled, she made a silent promise to herself to take things one step at a time and trust the journey. Whatever happened, she knew she had two amazing friends by her side, and that was all she needed for now.

The quiet morning Gunner had been enjoying was swiftly ended with a single phone call. He paced the length of his living room, boots scuffing against the hardwood floor as he pressed the phone tighter to his ear. Outside, the Montana mountains loomed, their snow-capped peaks holding his stare. His free hand clenched and unclenched at his side, tension coiling through his body.

When Tom couldn't seal the deal, Hank, head of the label, had stepped in. "I'm telling you, Gunner, this is it!" Hank's excitement crackled through the phone. "We want you in Nashville tomorrow. We saw the video and we're ready to record."

Gunner's heart raced, a familiar rush of adrenaline coursing through his veins. It was the same feeling he used to get before stepping on stage, before…

He shook his head, pushing away the memories of sold-out arenas and screaming fans and painkillers. But he'd done the work on himself. He had therapy if he needed it. He'd kept up with his physical therapy and would continue to do so. He had everything in place to ensure he stayed on the right path.

"Tomorrow?" Gunner echoed, his mind reeling. "That's short notice. I've got commitments here in Timber Falls, I can't just up and leave—"

But even as the words left his mouth, a part of him ached to say yes, to dive headfirst into the opportunity. The stage lights, the roar of the crowd—he couldn't deny he missed it. And life was different now. He had Aubrey. He had himself.

"Listen to me, Gunner." Hank's voice took on an urgent edge. "This isn't just any opportunity. We're Blackhawk Records. We don't wait around. If you're not here tomorrow, we'll move on to the next viral thing. You know how this business works."

Gunner's gaze drifted to the mountains again. This town was his home, the place where he'd healed and rediscovered himself. But was it enough? Could he really walk away from a second chance at his dreams?

"I hear ya, Hank," Gunner said, his voice thick with conflicting emotions. "It's just there's someone here. Someone important."

"Gunner, my boy." Hank's tone softened slightly. "I know you've been through hell and back. But this could be your ticket to redemption. Bring her, or whoever it is, with you. Don't let fear stop you."

Gunner flinched at the word *fear*. He wasn't scared, was he? No, he was cautious. Wary of falling back into old habits, of losing himself in the whirlwind of fame and addiction that had nearly destroyed him before.

"I ain't scared," Gunner muttered, more to himself than to Hank. "I just need some time to think, that's all."

"Time is the one thing we don't have, Gunner," Hank pressed. "The flight leaves at 11 a.m. Be on that plane or this deal is off the table."

Gunner closed his eyes, the weight of the decision pressing down on him like a physical force. In his mind's eye, he saw two paths stretching out before him. One leading to Nashville and all the glitz and glamour of his old life. The other winding through the peaceful streets of Timber Falls with Aubrey next to him.

But Nashville… God, Nashville. The call of spotlights and screaming crowds tugged at his heart, awakening a hunger he thought he'd buried.

He opened his eyes. "I'll try to make it work," he said finally, the words tasting bittersweet on his tongue.

"That's what I like to hear!" Hank exclaimed, his excitement palpable even through the phone line. "Now, let's talk logistics."

As Hank rattled off details of tomorrow's flight, Gunner's gaze drifted back to the snow-capped mountains outside his window. Even as he nodded along to Hank's instructions, a nagging voice in the back of his mind whispered doubts. Was he *really* ready to dive back into that world? And what about Aubrey? The thought of leaving her behind, of potentially losing the fragile connection they'd built, sent a sharp pang through his chest.

"Got it," Gunner said, when Hank finished.

"I'll see you tomorrow, then."

Hank ended the call, and Gunner let the phone slip from his grasp onto the couch. The silence that followed was overwhelming, filled with the weight of his decision and the countless what-ifs that swirled through his mind.

He crossed his arms, glanced at his framed photo of him and Aubrey on horseback. Her smile in that moment, carefree and genuine, tugged at his heart. "Dammit," he muttered.

His thoughts raced, painting vivid scenarios of potential

futures. In one, he saw himself on stage, bathed in spotlights, the roar of the crowd washing over him. In another,
he was here in Timber Falls, building a life with Aubrey,
finding peace in the simplicity of small-town living.

What if I lose her?

The sudden familiar rumble of a truck engine outside
broke through his thoughts. His shoulders sagged with relief at the distraction.

As he strode to the door, anticipation and trepidation
coursed through him. He knew Eli and Jaxon would have
opinions on his predicament, and part of him craved their
input while another part dreaded facing the reality of his
choices.

Gunner swung open the door, forcing a smile onto his
face. "You couldn't have picked a better time to show up,"
he called out, his voice carrying a forced lightness.

Eli and Jaxon sauntered in, their smiles easy and pos-
tures relaxed. The scent of leather and hay clung to them,
a reminder of the ranch life that Gunner adored.

"Figured you could use some company." Eli's eyes
scanned Gunner's face with a knowing look. He clapped
a hand on Gunner's shoulder, the gesture both comforting and grounding.

Jaxon followed Eli inside, his eyes twinkling with mischief. "That, and I know you might have some of that
fancy bourbon stashed away," he teased, his voice light
but—unless Gunner was imagining it—tinged with un-
derlying concern.

Gunner chuckled, the sound hollow even to his own
ears. "I just might," he said, leading them into the living

room. The familiar space suddenly felt claustrophobic, the weight of his decision pressing in on him from all sides.

As they settled onto the worn leather couch, Gunner's gaze flicked to that framed photo of him and Aubrey. His heart clenched, a physical ache that threatened to overwhelm him.

"Alright, spill it," Eli prompted, leaning forward, elbows on his knees. "We've heard the girls' version of what's happened, but you tell us yours."

Gunner ran a hand across the back of his neck. "I got a call from my agent yesterday, and then the head of the label this morning," he began. "They want me in Nashville. Tomorrow."

The words hung in the air, heavy with implication. Jaxon's eyebrows shot up, surprise and excitement crossing his features. "That's great news, isn't it?" he asked, his tone cautious.

Eli remained silent, his intense gaze fixed on Gunner, reading between the lines of what wasn't being said.

"It should be," Gunner replied. "But I can't help feeling like I'm standing at a crossroads, and no matter which path I choose, I'm gonna lose something important." His gaze drifted back to the photo of him and Aubrey, his heart heavy. "I should be over the moon about this chance, but all I can think about is Aubrey's face when I told her about the possibility yesterday." He swallowed hard, his voice raw with emotion. "It was like I could see her building walls right in front of me, protecting herself from the pain she's sure is coming."

Eli leaned back, his green eyes softening with understanding. "You're worried she thinks you're gonna leave her behind."

Gunner nodded, running a hand over his face. "It's more than that. I saw the doubt in her eyes, the fear. It's like she's waiting for the other shoe to drop, expecting me to be the same guy that walked away from her before." His voice cracked slightly. "I don't know how to convince her I'm not that guy, that I want her in my life no matter what, that I've got all the tools now to make sure I don't slip, that I've got the pain under control."

Jaxon shifted, his expression thoughtful. "Have you told her that? In those words?"

"I've tried," Gunner sighed, frustration evident in his tone. "But it's like she can't quite believe it. And now, with this opportunity, I'm afraid it'll just confirm her worst fears."

Eli leaned forward, his voice firm but kind. "You can't control Aubrey's fears or her past. What you *can* control is how you handle this situation." He paused, making sure he had Gunner's full attention. "You've got a shot at your dream again. A second chance that most people don't get. Don't throw it away because you're afraid of what might happen."

Jaxon nodded in agreement. "Eli's right. This doesn't have to be an either-or situation. You can pursue your career and still show Aubrey you're committed to her."

Gunner's heart thrummed with gratitude as he absorbed his friends' words. Their faith in him was palpable, a lifeline in the storm of his doubts.

"You make it sound so simple," he said. "But I can't

shake this feeling that I'm standing on the edge of something big, and one wrong step could cost me everything."

Eli's steady gaze met Gunner's. "That's because it is big,
brother. But you've got the strength to handle it. You've
overcome addiction, you've rebuilt your life here. This is
just another mountain to climb."

Gunner nodded slowly, feeling the weight of their support settle on his shoulders like a warm blanket. His mind
wandered to the life he'd built here in Timber Falls. The
quiet mornings, the nights filled with music at The Naked
Moose, the sense of belonging he'd found. And at the center of it all, Aubrey. Her fierce independence, her vulnerability, the way her eyes lit up when she laughed.

He could see it so clearly. A future here, with her. Mornings waking up to her smile, evenings spent on the porch
watching the sunset, building a life together, note by note,
day by day. The thought filled him with a longing so intense it was almost painful.

But there was that other pull too, the call of Nashville, of
stages and spotlights and crowds singing his lyrics back to
him. It was a part of him he couldn't deny, couldn't silence.

Jaxon added, "You said you wanted to fight for her,
right?"

"I did," Gunner said.

"Then fight for her," Jaxon declared.

Seventeen

Aubrey woke the next morning, a soft moan escaping her as she felt the gentle brush of warm lips against her neck. Her eyelids fluttered, confusion clouding her mind as she tried to make sense of the sensation. The familiar scent of sandalwood and leather enveloped her, and she inhaled deeply, her body instinctively relaxing.

"Mornin', darlin'," a husky voice whispered, sending shivers down her spine.

Her eyes snapped open, her heart racing as she realized it wasn't a dream. She turned her head slightly, her gaze meeting Gunner's intense eyes. His tousled hair fell across his forehead, and a tender smile played on his lips.

"Gunner?" she breathed, her voice still thick with sleep. "What are you—"

He silenced her with another kiss, this time on her cheek, his stubble grazing her skin. Her breath caught in her throat, her body melting into his touch.

Eventually, he moved away, his fingers tracing lazy circles on her hip. "Hope you don't mind the wake-up call."

She closed her eyes briefly, fighting the urge to lean into his touch. "It's…unexpected," she admitted, her voice softening despite herself. "But not entirely unwelcome."

She felt Gunner's smile against her skin as he placed another kiss on her shoulder. "That's what I was hopin' to hear."

As the last vestiges of sleep faded away, she found herself acutely aware of every point of contact between their bodies. The weight of his arm around her waist, the heat of his breath on her neck, the solid presence of his chest against her back. It was intoxicating.

"So, what's up?" she asked as she turned to face him.

He propped himself up on one elbow, his eyes searching hers. "How 'bout we take this moment and stretch it out a bit longer? Say…all the way to Nashville?"

Her brow furrowed, her mind struggling to catch up with his words. "Nashville? What are you talking about?"

His smile widened. "My label called yesterday. This is my one shot for a comeback. I've got two tickets to Nashville, and a recording studio waiting for me."

She pushed herself up on her elbows as she searched Gunner's face. "You're not serious," she said.

"Quite serious," Gunner replied, tracing a finger along her jawline. "We have a private plane waiting for us. I need to record that song and I want you to come with me."

Aubrey's mind raced, a whirlwind of questions and concerns battling against the thrill of spontaneity. "But the bar… My responsibilities…"

"Already taken care of," Gunner assured her, his tone

gentle but insistent. "Come on, Aubrey. When's the last time you did somethin' without thinking it through?"

She bit her lip, torn between her practical nature and the undeniable pull of adventure…and of Gunner himself. "I don't know if I can just drop everything and go."

"Sure, you can," Gunner said, his eyes never leaving hers. "You pack a bag, and we leave."

"But what about the bar?" she asked.

Gunner's fingers intertwined with hers, his touch warm and reassuring. "Charly and Willow have already agreed to cover for you," he said. "They practically pushed me out the door to come get you. Said it was high time you took a break."

Aubrey nibbled her lip. "They knew about this? And they're okay with it?"

"More than okay," Gunner chuckled. "Willow threatened to drag you to Nashville herself if I didn't follow through."

An easy comfort spread through Aubrey's chest, a feeling so foreign yet comforting that it almost overwhelmed her. She'd spent so long taking care of others, shouldering responsibilities, that the idea of someone—multiple someones—conspiring to do something just for her was almost too much to process.

"I don't know what to say," she whispered, her voice thick with emotion.

Gunner's thumb traced small circles on the back of her hand. "Say yes, darlin'. Let me whisk you away, just for a little while."

Aubrey felt a smile tugging at her lips, even as her practical side tried to resist. "You're impossible, you know that?" she said, shaking her head in wonder.

"Impossibly charming, you mean," Gunner said with a wink, pulling her closer.

She laughed, shaking her head. "What started all this?"

"I know I threw you for a loop at the talent show," he said, his voice gentle and coaxing. "I know you're thinking that I'm going to leave you, but I want you to know that's the furthest thing from my mind. This journey, this adventure, it wouldn't be complete without you by my side." He reached out and gently cupped her face, his touch both tender and reassuring. "We can make this work. I know it's not the conventional path, but together, we can do this."

Tears welled up in her eyes as she looked into his sincere, loving gaze. She had always been a planner, a person who liked to have everything mapped out and under control. But with him, she had thrown caution to the wind and jumped headfirst into the unknown. And now, she couldn't imagine going back to her old, predictable life.

"I don't want to lose you," she whispered, her voice choked with emotion.

"You won't," he promised. "Just as I refuse to lose you."

He would eventually go back on tour, and she couldn't bear the thought of being apart from him for so long. She finally gathered the courage to ask the question that had been weighing on her mind.

"But how will this all work?" she asked, her voice trembling with uncertainty. "When you go on tour, how will I see you?"

He paused, his thumb brushing over her cheek in a

gentle caress. "I don't have all the answers," he admitted. "But we'll take it step by step and make time for each other when we can. I can't give up music," he said, his voice filled with emotion. "It's a part of my soul, but so are you. I need you just as much."

She felt a wave of relief wash over her at his words, and she wrapped her arms around him, burying her face in his chest. They would find a way to make it work, she knew. They'd come this far. And as long as they had each other, they could weather any storm.

"So come, see Nashville with me," he said, taking her hand in his, "and see the other part of my life." His smile was sweet and inviting. "What do you say?"

Her eyes locked with Gunner's, searching for any hint of deception. Finding only sincerity and warmth, she felt something shift inside her. A grin slowly spread across her face as she made her decision.

"I say…" she purred, reaching out to grab the front of Gunner's shirt, "that Nashville can wait just a little longer."

With a swift tug, she pulled him back onto the bed, reveling in his surprised laugh. His strong arms encircled her, his warmth enveloping her as she pressed herself against him.

"Why, Miss Hale," Gunner drawled, "I do believe you're trying to make us miss our flight."

"How long do we have?" she asked, a sly smile playing on her lips as she looked up at him.

"Two hours," he murmured, his voice soft and low.

Her heart skipped a beat as she tilted her chin up, her lips dangerously close to his. She could feel the heat emanating from his body, and she couldn't resist the temptation any longer.

"Then maybe I just want to make sure this trip is worth leaving Timber Falls behind for a little while," she whispered.

Their lips met in a tender kiss that quickly deepened, sparking a passionate fire between them. She tangled her fingers in his hair as his hand gently cupped her face, his thumb brushing against her soft skin. The kiss was both familiar and exhilarating, growing more intense by the second.

Gunner eventually pulled away with a smile on his lips and whispered, "Guess I should show you what I've got then."

She laughed and ran her hands over his back, eagerly anticipating his next move. "Probably wise."

As their lips collided again, everything else faded away into the background and she became lost in the moment, completely consumed by his touch…and his worth.

Seated in the dimly lit recording booth later that evening, Gunner's heart was pounding in rhythm with the faint metronome ticking in his headphones. They'd run through the song, over and over again, and he'd repeated sections that the producer wasn't happy with. He adjusted the mic again, tilting it slightly downward to capture the raw emotion he knew would pour from his lips. With a slight nod to the producer behind the glass, Gunner signaled his readiness.

This is it, he thought, the moment that could make or break everything. His gaze flickered briefly to the couch where Aubrey sat, her presence comforting. Gunner's fingers tightened around the lyric sheet, the paper crinkling softly.

"Alright, Gunner," the producer's voice crackled through the headphones. "Whenever you're ready."

Gunner closed his eyes, drawing in a deep breath. The scent of polished wood and leather from his boots grounded him, reminding him of home, of Timber Falls and The Naked Moose. Of Aubrey.

This song is for her, he realized. *For us. Every word, every note—it's our story.*

As the intro began to play, Gunner opened his eyes, locking on to Aubrey's gaze through the glass. Her eyes mirrored his own, a swirl of hesitation and hope that matched the turmoil in his chest. Hope that this was the beginning of them making this work.

The first notes left his lips, his voice husky and tinged with longing. Each lyric felt like a confession, a piece of his soul laid bare for Aubrey and the world to hear. He poured every ounce of his being into the performance, determined to prove that he was more than his past mistakes, more than a washed-up country star looking for redemption.

As he sang, memories flooded his mind—their passionate night in Atlanta, the warmth of Aubrey's smile at The Naked Moose, the way her eyes lit up when she laughed. But with those sweet recollections came the bitter taste of his struggles, the weight of the addiction that had nearly cost him everything.

Never again, he vowed silently, his voice rising with renewed conviction. *I'm done running. I'm done hiding.*

The final chorus approached, and Gunner felt a surge of energy course through him. This was his moment of truth, his chance to show Aubrey—and himself—that he was capable of change, of love, of building something real and lasting.

As the song ended, he opened his eyes. His breath came in short gasps, his heart racing as if he'd just run a marathon. Through the glass, he saw Aubrey's eyes glistening with unshed tears, and he knew.

This was their beginning.

Gunner only looked away when he caught sight of the producer nodding along enthusiastically. The man's fingers danced across the soundboard, adjusting levels with practiced ease. A crackle in Gunner's headphones, and the producer's voice came through:

"That's it, Gunner! Keep that energy. We're capturing gold here."

Gunner's lips quirked into a half smile, his confidence surging. The final chorus approached, and Gunner felt a surge of energy course through him. As the late note faded, his opened his eyes.

He locked eyes with Aubrey once more, drawing strength from her presence. He'd given everything to that performance, laid bare his hopes and fears. Now, all he could do was wait, the future hanging in the balance between two worlds he longed to unite.

The last chords hung in the air, resonating through Gunner's body as he slowly removed the headphones. His hands trembled slightly, adrenaline and raw emotion coursing through him. He stepped out of the booth, his eyes immediately seeking Aubrey's.

There she was, her eyes shining with pride and something deeper, something that made his chest tighten.

"Darlin'," he drawled softly, his voice still husky from singing.

"That was absolutely incredible!" The producer's enthusiastic voice cut through the moment. The man's face was split with a wide grin, his hands gesticulating wildly. "Gunner, you've outdone yourself. The emotion, the depth… It's like you reached into your soul and pulled out pure gold."

Gunner felt a flush of pride mixed with humility. "I appreciate that, sir."

The producer clapped him on the back. "No, you don't understand. This isn't just good, it's career-defining. The way you captured the longing, the struggle, it's universal. Everyone who's ever been torn between two worlds is going to feel this in their bones."

As the producer continued to gush, Gunner's gaze drifted back to Aubrey. She gave him a small, knowing smile that spoke volumes. He thought, *She knows. She feels it too. This song, it's our story.*

The producer's voice faded into the background as Gunner's mind raced. He'd poured his heart into that song, opened up about his struggle to choose between Nashville and Timber Falls, between ambition and love. And now, with success potentially on the horizon, the choice loomed larger than ever.

Gunner extended his hand to the producer, his grip firm yet humble. "I'm grateful for the opportunity and your guidance."

The producer shook his hand enthusiastically, his eyes twinkling. "Son, with talent like yours, my job's easy. You just keep bringing that raw emotion, and we'll make magic. We'll work on this and get it to you when we're done."

Gunner nodded in agreement.

As the studio team began to pack up, he made his way over to Aubrey. She stood from the couch, her smile bright.

"So," Aubrey said, her voice soft but direct, "looks like another hit is coming."

"Maybe," he replied with a smile.

They moved to a quiet corner of the studio, away from the bustle. Aubrey's fingers brushed his arm, sending a jolt through him. "That song, Gunner, it was beautiful."

He met her gaze, seeing the vulnerability there that matched his own. "It's our story, Aubrey. Every word of it."

He smiled, feeling a sense of pride and satisfaction at her words. Creating music was his passion, his escape, his way of expressing himself in a world that often left him feeling misunderstood. And to have someone like her, someone who understood him on a level that no one else did, witness it was a rare and special gift.

"It is." She smiled.

"You know me too well," he said.

She laughed, a light and carefree sound that filled him with warmth. "I should hope so. After all, I am your muse."

He reached out, pulling her into his arms and holding her close. "And my heart," he whispered, pressing a kiss to her forehead.

The studio bustled around them, but Gunner felt a moment of clarity amidst the chaos. He straightened up. "All right, let's get out of here. Let me show you my Nashville. The real one, not just the glitz and glamour."

Aubrey's eyebrows rose in surprise. "You're not exhausted?"

He shook his head. "No, and we only have tonight here. Let's make the most of it." He grinned. "I want to share this part of my world with you."

Her lips curved into a soft smile. "I'd love that," she breathed, her voice tinged with a warmth that made his heart skip. "Show me your Nashville."

As the heavy studio door swung shut behind them, Gunner's calloused fingers intertwined with Aubrey's, sending a jolt of electricity up his arm. The neon lights of Lower Broadway flickered to life, painting the twilight sky in a kaleidoscope of colors. Gunner inhaled deeply, the familiar scents of whiskey and barbecue making him feel as at home as he did in Timber Falls.

They strolled down the bustling sidewalk, their joined hands swinging between them. Gunner's heart swelled with pride as he watched Aubrey take in the sights and sounds of Music City. He pointed to a weathered brick building with a faded mural.

"That there's where I played my first real gig," he told her.

Aubrey squeezed his hand. "I bet you were amazing."

Gunner chuckled, remembering his nervous, fumbling fingers. "Amazing might be a stretch, but I sure as hell gave it my all."

As they passed honky-tonks and cowboy boot shops, Gunner shared stories of late-night jam sessions and chance encounters with country music legends. Aubrey listened intently, her eyes wide with curiosity and a hint of something else—admiration, maybe?

"And over there," Gunner said, gesturing to a small park, "is where I wrote my first hit song. Sat on that bench for hours, pouring my heart out onto paper."

Aubrey's gaze softened. "What was it about?"

Gunner paused, his throat tightening with emotion. "Loss. The kind of heartache that changes a person."

He felt Aubrey stiffen beside him, and he wondered if she was thinking about her own past hurts. The air between them crackled with unspoken words and shared understanding.

"Sometimes," Aubrey said softly, "the most beautiful things come from our deepest pain."

Gunner's heart skipped a beat. In that moment, surrounded by the pulsing energy of Nashville and the warmth of Aubrey's presence, he felt a glimmer of hope for the future—*their* future. He had thought he had lost hope forever, but here it was, like a powerful light breaking through his darkest clouds.

He squeezed Aubrey's hand tight and felt a sense of peace wash over him. He had no idea what the future held, but in that moment, with Aubrey by his side, he could only say, "I'm damn glad you're here with me."

Her smile was sweet and warmed him from head to toe. "I'm happy too."

Eighteen

Aubrey couldn't fight her smile as she stepped into the legendary Bluebird Cafe, the pulsing energy of Nashville's music scene washing over her. It was a dimly lit space, filled with the warm hum of voices and the soft strumming of guitars. The stage was modest, but it held an unmistakable magic, like a portal to a world of endless possibility.

She glanced at Gunner, his rugged features softened by the amber glow, and felt a flutter in her chest. He had brought her here as a surprise, showing her more of his life. She couldn't believe she was actually standing in the heart of Nashville.

They weaved through the crowd, the air thick with anticipation and the faint scent of weathered wood.

As they placed an order and made their way to a small table near the back of the cafe, Aubrey couldn't help but drink in every detail: the faded posters on the walls, the worn hardwood floors, the intimate stage where history was made. She felt a thrill running through her, knowing that this was where legends were born.

"I can't believe I'm actually here," she whispered to Gunner, her eyes sparkling.

Gunner's lips curled into a knowing smile. "Welcome to the heart of country music, darlin'."

As she took her seat, Aubrey took in the intimate setting. The walls were filled with music history, adorned with signed guitars and faded photographs of legends who had graced this very stage.

"It's like stepping into a time capsule," she murmured, her gaze lingering on a black-and-white photo of Dolly Parton.

Gunner leaned in, his breath warm against her ear. "Every inch of this place has a story to tell."

Aubrey felt a shiver run down her spine, unsure if it was from Gunner's proximity or the weight of the room's history. She took a deep breath, trying to ground herself in the moment.

"I bet you have some stories of your own from here," she said, curiosity getting the better of her.

A shadow passed over Gunner's face, quickly replaced by his usual charm. "Darlin', you have no idea." He chuckled, but Aubrey caught a hint of something deeper in his blue eyes.

As the lights dimmed further, a reverent hush fell over the room. Aubrey felt it then—the magic of the Bluebird, the dreams and heartbreaks that had been poured out on that small stage. For a moment, she forgot about her own troubles, lost in the promise of the music to come.

Aubrey's fingers brushed against Gunner's as they both reached for a tortilla chip to dip into salsa. "These are so good," Aubrey whispered.

He leaned in, his voice low and husky. "Not as good as you look tonight, darlin'."

Aubrey felt her cheeks flush, grateful for the dim lighting. She took a bite of the chip, savoring the taste as she gathered her thoughts. "Flattery will get you everywhere, cowboy," she teased.

Gunner's laugh was a soft rumble that sent shivers down her spine. "I'm just tellin' the truth."

The emcee stepped onto the stage, his voice cutting through the gentle hum of conversation. "Ladies and gentlemen, welcome to open mic night at the Bluebird Cafe!"

Aubrey clapped along with the crowd as the first performer took the stage. A young woman with fiery red hair and a battered guitar, who began with a sweet country ballad.

"You know," Gunner said softly, his voice barely audible over the music, "this is where I got my start in Nashville."

Aubrey's eyebrows shot up. "Really? Here?"

Gunner nodded, a wistful smile playing on his lips. "Yep. I was just a kid with big dreams and an old guitar. Drove all night from Montana, slept in my truck and showed up here with nothing but hope."

"What was it like?" Aubrey asked, leaning in closer, captivated by this glimpse into Gunner's past.

"Terrifying," he chuckled, his eyes meeting hers. "But the moment I stepped on that stage, it felt like coming home."

Aubrey felt a surge of warmth in her chest, imagining a younger Gunner, full of nervous energy and raw talent. "I wish I could've seen that," she said softly.

As the current performer's set came to a close, a palpable excitement began to build in the room. Aubrey noticed people whispering, heads turning toward their table.

The host's voice rang out, "And now, ladies and gentlemen, we have a very special treat for you tonight. Let's see if we can get to the stage… Gunner Woods!"

A ripple of applause and excited murmurs swept through the crowd. Aubrey's eyes widened in surprise, her gaze darting between Gunner and the expectant faces around them.

"Gunner," she breathed, "did you know about this?"

Gunner's eyes widened, surprise and hesitation flashing across his face. He shook his head with a self-deprecating smile, his hand rubbing the back of his neck. "I swear, I didn't plan this, but I had to use my name to get us tickets."

The crowd's encouragement swelled, as the emcee said, "Come on, Gunner. Get on up here."

Aubrey watched as Gunner's Adam's apple bobbed, his fingers tapping an anxious rhythm on the table.

She nudged him playfully with her shoulder. "Get up there and show Nashville what they've been missing."

Taking a deep breath, Gunner nodded and stood up. As he made his way to the stage, Aubrey couldn't help but notice the subtle transformation. His shoulders straightened, his stride becoming more purposeful with each step. The dim lighting caught the planes of his face, highlighting the determination etched there.

Gunner took the stage, his presence immediately commanding attention. He adjusted the microphone, his fingers brushing against the strings of the guitar someone handed to him. In that moment, Aubrey saw the seasoned performer emerge, the man who had once set country music ablaze with his talent.

As he settled onto the stool, guitar cradled in his arms, his eyes found Aubrey's in the crowd. He gave her a small smile before turning to face his audience.

The first chord struck, and Aubrey's breath caught in her throat. Gunner's fingers danced across the strings, coaxing out a melody that seemed to wrap itself around her heart. His voice, smooth as honey, filled the room.

Aubrey felt a shiver run down her spine. The raw emotion in Gunner's voice transported her back to that night in Atlanta when they'd first met. The electricity between them, the connection that had sparked instantly, it all came rushing back, amplified by the power of his music.

Around her, the audience sat transfixed. A woman at the next table wiped away a tear, while a grizzled old man nodded along, eyes closed in appreciation. Aubrey glanced around, marveling at how Gunner's music seemed to touch each person uniquely.

"God, he's incredible." She swallowed hard, fighting back unexpected tears. She'd known Gunner was talented, but this, *this*, was something else entirely. His music spoke of pain, of hope, of redemption.

The patrons around her swayed gently, completely caught up in the spell Gunner was weaving. A couple nearby held hands tightly, exchanging meaningful glances.

In that moment, Aubrey understood the true power of live music, its ability to bring people together, to make them feel less alone in their struggles and dreams.

A beat passed. Then applause surrounded Aubrey. She found herself on her feet, clapping until her hands stung, her heart filled with hope that somehow, her being here in this moment meant that Gunner could mix his separate worlds of Nashville and Timber Falls.

A few hours later, the elevator doors slid open with a soft ping, revealing the sleek hallway of Gunner's Nashville condo building. Aubrey stepped out first, and she turned to flash Gunner a smile that made his heart skip.

"Ready for the grand tour?" Gunner drawled, fishing his keys from his pocket. His fingers trembled slightly as he unlocked the door.

Aubrey's eyes widened as they stepped inside. "Oh, Gunner," she breathed, taking in the open-concept space. "This is gorgeous."

He watched her intently, drinking in her reaction. The condo was a far cry from his rustic house back in Timber Falls, all clean lines and modern furnishings. He'd always loved how it blended country and city, much like himself.

"Make yourself at home," he said.

Aubrey moved farther into the space, her fingertips trailing along the back of a sleek leather couch.

"I can't believe this view," she murmured, approaching the floor-to-ceiling windows that dominated one wall. The Nashville skyline sprawled before them, all glittering lights against the night sky.

Gunner came up behind her, close enough to catch the faint scent of her perfume. "Pretty spectacular, ain't it?"

Aubrey turned to face him, and her smile beamed. The sight hit Gunner like a punch to the gut, memories of their week in Atlanta flooding back. Her eyes had held that same mesmerizing gleam then, in a different city, under very different circumstances.

"It reminds me a little of Atlanta," Aubrey said softly, as if reading his thoughts. "God, I've missed this so much."

Gunner swallowed hard. "The city?"

She nodded, a wistful smile playing at her lips. "The energy, the lights… It's intoxicating."

"Kinda like you," Gunner murmured before he could stop himself. He watched a blush creep up Aubrey's cheeks.

"Smooth talker," she teased, but there was a hint of vulnerability in her voice that tugged at Gunner's heart. He wanted nothing more than to pull her close, to show her that she belonged here too, in the city, in his arms, in his life.

Instead, he cleared his throat. "How about I show you the rest of the place?"

As they moved through the condo, he found himself seeing it through new eyes. The guitar mounted on the wall, little reminders of his past triumphs and failures. The collection of vinyl records, each holding a piece of his musical journey. The framed photo of Timber Falls Ranch, an anchor to his roots.

Aubrey took it all in, asking questions and offering genuine compliments. Her enthusiasm was infectious, and Gunner felt a weight lifting from his shoulders. He hadn't been back here since he left, a mess of a man. He'd been avoiding it, unsure if he could trust himself. But watching her in his space now, he realized how good it felt to come back here, healthy and happy.

"You know," Aubrey said, turning to face him with a playful glint in her eye, "I think we need to warm this place up a bit." Her fingers deftly unbuttoned his shirt, her touch leaving a trail of fire on his skin. She pushed the fabric off his shoulders, letting it fall to the floor. "God, you're so sexy," she rasped, her eyes darkening with desire.

Gunner's breath caught in his throat. He pulled her close, his hands roaming the curves of her body as he kissed her neck. "Not half as sexy as you, darlin'," he drawled, his voice husky with want.

They moved through the space in a heated dance, shedding layers with each step. The city's energy seemed to pulse through them, urgent and alive. Gunner's heart raced as Aubrey's hands explored his chest, her touch both tentative and bold.

"Aubrey," he whispered. "You're drivin' me crazy, you know that?"

She smiled against his lips. "Good," she teased, nipping at his lower lip. "That's the idea."

As they made their way toward the bedroom, Gunner couldn't help but marvel at how right this felt. Aubrey fit so perfectly in his arms, in this space, in his life. It was as if she'd always been meant to be here.

"What are you thinking?" Aubrey asked.

Gunner cupped her face in his hands. "I'm thinkin' that

you belong here, darlin'. With me. In this mixed-up life of mine."

Aubrey's eyes widened, a flicker of vulnerability passing through them. "Gunner, I—"

He silenced her with a gentle kiss. "Shh, we don't need to figure it all out right now. Just be here with me. In this moment."

As they crossed the threshold into his bedroom, Gunner's heart swelled with a feeling he couldn't quite name. All he knew was that Aubrey Hale had waltzed into his life and turned everything upside down in the best possible way.

The soft glow of the city lights filtered through the sheer curtains as they tumbled onto the plush bed. Their kisses deepened, each touch igniting a fire that he never wanted to end.

His hands trembled slightly as he caressed her skin, marveling at its softness. "You have no idea how much I want you right now," he murmured.

Her eyes locked on to his, passion and vulnerability swirling in their depths. "Show me," she whispered, her fingers tracing the contours of his face.

As they explored each other with tender urgency, he felt the weight of his past mistakes and regrets melting away. Here, in this moment with Aubrey, he was free from the pressures of fame, free from the chains of addiction that had once bound him.

"I want to give you everything," Gunner breathed, his voice rough, raw with emotion as he reached for a condom in the drawer of the nightstand. His hands moved quickly, but his heart still thundered in his chest. He looked down at her, bathed in the faint glow of the room, and for a moment, he couldn't breathe.

When he entered her, she arched into him, her body responding to his touch like she was made for him. Every curve, every soft sound she made, sent sparks through his veins. Their movements fell into a rhythm that was slow and deliberate, a dance he didn't need to think about because it was instinct. Her hands on him, her skin against his, felt like a fire consuming him from the inside out.

Gunner kissed her, deep and desperate, as if she might disappear if he didn't hold on tight enough. Her moan against his mouth sent a shiver through him, her fingers tangling in his hair and pulling him closer—always closer. Nothing existed beyond this moment, nothing but her. The world outside didn't matter; the past didn't matter. All that mattered was Aubrey and the way she looked at him like he was the only man who had ever touched her heart.

He moved within her, their bodies finding that perfect rhythm that felt like it had always been there, waiting for them to discover it. Every movement, every gasp, left him breathless, like she was pulling something out of him he hadn't even realized was missing. God, she was beautiful. He watched her, her face flushed, lips parted, and he felt the tension building between them—something wild, something he couldn't control.

When she trembled beneath him, her release crashing over her, Gunner followed, letting himself fall with her. It wasn't just physical—it was more. It was everything. His heart hammered as he collapsed beside her, pulling her into his arms, her body soft and warm against his.

For a long moment, they just breathed together, their hearts still pounding as if they were trying to sync. Gunner pressed a kiss to her hair, his voice rough in her ear. "Thank you for being here with me."

As he held her, Gunner knew this wasn't just another night together—it was a beginning. A promise. Aubrey was everything he'd ever needed, and he was going try his hardest to prove it to her.

Nineteen

Spring came fast. Too fast. Gunner stood in the heart of Timber Falls Ranch, a sea of motion and laughter swirling around him. The crisp spring air carried the scent of blooming wildflowers and fresh hay, mingling with the excited chatter of friends and cowboys bustling about. Jaxon and Charly's wedding was only days away, and the ranch had transformed into a hive of joyful preparation.

For a moment, Gunner let himself get lost in the scene. His eyes swept over the corral where Eli was helping string up fairy lights, past the weathered barn doors thrown wide to welcome guests and finally settled on the makeshift crafting area near the house. A smile tugged at his lips.

Soon one of his best friends would be getting married, and he couldn't have been happier for Jaxon.

He unconsciously fiddled with the worn leather bracelet on his wrist. The past few months with Aubrey had been a whirlwind of stolen kisses and late-night conversations, of rediscovering his passion for music and finding a place he truly belonged. The journey to Nashville happened a few months back, yet it seemed as if it were just yesterday. And now...

Gunner's gaze zeroed in on Aubrey as she laughed with Willow and Charly. Her nimble fingers wove delicate flowers into an intricate garland, each movement precise and graceful. Even from a distance, he could see the sparkle in her eyes, the way her smile lit up her entire face.

"I swear, if I have to make one more of these damn things, I'm gonna lose it," Willow grumbled good-naturedly, holding up a tangled mess of ribbon and wire.

Aubrey chuckled, reaching over to rescue the decoration. "Here, let me show you again. It's all in the wrist."

As he watched her patiently guide Willow through the process, just close enough to hear them, Gunner felt a familiar ache in his chest. How could he even think about leaving this? Leaving her?

But the call of the stage whispered in the back of his mind, reminding him of unfinished dreams. With a deep breath, he squared his shoulders and made his way toward the women, determined to savor every moment he had left in this little slice of heaven.

"Ladies," he drawled, tipping an imaginary hat as he approached. "I hear there's some decorating that needs doing. Any chance you could use an extra pair of hands?"

Charly let out a dramatic groan, leaning back in her chair and fanning herself with a half-finished paper flower. "Oh, Gunner, you have no idea what you're getting yourself into," she said with a wry grin. "I thought making our own centerpieces would be so romantic. Now, with the wedding just days away, I'm starting to think I should have let Poppy hire someone."

The group erupted in laughter, the sound warm and genuine. Aubrey's eyes crinkled at the corners as she nudged Charly playfully. "Come on, where's your sense of adventure? Besides, these will be way more meaningful than anything store-bought."

Gunner smiled, but his mind was elsewhere. He'd heard the label's offer from Tom an hour ago, and it weighed heavily on him. "Well, I could try my hand at this crafting business," he said, picking up a spool of ribbon. "Though I can't promise it'll be pretty."

As he sat down next to Aubrey, their eyes met briefly. The connection was electric, sending a jolt through Gunner's system. God, how was he supposed to leave Timber Falls? This was different from recording a single. He would need to stay in Nashville for a while and then go on tour. The thought of them being apart, of him missing moments like these, made his chest tighten.

Aubrey must have sensed something was off. Her brow furrowed slightly as she handed him a bunch of flowers. "You okay there?" she asked softly, her voice carrying a hint of concern.

He forced a smile, trying to shake off the worry. "Just fine, darlin'. Though I might need some of that patience you were showing Willow earlier. These stems are mighty tricky."

As he fumbled with the flowers, his mind raced. The label loved his new sound. They wanted him back in Nashville, promising studio time, a new album, a tour. It was everything he'd wanted again. So why did it feel like he was about to lose everything that truly mattered?

Charly snorted, leaning over to inspect Gunner's handiwork. "Looks like your fingers are better suited for guitar strings than flower stems, buddy," she teased.

Gunner laughed, the sound a bit hollow to his own ears. "You got that right. I should stick to what I know best, but here I am."

As the group continued their work, the easy banter flowed around him. Gunner found himself relaxing, drawn into the warmth of friendship. This was what he'd missed during his years chasing fame—the sense of belonging, of being part of something bigger than himself.

"Hey, Gunner," Aubrey called, her eyes meeting his. "Can you pass me that ribbon over there?"

Their fingers brushed as he handed her the spool, and for a moment, the world around them seemed to fade away. In that silent exchange, Gunner saw a future. Lazy Sunday mornings, shared laughter over pancakes, stolen kisses between sets at The Naked Moose. But he also saw the question in her eyes, the one he wasn't ready to answer.

Across the yard, Eli and Jaxon hefted a massive wooden arch, their movements in perfect sync as they maneuvered the unwieldy decoration.

"Little to the left, Jax," Eli grunted, his intense eyes focused on their task.

Jaxon adjusted seamlessly. "How's that?"

"Perfect," Eli nodded.

Gunner felt a pang of unease. He turned away, suddenly overwhelmed by the activity around him. Without a word, he slipped away from the group, his boots crunching on gravel as he sought a moment to himself.

At the edge of the property, he leaned against a weathered fence post, his gaze drifting to the distant mountains. The tranquil beauty of Montana stretched before him, but his mind was far from peaceful.

"Damn it," he muttered, running a hand over his face. The label's demands echoed in his head, a tempting promise of success and redemption. But at what cost?

He closed his eyes, picturing Aubrey's face. The thought of leaving her behind made his chest ache. Leaving Timber Falls before for a tour was easier. This, he nearly couldn't endure.

As he stood there, torn between love and ambition, Gunner realized that no matter what choice he made, something precious would be lost.

"Earth to Gunner!" Charly's playful voice snapped him back to reality. "Did you get lost in one of your country ballads again?"

Gunner turned, a sheepish grin tugging at his lips. "Just admirin' the view."

Charly rolled her eyes, but her smile was warm. "Well, come admire the view over a well-deserved beer."

As he followed her back to the group, Gunner felt the tension in his shoulders ease slightly. Charly's gentle teasing had a way of grounding him, reminding him of the simple joys he'd found here.

"Alright, folks," Jaxon called out, wiping sweat from his brow. "I think we've earned ourselves a break. Beers on ice."

A cheer went up from the group as they gathered around a makeshift picnic area. Gunner snagged a cold bottle, relishing the first sip as he settled onto a hay bale next to Aubrey.

"You okay?" she whispered, her fingers brushing his arm.

He nodded, forcing a smile. "I'm all right."

As conversation flowed around them, punctuated by laughter and the clinking of bottles, Gunner forced himself into the moment. These people, this place—he wanted to keep them all strong in his mind.

He took another swig of beer, letting the cool liquid chase away the bitter taste of indecision. For now, he'd savor this moment, surrounded by laughter and love, and pray that somehow, someway, he'd find a path that wouldn't lead to heartbreak.

He suddenly caught Jaxon's eye and saw him tilt his head slightly toward the barn.

Gunner excused himself from Aubrey and followed Jaxon behind the barn.

"Spill it," Jaxon said. "What's eating at you?"

Gunner sighed, leaning back against the barn. "The label loves the new tracks I sent. They want me back in Nashville, pronto. Album, tour, the whole nine yards."

Jaxon let out a low whistle. "That's great news, isn't it?"

"Should be," Gunner muttered. "But I can't stop thinking about what it means for me and Aubrey."

They'd paused near an old oak tree, its gnarled branches offering shade from the afternoon sun. Jaxon leaned against the trunk, facing Gunner, his expression thoughtful.

"Listen, man," he said, his tone gentle but firm. "Aubrey loves you. Anyone with eyes can see that. She'll support you, no matter what."

Gunner nodded, swallowing hard. "I know. That's what scares me. What if I'm making a mistake? Part of me doesn't even want to go. I want to stay here, with her, where everything finally makes sense."

"You can't run from who you are, Gunner," Jaxon said softly. "Music's in your blood. It's part of who Aubrey fell for."

Gunner sighed, rubbing the tension from his neck. "But what if I lose her? What if I lose all of this?" He gestured to the ranch, to the laughter echoing across the field. "What if I'm walking away from a good thing that saved me when I needed to be saved."

Jaxon placed a reassuring hand on Gunner's shoulder. "You won't lose anything. Home isn't just a place, it's the people who love you. And brother, you've got that in spades here. You and Aubrey are a good thing. You'll make this work. Timber Falls is all but a flight away. You can come home anytime, and now you know that you *should*. Being home grounds you."

As Gunner absorbed Jaxon's words, he felt a flicker of hope ignite in his chest. Maybe, just maybe, he could have both—his music *and* the life he'd built here in Timber Falls.

Twenty

Days had gone by, filled with all things wedding, and now Aubrey stood at the edge of the dance floor, her fingers lightly tracing the rim of her champagne flute as she watched Charly and Jaxon sway to the music. In the big white tent, the newlyweds moved in perfect sync, lost in each other's eyes, their faces glowing with unbridled joy, surrounded by all their friends and family. A bittersweet ache bloomed in Aubrey's chest.

They look so happy, she thought, a small smile tugging at her lips. *So certain.*

Her gaze drifted across the sea of smiling faces and twirling bodies, searching for one in particular. The absence of Gunner sent a ripple of unease through her.

"Have you seen Gunner?" she asked, turning to her mother beside her.

Her mom shook her head. "Not for a while. Perhaps he stepped out for some air?"

Aubrey nodded. "Thanks, I'll go check." It came as no

surprise that her mother loved Gunner. His charm could win anyone over.

She set down her glass and made her way to the edge of the tent, pausing to smooth the skirt of her cornflower-blue dress. The fabric felt suddenly constricting, matching the tightness in her chest.

I can't keep avoiding this, Aubrey thought, steeling herself. *We need to talk*. For days she'd been able to tell something was wrong. Maybe she didn't want to face it. Maybe she didn't want to admit there was trouble brewing, but she knew now—she couldn't avoid it any longer.

As she slipped out into the cool evening air, the sounds of laughter and music faded behind her. She took a deep breath, the scents of pine and wildflowers filling her lungs. She gazed out at the sprawling ranch, bathed in the golden light of the setting sun.

She started walking, her heels sinking slightly into the soft earth with each step. She moved with purpose, driven by a need to confront the truth she'd been dancing around for weeks. The weight of unspoken words and lingering glances had become too heavy to bear.

What if he's pulling away? The thought crept in, unbidden. *What if I'm not enough to make him stay?*

She pushed the doubts aside, focusing instead on the task at hand. Finding Gunner. Having the conversation they'd both been avoiding.

As she rounded the corner of the barn, her heart skipped a beat. There, silhouetted against the fading light, stood the man who had captured her heart.

She paused at the edge of the pasture, her breath catching in her throat. The mountains loomed in the distance, their jagged peaks painted in hues of purple and orange as the sun dipped lower.

Gunner stood alone. He seemed lost in thought, unaware of her presence. Her heart ached at the sight of him, so close yet feeling a world away.

Why does he look so…defeated? she wondered, her brow furrowing with concern.

Taking a steadying breath, she stepped forward. The grass rustled beneath her feet, breaking the stillness of the moment. She saw Gunner tense, his posture straightening as he sensed her approach.

"I thought I might find you out here," she said softly, her voice carrying on the gentle evening breeze.

Gunner turned, his eyes meeting hers. The intensity of his gaze made her pulse quicken, as it always did. "Aubrey," he breathed, her name a melody on his lips. "Shouldn't you be enjoying the party?"

She shrugged, stepping closer. "It didn't feel right without you there."

A flicker of guilt passed over Gunner's face. He ran a hand through his hair, a gesture Aubrey recognized as a sign of his inner conflict.

"I just needed some air," he explained, his voice tinged with an emotion Aubrey couldn't quite place. "To clear my head."

She nodded, her eyes never leaving his face. "And did it work?" she asked, her tone gentle but probing.

His gaze drifted back to the mountains, a wistful expression settling on his features. "I'm not sure anything can clear this particular fog, darlin'."

Her heart clenched at the pain evident in his voice. She closed the distance between them, her hand reaching out to touch his arm. The warmth of his skin beneath her fingers sent a familiar thrill through her, but she pushed the sensation aside, focusing on the matter at hand.

"Gunner," she said, her voice firm but laced with vulnerability, "what's been going on with you? You've been distant, troubled. I need to know what's wrong."

He turned to face her fully, his eyes searching hers. Weariness etched into his rugged features. For a moment, Aubrey thought he might deflect, but then his shoulders sagged slightly.

"I've been wrestlin' with something," he admitted. "Something that could change everything."

Aubrey's breath caught in her throat. She steeled herself, determined to be strong no matter what came next. "Tell me," she urged. "Whatever it is, we can face it together."

His hand came up to cup her cheek, his touch achingly tender. "You don't know how much I want to believe that," he murmured, his voice rough with emotion.

She leaned into his touch, her heart racing. "Then help me understand," she whispered. "No more secrets. Not between us."

He drew a deep breath, his hand falling away from her face. He turned slightly, gazing out at the Montana landscape as if drawing strength from the rugged beauty surrounding them.

"I got a call from my label," he confessed, his words

slow and deliberate. "They're offerin' me a chance to record a new album."

Aubrey's heart skipped a beat. "That's...that's amazing,"
she managed, her voice barely above a whisper.

He nodded, still not meeting her eyes. "It is. But it
means I'd have to leave Timber Falls. They want me in
Nashville for at least two months, maybe longer, to record
the album." His eyes finally locked with hers, filled with
a storm of emotions. "And after that, they're talkin' about
a tour to promote the album."

Aubrey felt as if the ground was shifting beneath her
feet. She struggled to keep her expression neutral, even
as her mind raced with the implications. "How long have
you known about this?" she asked, fighting to keep the
tremor from her voice.

"Just a few days," Gunner admitted, guilt flashing across
his face. "I've been trying to figure out how to tell you,
how to make this decision. It's everything I should want,
but..." He trailed off, his gaze drifting back to her.

Aubrey swallowed hard, forcing herself to focus on his
needs rather than her own tumultuous emotions. "But
what?" she prompted gently.

"But leaving Timber Falls for that long, leaving you..."
His voice cracked slightly. "It feels like I'm giving up something just as important."

Her heart ached at his words, even as a part of her soared
at the implication. She reached out, taking his hand in hers.
"Gunner, this is your dream," she said softly, surprised by
the steadiness in her voice. "You can't give that up, not for
anything or anyone."

His fingers tightened around Aubrey's, his touch electric even in this moment of uncertainty. He took a deep breath, his eyes searching hers with an intensity that made her heart race.

"Come with me," he said. "Join me in Nashville. And on tour. We could make this work, together."

Aubrey's breath caught in her throat. The offer hung in the air between them, tempting and terrifying all at once. For a fleeting moment, she allowed herself to imagine it. The excitement of life on the road, nights filled with music and passion, waking up each day in a new city with Gunner by her side.

But reality crashed in like a tidal wave. The Naked Moose. Her best friends. The life she'd painstakingly built here in Timber Falls. Her grip on Gunner's hand loosened as she took a step back.

"Gunner, I…" she started, her voice barely above a whisper. "I can't just leave everything behind. The bar, it's more than just a job. It's my home, my responsibility." She looked away, unable to bear the disappointment she knew she'd see in his eyes. "And Charly and Willow, they're counting on me."

Gunner's shoulders sagged, but he nodded slowly. "I understand," he said, though the pain in his voice was palpable. "You've built something real special here. I'd never ask you to give that up."

Aubrey felt tears pricking at the corners of her eyes. "I want to support your dream. I do. But I can't just abandon my life here." She reached up, cupping his face in her hand. "Is there no way we can find a middle ground?"

The tension between them crackled like electricity in the air. Her hand fell away from his face, and she wrapped her arms around herself, as if trying to hold herself together. His jaw clenched, his eyes stormy with conflicting emotions.

"Middle ground?" he echoed, his voice rough. "I don't know if there is one, darlin'. This tour, it's not just a few weeks. We're talking months."

Aubrey's breath caught in her throat. *Months.* The enormity of it hit her like a physical blow. She turned away, her gaze sweeping over the Montana landscape she'd grown to love.

"I can't ask you to wait for me," Gunner continued, his words barely audible over the pounding of Aubrey's heart.

Aubrey whirled to face him, frowning. "What are you saying, Gunner? That this is it? We just give up?"

He took a step toward her, his hands reaching out but stopping short of touching her. "I'm saying I don't blame you if you don't want to sit here and wait for me to come home."

Her eyes searched his. "And what about us? Aren't we part of each other too?"

A flicker of pain crossed Gunner's face. "Darlin', you know I love you. You've known that since that first day in Atlanta."

Aubrey's heart swelled in her chest. He'd never said those three little words, but she felt them too. She took his hand in hers. "And you know I love you too. I can wait for you. I can fly to see you when I can." She swallowed hard. "How long until you have to leave?"

"Two weeks," he replied.

The finality of it hit her like a physical blow. Two weeks was all the time she had left to hold on to.

As they stood there, hands clasped and hearts heavy, the sun dipped below the horizon.

She took a deep breath, squeezing Gunner's hand. "Well, these two weeks are ours. Let's make them count."

Gunner nodded, pulling her close and pressing a tender kiss to her forehead.

Twenty-One

Two weeks had come and gone in a blink of an eye, and Gunner stood frozen in the doorway of the state-of-the-art recording studio, his boots refusing to cross the threshold. The air hung heavy with the scent of leather and polished wood, a stark contrast to the crisp Montana breeze he'd left behind. His eyes darted from one unfamiliar face to another as musicians and producers bustled about, their energy palpable.

Aubrey. Nothing was the same without her.

He'd done his physical therapy this morning. While that managed the pain in his leg, it did nothing for the ache in his chest.

"Mr. Woods, we're all set up for you," a young assistant chirped, motioning toward the recording booth.

Gunner nodded, swallowing hard. This was it. The moment he'd been working toward for months. So why did it feel like he was walking to his own execution?

He forced himself forward, each step echoing his thundering heartbeat. The microphone stood before him. His fingers twitched, aching for the familiar comfort of his guitar. But today was all about vocals.

He rolled his shoulders to ease the tension. But as he stepped up to the mic, memories of Timber Falls flooded his mind. Aubrey's laugh. The warmth of her hand in his—

No. He couldn't think about her now. Couldn't let himself get lost in what-ifs and maybes. He took a deep breath, willing his mind to focus on the task at hand.

"Ready when you are, Gunner," the producer's voice crackled through his headphones.

Gunner nodded, his jaw set with determination. "Let's do this."

As the first notes filled the air, Gunner closed his eyes, letting the music wash over him. But even as he opened his mouth to sing, he couldn't shake the feeling that a piece of his heart was still back in Timber Falls, wrapped up in the arms of a certain blond-haired chef who'd stolen it without even trying.

"Perfect."

Gunner opened his eyes to catch the sound engineer's thumbs-up through the glass partition. A silent nod of encouragement from a stranger who had no idea of the emotional turmoil brewing inside him. "Sounds great on our end."

"Alright, let's take it from the top," Gunner said. He adjusted his stance, feet planted firmly on the studio floor, and focused on the sheet music before him.

The first chords of the melody filled the air, rich and resonant. It wrapped around Gunner like a familiar embrace, tugging at something deep within his chest. He closed his eyes, letting the music seep into his bones.

"I've been down this road before," Gunner began to sing. The words flowed from him, carrying a weight he hadn't anticipated. "Chasing dreams that always seem to slip away."

As he sang, Gunner's mind drifted. The lyrics, once just words on a page, now felt like they were etched on his heart. Each note carried a piece of his story, his struggles, his hopes.

He didn't falter. He couldn't. This was his shot at redemption, his chance to prove he still had what it took. So Gunner poured everything he had into every word, every note, letting the music carry him away from the doubts that had plagued him for so long.

His voice swelled with emotion as he reached the chorus, his thoughts drifting to Aubrey. Each memory fueled his performance, infusing the lyrics with raw longing.

"I can't shake the feeling that I left my heart behind," he sang, his voice cracking slightly with the weight of the words.

Through the glass, Gunner caught sight of the producer leaning forward, eyebrows raised in appreciation. The sound engineer nodded along, clearly impressed. But their admiration felt hollow, disconnected from the true source of his inspiration.

As he launched into the second verse, he closed his eyes again, picturing Aubrey's face. He felt a pang of loneliness. Here he was, pouring his heart out, and nobody truly understood the depth of what he was feeling. The irony wasn't lost on him—surrounded by people, yet feeling more alone than ever.

The melody swelled, and Gunner's rich baritone soared to meet it. But as the chorus approached, a tremor crept into his voice.

"Chasing dreams, but my heart's back home with you," he sang, the words catching in his throat.

Gunner's fingers tightened around the microphone stand, knuckles turning white.

"Cut!" The producer's voice sliced through the music. "Let's take five, folks."

Gunner stepped back from the mic, running a hand through his hair. He caught his reflection in the glass and saw a man torn in two.

"You okay in there, Woods?" the sound engineer called.

Gunner managed a weak smile and a thumbs-up. "Just need a minute," he replied.

As he leaned against the wall, memories of Timber Falls flooded his mind. The warmth of The Naked Moose, Aubrey's fierce blue eyes, the taste of her.

"What am I doing here?" he whispered, conflict etched across his face. His boots scuffed against the studio floor as he made his way to the corner, where his battered leather jacket hung. He shrugged it on, the familiar weight settling on his shoulders like armor.

"That was gold, Gunner," the producer's voice rang out, excitement evident in his tone. "We've got magic here."

Gunner turned, forcing a smile that didn't quite reach his eyes. "Appreciate it," he said. "I need some air."

The producer nodded, but Gunner barely registered

the response. His mind was already miles away, back in Timber Falls. He could almost smell the pine-scented air, hear the gentle clinking of glasses at The Naked Moose.

And Aubrey. God, *Aubrey*.

Her face swam before his eyes. Those striking eyes that could see right through him, the loose waves of blond hair that he longed to run his fingers through.

Success was within his grasp, but at what cost? The unanswered question echoed in his mind as he walked away, leaving a piece of his heart behind in that recording booth.

He gulped in the air as he stepped outside. Amidst the bustling crowd and constant flow of traffic, neon signs buzzed and flashed, each vying for attention. Towering buildings with vibrant exteriors housed a variety of establishments, from bars to eateries to live music venues. The air was thick with a blend of scents—the rich aroma of freshly brewed coffee intermingled with the sweet tang of Southern barbecue, with the unmistakable scent of car exhaust lingering in the background.

The memories of his dark past came flooding back as he thought about the times when he'd turned to pills for comfort to numb feelings like this.

Suddenly, he was snapped out of his thoughts by two women holding cell phones in front of him.

"Excuse me, are you Gunner Woods?" one of the women asked eagerly.

He looked up and nodded. "Ya. Nice to meet you."

"Can we take a photo with you?" the other woman chimed in, her eyes sparkling with excitement.

Gunner forced a smile and stood behind them as they took the photo.

"Thank you so much!" the woman exclaimed with gratitude.

He gave a small nod before walking away, the taste of his past troubles lingering in his mouth. It was a stark reminder that even in a city bursting with life, he could still feel completely alone.

The bell chimed as the door of The Naked Moose swung shut behind Aubrey with a resounding thud, her boot heels clicking against the worn floorboards as she began closing for the night. The silence enveloped her like a thick blanket, a welcome relief from the boisterous energy that had filled the space just hours ago. Her gaze swept across the empty tables, lingering on the stage where Gunner had once stood, his voice weaving magic through the air.

They'd texted all day long, and into the night. When they weren't texting, they FaceTimed, but it didn't feel like enough. Timber Falls felt empty without Gunner there. And Aubrey felt like she was torn in two. Timber Falls seemed even quieter now. She missed Atlanta. The sense of life there. And the bar was too damn busy for her to fly out to see Gunner.

A familiar ache bloomed in her chest as she made her way behind the bar, her fingers trailing along the polished surface. "Another night over," she murmured to herself, reaching for a rag to wipe down the counter. The motions were automatic, ingrained now.

As she worked, her mind wandered to the day's events, replaying moments like a worn-out record. The laughter of patrons, the clink of glasses and always, always, Gunner's missing presence, magnetic and undeniable. She paused, gripping the edge of the counter as a wave of longing washed over her.

"Get it together, Hale," she chastised herself, but her voice lacked its usual edge. The tough exterior she'd cultivated since fleeing Atlanta felt paper-thin tonight, barely concealing the vulnerability beneath.

Her gaze drifted to the bottles of beer in the fridge, Gunner's favorite. Without thinking, she reached for one, cracked it open. The amber liquid caught the low light, reminding her of the warmth in his eyes when he smiled at her.

"What are you doing to me, cowboy?" Aubrey whispered, bringing the glass to her lips but not drinking. The scent of the beer enveloped her, and suddenly she was back in Atlanta, that first night when their paths had crossed, and their journey began.

She set the bottle down with a soft clink, her hand trembling slightly. "This isn't me," she said aloud, her voice echoing in the empty bar. "I had a plan. Move to Timber Falls. Be happy."

But even as the words left her lips, Aubrey knew they were a lie. She had never been happy with small-town life. Not truly. She missed the big city, and Gunner had burrowed his way into her heart, past all her carefully constructed defenses. He understood her in a way no one else had, seeing past the tough-as-nails exterior to the woman beneath who longed for connection, for home.

"Damn it," she muttered, running a hand through her hair. When did Timber Falls become home? When did *he*?

Nothing felt right. Everything felt…*messy.*

The questions hung in the air, unanswered, as Aubrey resumed her cleaning. But try as she might, she couldn't shake the feeling that something fundamental had shifted. The life she'd built here, the walls she'd erected—they were crumbling, and at the center of it all stood Gunner Woods, guitar in hand and that crooked smile on his lips, beckoning her toward a future she'd never dared to imagine.

One where she might just be able to have everything that she ever wanted, if only she dared to trust him.

And she realized in the very depths of her heart, she *could* and *did* trust him. He wasn't her father. He wasn't Chef Bisset. He was… *Gunner*—strong, kind and fighting for the same happiness she was.

The soft creak of the back room door broke through Aubrey's thoughts. She looked up, her eyes widening as Willow and Charly emerged, their faces etched with concern.

Willow exchanged a knowing glance with Charly. "You okay?" she asked, her voice gentle but laced with the strength that had seen her through her own struggles.

Aubrey's fingers tightened around the rag she'd been using to wipe down the bar. "I'm fine," she said automatically, the words feeling hollow even as they left her lips.

Charly moved closer, her warm eyes searching Aubrey's

face. "You don't look fine," she said softly. "Is this about Gunner?"

The name sent a jolt through Aubrey's system. She took a deep breath. "I…" she began, her voice catching. "I miss him. God, I miss him so much it hurts."

The admission hung in the air, heavy with vulnerability. Her mind raced, torn between the urge to backpedal and the desperate need to unburden herself.

"Nothing feels right without him here," she continued, the words tumbling out now. "I keep expecting to hear his guitar, to see that charming grin of his. And I hate it. I hate feeling this dependent."

Willow reached across the bar, her hand covering Aubrey's. "It's okay to need someone. It doesn't make you weak."

Aubrey met her friend's gaze. "Doesn't it, though?" she whispered, voicing the doubt that had been gnawing at her since Gunner's departure.

Willow's eyes softened, her protective nature shining through as she offered Aubrey a reassuring smile. "No, it doesn't," she said firmly. "Feeling deeply for someone, missing them, that's strength. It means you've opened your heart enough to let him in, despite everything you've been through."

Aubrey's chest tightened at Willow's words. She thought of the walls she'd built after fleeing Atlanta, the way she'd kept everyone at arm's length. Until Gunner. His soulful eyes and that damned charming drawl had wormed their way past her defenses.

"But what if—" Aubrey started, her voice catching.

"What if he doesn't come back?" Willow finished gently. "That's a risk we all take when we let someone in. But Aubrey, you can't let fear stop you from living."

Charly nodded, her calming presence seeming to fill the room. "Willow's right," she said, her voice soft but sure. "And maybe...maybe this longing you're feeling is telling you something important."

Aubrey raised an eyebrow, curiosity momentarily overriding her emotional turmoil. "What do you mean?"

Charly leaned against the bar, her expression thoughtful. "Well, think about it. You miss Gunner, yes, but it's more than that, isn't it? You miss the way you felt when he was here, the possibilities he represented."

The words hit Aubrey like a physical blow. She closed her eyes, remembering the spark of excitement she'd felt every time Gunner took the stage, the way her world had seemed to expand beyond the borders of Timber Falls.

"Maybe," Charly continued, her tone gentle, "this is a sign that you need to reevaluate what truly makes you happy. Both here in Timber Falls and beyond."

Aubrey nodded slowly, her fingers tracing patterns on the polished wood of the bar. The truth of Charly's words resonated deep within her, unlocking a floodgate of emotions she'd been desperately trying to keep at bay.

"You're right," she admitted, her voice barely above a whisper. "It's not just Gunner I'm missing. It's everything." She looked up, her eyes shimmering with unshed tears. "I love Timber Falls, I do. The simplicity, the sense of community. But sometimes I feel like I'm suffocating."

She took a shaky breath, the words tumbling out now.

"I miss the buzz of the city, the endless possibilities. The thrill of creating a new dish and seeing it come to life on a plate." Her hand clenched into a fist. "But then I think about leaving all this behind, leaving you both, and it feels like I'm tearing myself in two."

Willow pushed herself off the bar, her eyes intense as she studied Aubrey. "Why does it have to be one or the other?" she asked, her tone challenging but not unkind.

Aubrey blinked, caught off guard. "What do you mean?"

Willow leaned forward. "Why can't you have it all? The excitement of the city and the peace of Timber Falls? Your culinary passion and the bar? Us and Gunner?"

The question hung in the air, electric with possibility. Aubrey felt a flicker of something unfamiliar in her chest. Hope, fragile but undeniable.

"It's the logistics of making it all work," she murmured, her mind racing. "It just seems...too complicated."

Willow raised her brows. "Is it really? Because it seems pretty easy to me."

Could she really blend these two worlds? As the idea took root, Aubrey felt a smile tugging at her lips for the first time in weeks. It was unconventional, impractical even, but the more she considered it, the more right it felt.

Maybe she didn't need to give up the side of herself that she felt like she'd left behind in Atlanta after all...

She looked up at her friends, gratitude washing over her. "You really think I could make this work?"

Charly's eyes crinkled as she smiled, her calming presence filling the space between them. "Of course you can, Aubrey," she said, her voice soft but sure. "Your journey doesn't have to be about choosing one life over the other. It's about finding a way to weave together all the things you love."

Her heart quickened at the thought. She twisted a strand of her hair. "Even Gunner?" she asked, her voice barely above a whisper.

Charly nodded, reaching out to squeeze Aubrey's hand. "Especially Gunner. You love him. You shouldn't have to miss him like this."

Heat filled Aubrey's chest, melting some of the ice that had formed around her heart. She closed her eyes, allowing herself to imagine a future where she didn't have to choose. Where the thrill of the city could coexist with the comfort of small-town life, where Gunner's music could blend with the familiar sounds of The Naked Moose.

When she opened her eyes, they were brimming with tears. "I don't know what I did to deserve friends like you," she said, her voice thick with emotion.

Willow snorted, breaking the tension. "Oh please, you put up with our drama on a daily basis. We owe you."

Aubrey laughed, the sound echoing in the empty bar. It felt good, like shedding a weight she'd been carrying for too long. She looked at her friends, these women who had become her family, and felt a surge of determination.

"You're right," she said, straightening her shoulders. "I can have it all. Now I just need to figure out how."

Willow grinned. "And we'll help you."

Twenty-Two

The audience in Nashville was alive with energy, the crowd's cheers and applause washing over Gunner like a warm tide. The theater was a sight to behold, with its grand marquee lit up in neon lights. The old brick building stood tall and proud, its entrance lined with posters of past performances. The large stage was decorated with cowboy boots and guitars.

He had been back in Nashville for a week now, but it still felt surreal. He had brought two suitcases with him, not admitting to himself that it felt like he was moving back and leaving Timber Falls behind…and leaving Aubrey behind.

But as the spotlight hit him and he began to strum his guitar, all thoughts of the past were replaced with the joy and passion of performing. And as he sang his heart out on that legendary stage, Gunner knew that he was exactly where he was meant to be, which brought a world of confusion with it.

How could he feel so torn and comfortable at the same time?

The label had set up a show for him to play some new songs live along with the old. His fingers danced across the guitar strings, muscle memory taking over as he lost himself in the music. The newest song flowed from him, raw and honest, laying bare the struggles he'd faced.

Gunner's lips curved into a smile as he sang, watching the crowd react to his music. This was what he lived for. This connection, this ability to touch hearts with nothing more than his words and melodies. The label had been right; trying out the new material live was electrifying.

As the chorus hit its peak, Gunner's gaze swept across the sea of faces before him. His breath caught in his throat, the next lyric dying on his lips as his eyes locked on to a strikingly familiar face. His fingers stumbled, the guitar emitting a discordant twang that pierced through the music.

"Aubrey," he said into the microphone. What was she doing here? His heart raced, a mixture of hope and disbelief coursing through him.

Gunner blinked, willing himself to focus on the performance, but his eyes kept drifting back to her. She looked as beautiful as ever, her blond waves framing her face, her expression a mix of determination and vulnerability that tugged at something deep within him.

"Sorry, folks," he said into the microphone, forcing a chuckle. "Guess these new songs are still a bit rusty."

The crowd laughed good-naturedly, but Gunner barely heard them. His mind was reeling, memories of their days and nights together flooding back. The taste of her lips, the softness of her skin, the way she'd looked at him like he was the only man in the world.

As he strummed the opening chords of the next verse, his gaze remained fixed on her. She was moving through the crowd now, each step bringing her closer to the stage. His voice wavered slightly as he sang, the lyrics taking on new meaning in her presence.

"I've been runnin' from my demons, but they always catch up," he crooned. "Maybe it's time I turned and faced 'em, let 'em set me free."

Aubrey was at the edge of the stage now, her eyes never leaving his. His heart thundered in his chest, drowning out the music, the crowd, everything but her. He knew, in that moment, that whatever happened next would change everything.

The final chord hung in the air, suspended like a held breath. Gunner's fingers stilled on the strings, the silence that followed shocking in its suddenness. The crowd's excited chatter dissolved into confused murmurs, a ripple of uncertainty spreading through the packed room.

"What's going on?" someone called out.

Gunner barely heard them. His focus was entirely on Aubrey, her presence magnetic. She stood at the edge of the stage, her eyes locked on his, a storm of emotions swirling in their depths.

"Aubrey," he said again.

In the crowd, Aubrey took a deep breath, squaring her shoulders. The sea of people seemed to part before her as she moved forward with purpose, each step deliberate and sure. Gunner watched, transfixed, as she drew closer.

"Is this part of the show?" he heard someone ask.

Gunner's heart raced. He wanted to run to her, to sweep her into his arms, but he remained rooted to the spot, his guitar a barrier between them.

As Aubrey reached the foot of the stage, Gunner found his voice. "Folks, I'm gonna need a moment here," he said into the mic.

The crowd's confusion was palpable, but Gunner couldn't bring himself to care. All that mattered was Aubrey, standing there, looking up at him with a determination that made him unravel.

His heart thundered in his chest, a wild rhythm that threatened to drown out the confused murmurs of the crowd. He felt pulled toward Aubrey like a magnet, every fiber of his being aching to close the distance between them. But doubt and fear held him in place, his fingers still frozen on the strings of his guitar.

She went to climb up on the stage, but security stopped her.

"Let her up," he said, sliding his guitar onto his back.

As Aubrey took his hand, he marveled at how perfectly it fit in his. He helped her onto the stage, pulling her close, their bodies fitting together like they were made for each other.

"Hi," she said, smirking.

He chuckled. "Hi."

The crowd fell silent, a collective hush blanketing the venue as Aubrey stood before Gunner. Her chest heaved with each breath, her eyes never leaving his. The air crackled with electricity, heavy with anticipation.

"I can't do this. Being away from you, it's not work-ing." She glanced back at the crowd. "I know the tim-ing is terrible, but I couldn't wait to say all this to you." She stepped closer, and he wrapped his arms around her as she said, "I'm tired of being left behind. This time, I'm choosing to chase after what I want. And what I want is you, Gunner Woods."

The raw emotion in her voice made Gunner's breath catch. "Darlin', are you sure?"

Aubrey's lips curved into a soft smile. "I've never been more sure of anything in my life. I can't do life without you." She paused, cocking her head. "Well, I *can*. But I don't want to."

Gunner's heart soared, hope and joy flooding through him. He cupped her face. "I've missed you something fierce," he murmured, his voice thick with emotion. "But how're we gonna make this work?"

Aubrey's gaze never wavered. "I'll work remotely with Chef Miguel to create cocktail and app recipes for the bar when we're in Nashville or on tour. Charly and Willow have agreed to hire another bartender to replace me. The rest of the time, we'll be in Timber Falls." She paused, a hint of vulnerability creeping into her voice. "And maybe when I'm in Nashville, I can find a restaurant to work at, so I can see if that dream I once had is worth chasing again."

Gunner's breath caught. "You'd do that? For me?"

"For us," Aubrey corrected, a smile playing on her lips. "Besides, I love the city. It's part of who I am, just like you are, so this would be good for me too. I kept think-ing I had to give something up to be happy, but I know

now, I don't. I can have it all. We can make this work—
our perfect, messy life. We'll be home, as long as we have
each other."

He didn't need to hear more, pulling her into a tight
embrace. The warmth of her body against his felt like coming home, her curves fitting perfectly against the planes
of his chest. He buried his face in her hair, inhaling the
scent of lavender and something uniquely Aubrey, as the
crowd went wild.

"I love you so damn much," he murmured, his voice
thick with emotion.

Aubrey's arms tightened around him, her fingers digging into his back. "I love you too," she whispered, her
breath hot against his neck.

Not quite sure how he got so lucky, he leaned away and
then dropped his mouth to hers. The noise of the crowd
and the music of his band faded into the background, his
focus solely on her.

She tasted like sweet honey, her lips soft and plump
against his, her body warm and inviting. He held her
tightly, wanting to never let her go.

For a bit, they were lost in the moment, the heat and
electricity between them palpable. It was as if they were
the only two people in the world, completely consumed
by each other.

But all too soon, the kiss ended, and he pulled away,
still holding her close. They looked into each other's eyes,
both of them breathless and exhilarated.

Not wanting to break the spell, he leaned in and whispered, "I need to finish the show. Then we can go somewhere quieter so we can continue this."

She smiled and replied, "Wherever you go, I'll follow and bring my dreams with me."

Epilogue

The Naked Moose stood transformed, its rustic charm now covered in twinkling lights and colorful banners. Standing outside of the bar, Aubrey held the door open, greeting the arriving family members of the talent show kids with a warm smile. Gunner had recently finished a tour across America, promoting his latest album, and Aubrey was happy that they were both back in Timber Falls for the summer months. She loved her time traveling and the big cities, but Timber Falls was home.

"Welcome, Brooks! Anna, that dress is adorable," Aubrey exclaimed, kneeling to admire a little girl's frilly dress. As she stood, she caught sight of the Millers approaching. "John, how's that leg healing up?"

The older man chuckled, patting his knee. "Right as rain, thanks to your famous chicken soup, Aubrey."

"We're so excited for the talent show," a young mother gushed, her toddler clinging to her leg.

Aubrey nodded, a sense of pride washing over her. "It's

our favorite event here too." She glanced inside the bar, catching a glimpse of Gunner setting up the stage.

Inside, he carefully tuned a small guitar, his strong hands moving with practiced ease. A group of wide-eyed children gathered around him, their excitement palpable.

Aubrey shut the door and headed toward the stage. The talent show was a yearly tradition now at the bar. And Gunner mentored all the musical kids every year, even when he was on the road.

"Alright, kiddos," Gunner said, his eyes twinkling. "Who wants to give this beauty a strum?"

A chorus of "Me! Me!" erupted, and Gunner laughed, the sound rich and warm. He handed the guitar to a shy boy hanging back from the group.

"Here you go, partner. Give it a try."

The boy hesitated, then plucked a string. The note rang out, clear and true, and a smile spread across his face.

"There you go!" Gunner encouraged, his voice filled with genuine enthusiasm. "You're a natural."

As Gunner continued to interact with the children, Aubrey found herself watching him, struck by the easy way he put everyone at ease. It was a far cry from the troubled man who had returned to Timber Falls seeking redemption and a fresh start.

"Alright, folks," she called out, her voice carrying over the excited chatter. "Let's get this show on the road!"

As the families settled in, Aubrey caught Gunner's eye. He winked, and she felt a flutter in her stomach as she took in the moment.

Charly knelt down in front of her twins, Emma and

Ethan, smoothing their matching cowboy hats and adjusting their little bolo ties. The five-year-olds fidgeted, their eyes darting nervously around the bustling room.

"Remember," Charly said, her eyes radiating calm, "it's just like we practiced at home. You two are going to be amazing."

Jaxon squatted beside them, giving his easygoing smile. "And even if you forget the words," he added with a wink, "just keep on singin'. That's what real cowboys do."

Emma's bottom lip quivered. "But what if everyone laughs at us, Mama?"

Charly pulled her daughter into a gentle hug. "Oh, honey, they won't. They're all here to cheer you on. And you know what?" She leaned in close, as if sharing a secret. "Even if they did laugh, it wouldn't matter. Because you're brave enough to get up there and try."

Ethan puffed out his little chest. "I ain't scared," he declared, though his trembling hands betrayed him.

Jaxon tapped his son's hat. "'Course you're not. You're a Reed, through and through."

Aubrey smiled at them, and then looked next to her at Willow, who turned to Eli, who stood stoically beside her, with his eyes fixed on their daughter, Sophie.

"You okay?" Willow asked softly, reaching for his hand.

Eli's jaw clenched, then relaxed. "Yeah," he said gruffly. "Just never thought I'd be here, you know? Watching my little girl recite poetry." He gave a small smile. "No one better laugh at her."

Willow slowly shook her head. "I'm sure they know better than to do that."

Sophie skipped over then and looked up at them, her green eyes—so like her mother's—wide with anticipation. "Do you think they'll like my poem, Daddy?"

Eli knelt down, his usual reserved demeanor softening as he looked at his daughter. "They're gonna love it. Just like your mama and I do."

Aubrey's heart melted into a puddle on the floor.

A hush fell over the crowd as Willow and Eli's daughter, Sophie, stepped onto the small stage. Her auburn hair, braided neatly, swung as she adjusted the microphone. Aubrey held her breath, remembering how nervous the little girl had been during rehearsals.

Sophie's clear voice rang out, strong and steady. "'The Cowgirl's Heart,' by Sophie Cole."

Aubrey's gaze flicked to Willow and Eli. Willow's fingers were intertwined tightly with Eli's, her knuckles white. Eli's jaw was set, but his eyes shimmered with emotion.

Sophie's words painted vivid images, and Aubrey found herself transported. The crowd hung on every word, captivated by the young girl's talent and poise.

As Sophie finished, silence lingered for a heartbeat before thunderous applause erupted. Willow let out a choked laugh, tears streaming down her face. Eli pulled her close, pressing a kiss to her temple, his own eyes suspiciously moist.

"Did you see that?" Willow whispered, her voice carrying to where Aubrey stood. "She did it, Eli. Our baby girl did it."

Eli nodded, a rare full smile spreading across his face. "She's got your spirit. And your talent."

Aubrey felt a lump form in her throat. She remembered the day Willow had confided in her about her fears surrounding motherhood, worried her past trauma would overshadow her ability to love. Yet here she was, radiating pride and joy.

As the next act prepared, Aubrey slipped to the back of the room. She leaned against the wall, taking in the scene before her. The Naked Moose, once just a run-down bar, now pulsed with life and laughter. The bar hadn't only become successful, it was magical.

Her gaze swept over her friends. Willow and Eli, their heads bent close together as they whispered words of love and pride. Charly and Jaxon, surrounded by their growing family. And Gunner, his eyes meeting hers across the room, a question in their depths that made her heart race.

We did it, Aubrey thought to herself, running a hand over the smooth wood of the bar. *We turned this place into something beautiful. Something that matters.*

As if sensing her moment of introspection, Gunner made his way to her side. "Penny for your thoughts, darlin'?" he drawled, his hand finding the small of her back.

Aubrey leaned into him. "Just thinking about how far we've come. How The Naked Moose has become…well, everything I never knew I needed."

Gunner's arm tightened around her. "It's not just the bar that's become something special, hmm?"

Aubrey felt a blush creep up her neck. She turned to

him, keeping her voice quiet as the next act took the stage. "I need to tell you something."

His eyes locked on to hers, concern flickering across his face. "Everything alright?"

Aubrey took a deep breath, steadying herself. "I've been watching you with the kids today, and it just melts my heart." She placed a hand on his chest, feeling the steady thrum of his heartbeat. "The way you connect with them, how patient and kind you are."

Gunner's brow furrowed slightly, a question forming on his lips. Before he could speak, Aubrey pressed on.

"I'm so glad you're good with children, because..." She paused, her voice catching. "Well... I'm pregnant."

For a moment, time seemed to stand still. Aubrey searched his face, trying to gauge his reaction.

Until Gunner's eyes widened, heady emotions flashing across his features. Then, slowly, a smile spread across his face—one that reached his eyes and lit up his entire being.

"Aubrey," he breathed, his voice thick with emotion. "We're gonna have a baby?"

She nodded, tears pricking at the corners of her eyes. "We are."

In one fluid motion, Gunner pulled her close, enveloping her in his strong arms. "Oh, darlin'," he murmured into her hair.

Aubrey melted into his embrace, relief and joy washing over her. "You're happy?" she asked, her voice muffled against his chest.

Gunner pulled her in close, holding her face tenderly in his hands. "This is more than just happiness," he whispered as he placed a hand on her stomach. "This baby is our future, our legacy. And I swear to you, right now, that I will love and protect both of you with every fiber of my being."

She returned his smile with one of her own. "And we will love you endlessly."

★ ★ ★ ★ ★

LET'S TALK

Romance

For exclusive extracts, competitions and special offers, find us online:

f MillsandBoon

X @MillsandBoon

O @MillsandBoonUK

♪ @MillsandBoonUK

Get in touch on 01413 063 232

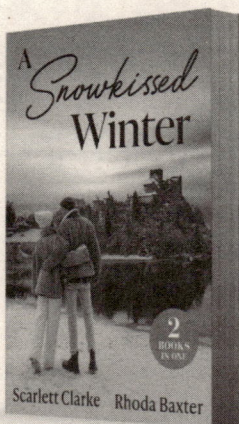

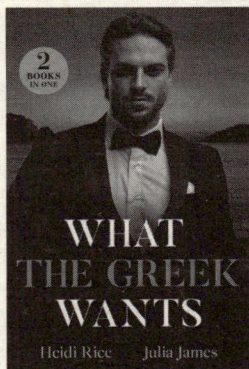

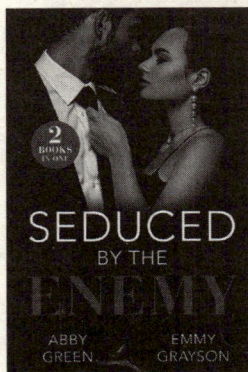

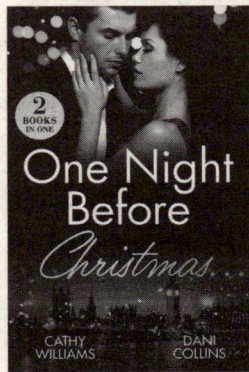

MILLS & BOON

THE HEART OF ROMANCE

A ROMANCE FOR EVERY READER

MODERN

Prepare to be swept off your feet by sophisticated, sexy and seductive heroes, in some of the world's most glamourous and romantic locations, where power and passion collide.

HISTORICAL

Escape with historical heroes from time gone by. Whether your passion is for wicked Regency Rakes, muscled Vikings or rugged Highlanders, awaken the romance of the past.

MEDICAL

Set your pulse racing with dedicated, delectable doctors in the high-pressure world of medicine, where emotions run high and passion, comfort and love are the best medicine.

Love Always

Celebrate true love with tender stories of heartfelt romance, from the rush of falling in love to the joy a new baby can bring, and a focus on the emotional heart of a relationship.

HEROES

The excitement of a gripping thriller, with intense romance at its heart. Resourceful, true-to-life women and strong, fearless men face danger and desire - a killer combination!

afterglow BOOKS

From showing up to glowing up, these characters are on the path to leading their best lives and finding romance along the way – with plenty of sizzling spice!

To see which titles are coming soon, please visit

millsandboon.co.uk/nextmonth